Praise for Stephen Greenleaf

"Mr. Greenleaf is a real writer with real talent!"

The New Yorker

John Marshall Tanner

"The long-sought heir of Sam Spade, Marlow and Archer."

San Francisco Examiner

and *Toll Call*

"One of his best . . . An extremely satisfying story."

The Orlando Sentinel

Also by Stephen Greenleaf
Published by Ballantine Books:

TOLL
CALL

STEPHEN
GREENLEAF

BALLANTINE BOOKS • NEW YORK

All rights reserved under International and Pan-American Copyright
Conventions. Published in the United States by Ballantine Books, a
division of Random House, Inc., New York, and simultaneously in
Canada by Random House of Canada Limited, Toronto.

Library of Congress Catalog Card Number: 86-40351

ISBN 0-345-35349-8

This edition published by arrangement with Villard Books, a division of
Random House, Inc.

Manufactured in the United States of America

First Ballantine Books Edition: October 1988

For Marge and Doc

"State your name, please."

"John Marshall Tanner."

"Are you a resident of the city and county of San Francisco?"

"Yes, I am."

"What is your business, Mr. Tanner?"

"I'm a private investigator."

"Licensed by the State of California?"

"Yes."

"How long have you been a private detective?"

"A little over ten years."

"And what did you do before that?"

"I was a lawyer."

"In this city?"

"Yes."

"How long did you practice law?"

"Approximately eight years."

"Are you still a member of the bar of this state, Mr. Tanner?"

"Yes."

"But you no longer practice law."

"That's correct. But I occasionally accept a retainer."

"Why is that?"

"It allows me to keep certain information confidential pursuant to the attorney-client privilege. I find that useful, and my clients find it reassuring."

"I see. Now, let me turn your attention to this past October, approximately a year ago. At that time did you have occasion to discuss certain business affairs of the plaintiff in this case, Mr. Malcolm Halliburton?"

"Yes, I did."

"With whom did you have that discussion?"

"With you, Mr. Stacey."

"Pursuant to that discussion, were you engaged in your professional capacity to perform services for the defendant in this case, the Arundel Corporation?"

"I was."

"And what were those services?"

"I was given a copy of the resumé Mr. Halliburton had included with his application for the position of vice-president of international marketing for Arundel Corporation, and I was asked to verify certain items of personal history listed on that resumé."

"Were you told why?"

"I was."

"What were you told?"

"Objection. Hearsay."

"It goes to his state of mind, Your Honor."

"The jury is cautioned that the answer will be admitted solely to show the state of mind of the witness, and not for the truth of the matters asserted. You may answer the question, Mr. Tanner."

"Thank you, Your Honor. I was told that Mr. Halliburton had been hired by Arundel in 1979; that his contract contained certain bonus and incentive provisions which were highly lucrative; that over the next five years Mr. Halliburton had not performed pursuant to Arundel's expectations in that certain of his activities were being investigated for possible illegalities, including embezzlement and bribery; that in view of these irregularities the company had decided to terminate Mr. Halliburton's employment; and that shortly after his termination Mr. Halliburton had filed suit to collect the amounts he felt were due and owing to him pursuant to his employment contract. As part of its defense to that lawsuit, the corporation wanted to ascertain whether Mr. Halliburton's employment application had been truthful and complete in all respects, or whether it had been fraudulent and misleading in certain particulars."

"So essentially you were asked to verify the employment application."

"Right."

"And if you found any errors or omissions what were you to do?"

"Report them to you and try to ascertain the correct information."

"How long did you work at this project, Mr. Tanner?"

"For two months, on and off. For a total of seventy-five hours, approximately."

"Did you incur significant expenses?"

"Yes. There was a good deal of travel involved. I went to Durham, North Carolina; Providence, Rhode Island; Washington, D.C.; and to Massachusetts, Missouri, and Iowa as well."

"Now, I show you a copy of what has been marked Defendant's Exhibit D. Can you identify that for me?"

"That is what you have given to me and described as the resumé attached to the employment application that Mr. Halliburton submitted to Arundel Corporation back in 1979."

"Tell me, Mr. Tanner. What items on that resumé did you find to be true?"

"Objection, Your Honor. No foundation."

"Your Honor, plaintiff has previously admitted pursuant to Section 2033 of the Code of Civil Procedure that certain affidavits and other documents obtained by Mr. Tanner during his investigation were authentic and genuine. Those documents will be offered into evidence after Mr. Tanner completes his testimony, as providing the foundation for that testimony. If at this late date counsel for Mr. Halliburton seeks to challenge the authenticity of these documents, I assure him that we will move pursuant to CCP Section 2034(c) for an order requiring plaintiff to pay the expenses of any and all affiants and records custodians forced to travel to this court to authenticate the documents, and for reasonable attorneys' fees as well. Are you making such a challenge, Mr. Kinlaw?"

"Our position regarding the documentation will be asserted when and if they are offered into evidence, Mr. Stacey, and not before."

"May I proceed, then, Your Honor?"

"You may, Mr. Stacey. Subject to a motion to strike if a sufficient foundation is not forthcoming."

"Thank you. So, Mr. Tanner. Tell us, for example, what you learned of Mr. Halliburton's place and date of birth."

"His resumé says he was born in Paris, France, in 1939. Actually, he was born in What Cheer, Iowa, in 1945."

"How big a city is What Cheer?"

"In the 1980 census the population of What Cheer was eight hundred and three."

"How about Mr. Halliburton's education?"

"His resumé states that he attended Governor Dummer Academy in Massachusetts, then Brown University, the London School of Economics, and the graduate school of business at Duke University. It also states he was awarded the degrees of Bachelor of Arts, a Master of Arts in Economics, and a Master of Business Administration. Actually, Mr. Halliburton graduated from high school in Moravia, Iowa, and attended Northeast Missouri State Teachers College in Kirksville, Missouri, on a football scholarship. He dropped out after two years when a knee injury ended his athletic career. Mr. Halliburton is still remembered by several merchants in Kirksville, as owing them sizable amounts for food, clothing, and other necessaries which were extended to him on credit during his college days."

"Your Honor, move to strike the final portion of that answer as hearsay. I know of no affidavits on that point. The matter is also immaterial."

"Read the answer please, Mr. Reporter. Thank you. The objection is sustained, Mr. Kinlaw. The jury will

4

disregard everything following the word *career.* You know better, Mr. Tanner."

"I'm sorry, Your Honor. I got carried away by my intrepidity."

"Continue, Mr. Stacey."

"Thank you, Your Honor. So Mr. Halliburton has no college degree, to say nothing of a Master's in Business Administration?"

"He has no degrees from the institutions he listed, and I found no evidence that he attended any educational institutions other than Northeast Missouri State and Moravia High."

"How about his employment record?"

"His resumé states that he was employed by Exxon Corporation, and he was, but not as an assistant vice-president of bulk product marketing, as he represented."

"In what capacity was he employed?"

"As a gas station attendant in Washington, D.C. The station was on Connecticut Avenue."

"How about his other position, that of Chief Executive Officer of Halliburton, Incorporated?"

"That much is true. He did hold that position in that company. But the company did not have assets in excess of thirty million dollars and it did not have more than one hundred employees and it did not engage in the manufacture and distribution of computer software."

"What were its assets and what was its business, Mr. Tanner?"

"Halliburton, Incorporated owned a 1973 Dodge Challenger and not much else. What it did was sell the contents of its trunk—which ranged from Gucci shoes from Mexico to Navajo jewelry from Taiwan—at various outdoor locations in the Washington-Baltimore corridor. Most of the locations were vacant lots."

"I see. Was there anything at all on that resumé that was the truth, Mr. Tanner?"

"Well, Mr. Halliburton said he was a skilled and experienced salesman, and I'd say there was some truth to that."

"Why?"

"He did a damned good job of selling himself to the Arundel Corporation."

"Thank you, Mr. Tanner. Your Honor, I submit the aforementioned affidavits and other documents which support Mr. Tanner's testimony, which have been stipulated as authentic and which have been collectively marked as Defendant's F."

"Any objection, Mr. Kinlaw?"

"Ah . . . no, Your Honor."

"It may be admitted."

"No further questions, Your Honor."

"You may cross-examine, Mr. Kinlaw."

"Thank you, Your Honor. Mr. Tanner, you're a private eye, right?"

"Right."

"For sale to the highest bidder."

"Not always."

"But usually?"

"Maybe not even that. I look at the bidder as well as the bid."

"Come now, Mr. Tanner. You testify in court quite often, do you not?"

"I suppose I do."

"And you get paid for it, true?"

"Yes."

"You're being paid for the testimony you just gave, aren't you, Mr. Tanner?"

"I'm being paid for my time, Mr. Kinlaw, not for my testimony."

"At what rate?"

"Forty dollars per hour."

"That's quite a lot, isn't it?"

"I happen to know it's only one fifth of what you charge for *your* time, Mr. Kinlaw."

"That's hardly the point, is it?"

"I don't know. You brought it up."

"I . . . Now, you've testified for Mr. Stacey several times before, have you not? In other cases?"

"Twice."

"How did those come out?"

"Won one, lost one."

"Did you receive a bonus afterward, in either case?"

"No."

"Are you sure?"

"I am. And so is my banker."

"I see. Now, you don't know of your own personal knowledge or experience that Mr. Halliburton lacks an MBA degree, do you, Mr. Tanner?"

"No."

"And you don't know whether he ever sold computer software for a living, do you?"

"No. I just know he didn't sell it for Halliburton, Incorporated."

"So as far as you know, the essential parts of Mr. Halliburton's resumé may well be true, isn't that right?"

"I guess it depends on what you mean by essential. He got his name and address right. And the color of his eyes. But I imagine the Arundel Corporation sees that resumé as a rather expensive hoax."

"Move to strike as nonresponsive, Your Honor."

"Overruled."

"But—"

"Proceed, Mr. Kinlaw."

"Very well. Let's turn to your previous profession, Mr. Tanner. You say you used to be a practicing attorney, but now you're not. I wonder if you can tell me why you're not a lawyer anymore."

"There's not an easy answer to that. A lot of it had to do with not liking to talk on the telephone, I think."

"Come now, Mr. Tanner. There was more to it than that, was there not?"

"I suppose there must have been."

"You got in some trouble, didn't you? Trouble that resulted in a jail term."

"What I got into was a situation in which I felt it necessary to make certain observations in order to protect my client's rights. The person to whom I made those observations didn't take them kindly. Since he happened to be a judge, he sentenced me to six months in jail for contempt of court. I served the time rather than apologize. After I got out I decided that since none of the reasons for my contemptuous outburst had disappeared, I'd try to get into a more respectable line of work."

"More respectable? Surely you don't expect me to believe that a private detective pursues a more respectable calling than an attorney-at-law."

"No, Mr. Kinlaw. I don't expect *you* to believe that. But I think the jury might."

Just another day in Superior Court—predominantly bor-
ing, with intermittent flashes of wit or tension; periodi-
cally entertaining or even enlightening if either of the
lawyers is any good; marginally productive; and in this
case, since my client was a lawyer and his was a corporation, a day more profitable than normal.

It was warm and sunny—typical San Francisco sum-
mer-in-fall—so I decided to stroll back to the office instead
of hailing a cab. Along the way I dodged the drunks and
the ravers as I considered what to do with the proceeds of
the Arundel account. I needed a few big-ticket items—a
refrigerator, a couch, a valve job—and countless smaller
conveniences as well—a floor lamp, a shower curtain, a
belt. But what I needed more than anything was to patch
things up with my secretary, so along the way I stopped
at the Neiman-Marcus perfume counter and bought Peggy
a quarter-ounce of Obsession, which the salesclerk assured
me was the latest thing. I had no idea if the scent was to
her taste, I just hoped the same thing the manufacturer
hoped—that with that name and that label it didn't have
to be.

The little box—gift-wrapped in glass and paper worth
more than the fragrance itself—was concealed behind my
back as I let myself into the outer office, but there was no
one there to give it to. I surrendered my contrite smile and
did a quick calculation: it was Monday and it was afternoon, so Peggy was definitely scheduled to be on duty and
Peggy always did what she was scheduled to do. I consid-

ered the possibilities, shrugged, put the little box on top of her typewriter, then went into my private office and sat down at my desk prepared to glide to the end of the day on the wings of my triumphant court appearance.

I was slitting open the top envelope from the stack of mail in front of me before I noticed her. She was lying on the couch, one arm a shield across her eyes, the other a sash across her chest. One leg was stretched out straight but the other dangled awkwardly off the cushion, and that single ungainly image was enough to make me hurry to her side, propelled by the sudden, sweaty conviction that Peggy Nettleton was dead.

Perhaps it was Malcolm Halliburton's hateful stare that had so attuned me to catastrophe, perhaps it was the persistent fog of dread that clouds my profession, perhaps it was merely a temporary tic of fear, but whatever it was I was firmly in its grip as I knelt by Peggy's side and touched her shoulder. It was warm and yielding, definitely alive, a much more precious gift than the one I'd left atop her desk. I saw no blood, no blue-black smear of violence, and beneath my searching gaze Peggy's chest ballooned with a placid breath. I pressed her flesh more firmly, then shook her till she stirred.

She groaned and rolled away from me, so covetous of sleep she convinced me she was imperiled only by a nightmare. I mouthed an inchoate prayer of thanks and went back to my desk, lightened of most but not all of the apprehension of the previous moment, uncomfortably aware of how vulnerable I was to fate and mischief. To subdue such musings I continued through the mail, which was entirely routine and thus unable to keep my mind from casting stark, bleak images of life without the woman on the couch.

Our history was neither complex nor fantastic. She'd answered my ad in the Sunday *Chronicle*—the one I placed when I was finally in a position to afford some help—and had sailed through the interview as though I were the applicant and she the jaded boss. She accepted my offer of employment only after establishing some ground rules: half-time only, no nights, no demeaning personal services such as fetching lunch or laundry, the immediate replacement of my manual typewriter with a new Selectric, and the equally immediate cleansing of the office carpet and painting of the office walls. I'd accepted her conditions gratefully, and she'd begun work the next day. Suddenly, somehow, it was eight years later and the rules were less precise.

It was a unique relationship, at least for me. She was my only audience, my only motive to verbalize a thought or express an emotion. The rare and random epiphanies of my life would go unremarked if not for Peggy, yet there was nothing sexual between us, though once I'd made a halfhearted try that was wholeheartedly rebuffed on the sensible ground that we needed each other as friends more than we needed each other as lovers. There was a whole lot of respect on each side of the association, and an equal measure of affection, and maybe in each of us there was a sense that, whatever heated little exercises we might have going on the side, this was the alliance in our lives that mattered most. It was not something I viewed as an achievement, but my best times were the times I spent with Peggy.

Her measured breathing continued to sweeten time, so I went back to my business. I'd worked my way down to an urgent appeal from the Native American Rights Fund when Peggy struggled to a sitting position and looked at me. Startled, she rubbed her eyes, groaned, and looked at me again. "Hi," she said thickly.

"Hi."

"I guess I fell asleep."

"I guess so."

"I've never done that before. I'm sorry. I . . ."

I waved at her apology. "Don't worry about it."

"No. I'll come in early tomorrow to make up the time."

"Don't be silly. Go back to sleep if you want. I don't have anything that needs doing right away. Except this."

I trotted to the outer office and retrieved the little package and went back and presented it to Peggy.

"What's this for?" she asked, frowning. "My birthday's in June. You even remembered this year."

"A little peace offering. So we can forget our little fight."

"What fight?" she asked, her words still slow and fuzzy. "Oh. That. I tried, Marsh, but about midnight my fingers broke off relations with my brain and the strangest things started to show up on the page. I just couldn't send out those reports with typos in them; it's so . . . tacky. I—"

"It was my fault," I interrupted. "I shouldn't have pressed you. Thank God someone around here has standards. Another day didn't matter anyway. I was unreasonable."

"No you weren't. I was incompetent."

I grinned. "Let's have another fight about whose fault it was. You take my side and I'll take yours. Like those horse races where you ride my horse and I ride yours and the money goes to the one that comes in second."

Peggy smiled, yawned, and opened her present. "Obsession. I've always wanted to try it." She looked up from the package at me. "You can't afford this."

"Today I can."

She took a moment to decipher, then nodded. "The Arundel trial. How'd it go?"

"Okay, I guess. As I left the stand, Halliburton tossed me a look that activated my acne, so I suppose I did what I was hired to do."

Peggy gazed back at the tiny cruet as though it had been filled from the fountain of youth. "Shall I put some on?"

"Sure."

She opened the bottle, tipped the essence of something or other onto a fingertip, and dabbed it behind her wrists and ears. "Want to smell?"

I went to the couch, leaned down, and took a sniff. My nose wriggled in self-defense, and I suppressed a sneeze as I tried and failed to identify the scent. I doubt that it existed anywhere but on the flesh of wealthy women. "You don't have to wear it, you know," I told her. "I didn't know what kind you use."

"But I like it I think," she said, inhaling. Then she grinned. "My usual brand's Norell, if the question ever comes up. In Trivial Pursuit, or something."

We exchanged flirtatious peeks, then Peggy closed her eyes and leaned back against the couch, giving me a chance to examine her more closely.

Tall, angular, she was darkly and archly handsome, with long brown hair that curled at her shoulders and black-brown eyes that were customarily narrowed in a dedicated skepticism. Below the eyes, her sharpened chin and nose seemed always to be accusing me of being less fervid than I ought.

At quick glance, Peggy had aged not a whit from the moment she first entered my office eight years before, but closer inspection revealed minor flaws. Her hair seemed limp and neglected, her cheeks two shades too pale, her eyes in danger of drowning in the big black pools that spread beneath them. Her shoulders sagged; her hands lay lax; a stocking puckered at the knee. Her entire aspect was that of an extremely efficient appliance that had recently been unplugged.

The contrast from a few short weeks before was so disturbing I asked a question. "Is anything wrong?"

I asked it casually, gently, my eyes back on my mail, all to belie my concern. But as usual I didn't evade her defenses.

She opened one eye. "What?"

"I asked if anything was wrong."

"What makes you think anything's wrong?"

"You do."

She closed the eye. Her smile was arid and forbidding, and succeeded a sigh. "The perfume doesn't give you a license to be candid, Mr. John Marshall Tanner." Her words were as stiff as steel.

"You're exhausted," I persisted. "You've been on edge

for over a month. Usually you handle my more boorish outbursts without a ripple, but lately you've been giving me exactly what I deserve. Which is your right, but not your style."

"So?" Anger barbed the word. "Maybe I've decided to become more assertive. They give classes in it, you know. Someone's decided the world *aches* for more assertive women."

I ignored the snap. "Maybe I can help with whatever it is. I'd like to, if you think I could."

She shook her head, her eyes still closed, as though that made me insignificant. "It's nothing. I've gotten myself into a situation, is all. Now I've got to get myself out."

"That's the kind of thing I do for a living, you know."

She hesitated, then shook her head. "This isn't that big a deal, Marsh. Really. I'll be fine."

"Great. When you are I hope you'll let me know."

I was insulted and angry and she knew it from my tone. We slid into a huffy silence. Peggy seemed even more deflated than before, more churlish and reluctant. I wanted to help, but I knew her well enough to know she couldn't be pushed effectively. Every time I'd tried it in the past I'd only solidified her obstinance to the approximate hardness of a diamond.

I guessed the problem was a man—she'd gone through several of them in the years she'd worked for me, not surprising in a city where the vast majority of men are either gay or married or revoltingly narcissistic, and not surprising in a woman who'd told me several times that her one failed marriage was more than enough, that since she was self-sufficient financially and had already birthed a child and was past the age of safely bearing more, there seemed little reason to revisit the altar or even the justice of the peace and even less reason not to sample a wide variety of what came in the box marked MALE. But whatever the problem, there didn't seem to be a place in it for me. Not yet. So I asked if there had been any calls while I was out.

14

She shook her head, but for some reason my question prompted one of her own. "Tell me something, Marsh."

"What?"

"When you go to all the trouble to change your telephone number, how does someone learn the new one so goddamned fast?"

I spent the rest of the day fretting over Peggy. The new telephone number she'd given me a few weeks earlier seemed suddenly an ominous incident, but she dodged all my efforts to discover why she'd changed her number and who had upset her by managing to learn the new one. She had, in fact, voided my every attempt at conversation of any sort until it was time for her to leave for home. As we bid each other a carefully perfunctory good-bye her face seemed frozen in a timorous mask, as though where she was going was even worse than where she'd been, which was with me and my awkward, aimless questioning.

I was so concerned about her I considered tailing her after she left the office, in a blind grasp at some hint of what was gnawing at her. But Peggy usually stopped for a drink somewhere, then took the bus home. Even in the evening crunch there was no way I could keep her in sight without being spotted and running the risk that she would seal off the infected portion of her life forever.

Soon after Peggy left I went home myself, fixed an early dinner of tomato soup and day-old pizza, and stewed some more about my secretary. It wasn't so much that I felt she was a candidate for a serious predicament as it was my certainty that if one in fact confronted her she would wait too long before asking for help. Like many virtues, doggedness has a second side, and Peggy's gritty self-reliance could make Pete Rose look like a shirker. During the course of the evening I debated and discarded a host of approaches to the problem, from confrontation to secret surveillance, and in the process I realized I still didn't know all that much about the woman who had brightened my life more than anyone in the past eight years.

She had grown up back east—New Hampshire, I thought—and had gone to Bennington for a while before dropping out to marry a "swashbuckler," as she called him, a structural engineer who had impregnated her in their third year of marriage and abandoned her the next. Her family was so upset when she left college that they cut her off without a cent, and after the divorce Peggy had gone to work as a self-taught secretary to support herself and her baby daughter, Allison. By the time she came to work for me, Peggy's mother had died and her father had been put in a rest home with Alzheimer's and Allison was in the corps de ballet in some avant-garde dance company in the SoHo section of New York. As far as I knew, Peggy had never heard from the swashbuckler again.

Matters had stood that way until a little less than a year ago, when her father had died and left her some insurance money, which in turn had financed her daughter's move from New York to San Francisco. Allison had brought along a rather disreputable companion, an actor who was equally into drugs and sponging off his mate, and for that reason or some other a degree of tension had developed between Peggy and her daughter, a tension whose precise source was still a mystery to me, and possibly to Peggy as well.

The rest of my knowledge was made up of those quirky odds and ends that define us to the portion of the world that's interested. Peggy had a cat she loved and a neighbor she was friends with. She worshipped Doris Lessing and Nadine Gordimer, loved Richard Strauss and Gustav Mahler, collected copies of Matisse and Mary Cassatt. Her favorite color was red; her favorite flower the California poppy; her favorite place in the city the Palace of the Legion of Honor. She appreciated food and wine to the extent that a couple of birthday dinners she'd fixed for me at her apartment ranked among my all-time favorite meals. She liked to visit art museums in her spare time, though she bemoaned the great gulf between San Francisco's public art and that available in New York and LA. She was a perfectionist about her work and about most other areas of her life as well, with the apparent result that sooner or later her boyfriends all fell short of her ideals and more than one of her female friends had ended up committing what Peggy had viewed as private treason.

Peggy demanded much of the world and more of herself, and I felt fortunate to have held on to her as long as I had. I think I had succeeded for eight years because my life was so spare and simple I was relieved of making the imperfectible choices that more ambitious men are faced with, and because I could make her laugh. Still, I was afraid that sooner or later I would make what in Peggy's eyes was a mistake so basic and unforgivable that she would vanish from my life as suddenly as she had appeared, leaving me as desolate as a jilted spouse. In the meantime, though, I intended to continue to enjoy what amounted to a first for me—an important relationship with a woman that floated on friendship rather than on lust.

I fretted in forms that progressed from the abstract to the concrete until ten o'clock that evening, when my imagination was raging so ungovernably I decided to give Peggy a call, to make sure she was okay. I got a busy signal that relieved me, though not entirely. I tried again ten minutes later. Still busy. Twenty minutes after that her phone was busy yet again, and by then I was not relieved at all.

I put on my shoes and tucked in my shirt and got ready to drive to Peggy's. There were plenty of innocuous reasons for the phone being tied up for so long, of course, but there were some fearsome ones as well, and it was those that were shoving me toward the flat expanse of the Marina District, where Peggy rented an apartment.

When my hand was on the door knob my phone rang. After a quick debate I retreated to answer it.

"Marsh? Hi. It's Peggy."

I kicked off my shoes and sagged back onto the couch. "How are you?"

My voice must have grown an irritated burr, because Peggy hesitated before she answered. "I'm fine. Why?"

"I've been trying to call you. The line was always busy. I was starting to get worried."

"About what?"

"I don't know. About whatever's been bothering you lately, I guess."

"*Nothing's* bothering me, Marsh. Stop playing mother hen."

"I'm not playing." The words were truthful, but more dramatic than I intended.

Peggy started to say something, stopped, then began again in a bantering lilt that was supposed to deflect my concern. "The reason I called was, you remember I said I'd come in tomorrow first thing to make up for falling asleep on the job? Well, I just remembered I can't make it in the morning. But I'll be in after lunch, and Wednesday I'll be in all day. Promise. So relax; you'll get your money's worth."

"I'd get my money's worth if you only came in three hours a month."

"Why, I think that's almost a compliment, Marsh Tanner. You'd better be careful or they'll throw you out of the Grand Order of Confirmed Misogynists."

She was urging me to collaborate in the jest but I wasn't quite ready to. "Who were you talking to?" I asked, as close to a demand as I'd ever made of her.

"When?"

"Just now. On the phone."

"Kind of nosy, aren't you?"

"Who?" I repeated.

She paused again. "A friend."

"Anyone I know?"

"No."

"Anyone I'd *want* to know?"

This time I was the one grasping at a laugh, but now it was Peggy who demurred. "No," she snapped.

I kept trying, this time in Peggy's preferred pretext. "Speaking of friends, how come you never fix me up with one of them?"

Peggy's laugh was leaden, still hinting of bitter memory. "I'm not sure she'd appreciate the subtleties of your life-style."

"What is my lifestyle, Miss Expert?"

"Oh, if I had to label it I suppose I'd call it a couple of degrees short of laid back."

"Laid out, you mean."

"You said it, I didn't."

"But I can change. I'll buy a BMW. I'll take up wind-surfing. I'll eat raw fish and drink raw milk and wear raw silk."

Peggy was giggling like her self of six months ago. "No, Marsh. I won't give you a chance. If you went Yuppie I couldn't keep your precious personality a treasure just for me."

"Why does the word *antique* come to mind when you say that?"

We exchanged a set of matching chuckles, and I forgot the hot round slug of worry that had burned in my gut a few short minutes before, but only momentarily. "So you won't tell me who you were talking to."

"No."

"Why not?"

"Because it's private. Signing my paychecks doesn't give you the right to know *all* my little secrets. You already know too many of them as it is."

I started to say good-bye, then didn't. Several years ago, a man had been trying to kill me because he thought I'd known some things I hadn't, and at one point it occurred to me that he might decide to lie in wait for me in my office, with Peggy under a gun, to take me out the minute I walked in the door. So Peggy and I developed a code, to use whenever I called in, that would let me know if there was any danger lurking behind the door marked TANNER INVESTIGATIONS.

With that in mind, instead of saying good-bye I said, "Okay, Peggy. I'll take your word for it that nothing's wrong. There's just one last thing."

"What?"

"Did you remember to water the plants today?"

Peggy paused long enough to dredge the code words into her consciousness. "Yes, I did remember, and yes, there really isn't anyone here, code or no code. Now do you believe me?"

"I guess I have to."

"You've been reading too many mystery books."

"Mystery books aren't half as scary as the morning paper, Peggy. And if there's anything at all to ESP, then there's something wrong over there no matter what you say. I still hope you'll tell me what it is."

Peggy sighed. "Will you go to bed or do I have to start humming Brahms' Lullaby?" She hesitated, then spoke in the mildly mocking tone I knew so well. "Or maybe there's someone over there with you. Have *you* watered the plants today, Mr. Tanner?"

"Hell, if I had someone here with me I'd have left you to your troubles no matter *what* they were."

Mercifully, Peggy chose not to discuss my love life. "Don't forget the Grantland deposition tomorrow afternoon."

"Transamerica Building at two."

"Right. Marsh?"

"What?"

"I'm not real big on gratitude, you know? I mean, anything I get in life I figure I pretty much deserve and then some. But thanks for checking on me."

"Sure."

"And thanks for caring. Lately I've found it's real easy to convince myself that no one does."

4

The phone call calmed my fears, but my sanguinity only endured till three A.M., when I woke up in a cold room with a hot sweat that emanated from my certainty that Peggy Nettleton was in serious and mounting jeopardy no matter how firm or funny her denials. I got up, fixed myself a drink, and lay awake the rest of the night formulating a plan, which at the ungainly hour of seven o'clock had me and my Buick parked a block down the street from the door to Peggy's apartment building. I wasn't fully certain why I was there, I was just certain that I had to do something to deflate my apprehensions, for my own peace of mind if not for Peggy's.

She didn't emerge till ten. I spent the interim avoiding meter maids and reading Louis Auchincloss and watching drivers cruise the street in a desperate search for a place to park. One guy in a gray Ford went by five times before he found one. Each time he passed, his face was a darker shade of crimson, as though he had a divine right to my slot.

Between the book and the traffic I wondered why I had become so alarmed from so little stimulus. The only thing I knew for certain was that Peggy looked tired and seemed distracted. Common enough symptoms, though not common to her. Still, the scope of my concern was surprising, so much so that I began to wonder if it was a window to a deep desire that I had denied for far too long. Perhaps Peggy had become more than a friend to me; perhaps I had fallen in love.

Not impossible, since I'm often in love long before I know it. And not an unpleasant prospect, since being in love is usually better than being out of it, even though at my age love doesn't sustain itself but needs a lot of work, a labor that's increasingly easy to shy away from. And not unintriguing, since if I confessed my sentiments to Peggy I could see if they were shared.

But if they were shared, what? Dating. And we who had communicated with an easy rapport over eight years of professional partnership would immediately become tongue-tied. After dating—sex. Not that I didn't want it. Not that I hadn't dreamed of it. Just that sex places a relationship under a moral microscope, and when viewed through such a lens such matters can loom grotesque and unappealing. And after sex . . . ? Decisions. Commitments. Responsibilities. Change.

Easy to shy away from.

By the time the garage door opened and Peggy and her Subaru emerged, I was as tired and confused as Peggy seemed to be. Still, I managed to remember why I was on Fillmore Street instead of Jackson Square in time to start my car and tag along as she drove off.

She turned left on Lombard, took a right on Van Ness and headed downtown, then surprised me by passing up the left on Broadway and continuing on Van Ness until she reached the Civic Center. When she joined the line of cars that was descending to the underground garage, I suspected she was on a municipal errand of some sort, mundane and unrevealing. I almost broke off my pursuit and headed for the office, but when serendipity presented me with a parking place in front of the city library I hurried to occupy it, then waited for Peggy to emerge from her subterranean shelter.

It took eight minutes. She came out of the pedestrian entrance at a trot, dressed in a tweed skirt and camel jacket, her purse slung over her shoulder and clutched to her side as though it was full of secrets.

She turned up Larkin Street immediately, presumably

23

heading for the Federal Building. A thousand things, benign and private, could have prompted the journey, and that realization made me lag behind. Luckily, as it turned out, because Peggy looked back several times, as though she suspected someone was in her wake.

When she didn't turn toward the Federal Building, but crossed Turk and continued up Larkin, I quickened my pace. This time my luck ran out, because in the time it took me to look both ways before I crossed the street, Peggy managed to disappear.

I trotted to the last place I'd seen her, but encountered only strangers' faces, most of them Asian. I looked up and down the block, at the Hotel Yogi and the Phnom Penh Café and the other nondescript businesses and apartments far removed from the Manhattanized downtown, and gradually realized that the building at my back was one I'd visited many times over the past ten years, and hoped to visit many more.

I peered through the barred glass door. Peggy wasn't in the vestibule, but the elevator indicator was on the rise. When it stopped at the second floor I knew where Peggy had gone. What I didn't know was why.

I retreated to the Federal Building and sat next to the defunct fountain in position to see Peggy when she returned to reclaim her car. While I waited, I considered what her visit to the second floor of the Larkin Street building might mean, and decided that at the very least it meant I'd been right to worry through the night about what was haunting her.

Thirty minutes later, Peggy retraced her steps, hurrying past the Federal Building without looking my way, her expression intent, determined, wary. I waited until she was out of sight, then walked back up Larkin to the building she had vacated. I didn't wait for the elevator, but took the stairs two at a time, the way I always did, and came to a stop when I was face to face with the door to apartment 10, the one with the door knocker fashioned from a silver spur.

I knocked twice. "Did you forget your—"

My presence cleaved her question. She froze for a moment, mouth agape, then cackled twice and grinned her Class A grin, the one that came with a healthy dash of sass. "Marsh Tanner. What the . . . How the hell *are* you, sugar bear?"

"Hello, Ruthie. Long time, no see."

"A coon's age and then some, you mangy coyote."

"So how are you, Ruthie?"

"Well, I still got my teeth and my hair, and my plumbing works if I give it some lubricant from time to time, so I guess I can't complain. Not that *you're* interested, you illegitimate son of a snake. I don't suppose you care to tell me why you haven't been by to see me since poor Ralphie had his stroke."

Ralphie was Ruthie's parakeet. The night he died, Ruthie had called me almost as deep in tears as she'd been the day they told her Harry, her husband, had been murdered in a valley town named Oxtail and I'd spent several hours comforting her as best I could, until she was in shape to comfort me.

Harry Spring had been a friend and mentor, a former sheriff's deputy who became the best private investigator in the city and who had told me what I needed to know to get me through my first year in the trade. After that I'd begun to figure most things out for myself, but it had hit me hard when Harry died, and a little harder after I found out who had killed him. But that had all washed out years ago. Ruthie had taken over Harry's business, specializing in domestic wrangles of one kind or another, the kind of wrangles I tried to avoid by referring such stuff Ruthie's way as often as I could. But Ruthie took on other causes as well, and I wondered if one of them might be whatever it was that was plaguing Peggy.

Ruthie was a friend, and I owed her for nurturing me through a lot of lonely nights in ways both bawdy and maternal, so I always felt guilty when I saw her and was reminded of how long it had been since I'd given her a call.

And in a few minutes I was going to feel even more unworthy, because I was going to try to persuade her to do something she wouldn't want to do.

"Well. I'm waiting for your excuse," Ruthie declared, hands on denim hips, feet in pointed boots, her deep-dish smile displayed above a fringed shirt held together with snaps instead of buttons and dripping fringe from the wrists and pockets.

"I've been sick," I said. "Old Hawaiian disease."

Ruthie barked a laugh. "Lackanookie, my wrinkled ass. I told you anytime you want your ashes hauled I can fix you up with the sweetest thing you've ever laid your tongue on, and she won't charge you the yard-and-a-half she gets from her regular admirers, either."

"I don't know, Ruthie. Store-bought sex is more risky than Russian roulette in this town."

Ruthie's smile slipped away as though it had been stolen. "AIDS. Yeah. Friend of mine just died of it. I'd rather be chewed on by a shark than go that way, I really would. Some say it's the wrath of God." Ruthie closed her eyes. "Well, if the good Lord cooked this one up then He's a flaming sadist. I used to smuggle him in some heroin at the end. To ease the pain a little. The boys at the jail always got a little spare sitting around, stuff that don't quite make it to the evidence locker."

Ruthie spit out a mordant laugh, then opened her eyes. She had been a deputy, too, once upon a time, and she still had scads of friends on the force who would swim to Alcatraz if she asked them to, and I believed every word she said about the heroin. Ruthie had been a nurse in Korea before she joined the sheriff, and she'd decided at some point that there was no reason in the world not to make dying as easy as possible for those with a one-way ticket. Ruthie Spring was as moral an individual as I knew, an actor upon belief rather than merely a sloganeer, but her code was all her own.

"Cassie's clean, Marsh," she was saying. "She's clean

and she's careful and she sees a doctor once a month. Want me to give her a buzz?"

I shook my head. "Some other time, Ruthie. But how about you? You getting your fur stroked enough these days?"

Ruthie's eyes softened and her voice followed suit. "That's a long story, sugar bear. Why don't you come in and let me bore you with it?"

She led me into the apartment. The front room was still converted to an office, the way it had been when Harry was alive, the desk and file cabinets and bookshelves cluttered with memorabilia from Ruthie's rather outsized life, with Harry and before and after as well. A quick glance told me the place was much the same except for the empty cage that had housed the dearly departed Ralph and an 8 x 10 glossy in a silver frame that pictured Ruthie arm-in-arm with the lady mayor, smack in the middle of Haight Street.

Across from me, Ruthie stood tapping the toe of her boot, waiting for my attention to return. "How about a drink? Cut the dust a little."

"Not before noon, Ruthie."

"It's noon in Dallas, sugar bear."

I shook my head.

"Since when?"

"Since I learned what a prostate is."

Ruthie chuckled. "Hell, Marsh, it's never too early for a snort. The other morning I was out of milk so I tried Hamm's on my corn flakes. Not half bad, till I screwed up and added sugar. How about coffee?"

"Sure, if it's ready."

"Why, them little crystals are just chomping at the bit to hop out of the jar and into your cup, doll. And I got one of them little dealies that boils water quicker than you can take a piss."

I kept myself from shuddering.

"Be back in two shakes of your pecker."

Ruthie went off to the kitchen and I leaned back in my

chair and enjoyed being nestled in Ruthie's ample bosom once again, amid the memories and the mementoes and the tangible ether of energy and accomplishment that permeated the place. I always felt good around Ruthie, because Ruthie herself was good and was salty enough to tolerate nothing less than a peer in her ambit.

"So what's this about your love life?" I called out to her. "Sounds like you've got something torrid going."

"I got me a boyfriend, if you can believe it," she yelled back. "Put my brand on the critter about six weeks ago."

"So tell me about him."

Ruthie waited till the coffee was ready before she answered. After she returned to the front room and handed me my cup she took a seat across from mine. "Well, the first thing you got to know is, he's pint-sized. Everything about him's tiny but his wallet and his dick. They say money can't buy happiness, Marsh, but I'm here to tell you that money and a big twanger can damned sure get a woman within roping distance of it."

As usual, Ruthie's words were as rough as a cob, but her eyes stayed as soft as her heart. She patted the frizz in her brassy blond head, took a gulp of coffee, and crossed her legs, giving me a good look at a boot made from the fresh-plucked flesh of an ostrich.

Ruthie hadn't been in Texas for years—she said it was because she didn't like the way the oil people had pushed the cattle people aside and had taken over everything from politics to football—but she was stamped to her soul with that heritage and she'd decided long ago not to fight it but to let it rip. I'd seen a few of San Francisco's pseudosophisticates look down their noses at her over the years, after one or another of her earthy outbursts, but no one who knew her well looked anywhere but up. "It's the real thing, huh?" I said.

"It's real enough to tingle my titties, Marsh, and that's as real as it gets for a woman who's left menopause about twelve miles down the road."

"I'm happy for you, Ruthie."

"Hell, I'm happy for me too. And old Caldwell—Caldwell Rakes, he's my fella—he's just as tickled as a rat in a dumpster. Can't get enough of me, he says. What I don't tell him is he gets all of me I can bear to give."

Ruthie's eyes flicked to the wall, where a framed photograph of Harry—smiling, strutting, displaying a huge coho he'd landed out of a river up in Oregon—hung where she could see it anytime she wanted or needed to. Caldwell Rakes might have a lot of her, but there was still a nugget deep inside that would remain forever Harry's.

"You're out and about at an odd hour, aren't you, Marsh?" Ruthie's hearty friendliness had evaporated, leaving a steel-eyed stare in its stead. "Been down in federal court?"

"I'm here on business, Ruthie."

"Yeah? Whose business?"

"Yours. And mine."

"That so?" Ruthie recrossed her legs and tugged on a wisp of hair that dangled beside an ear that sported an earring shaped like a horseshoe. "You referring something my way?"

I shook my head. "It's about one of your clients."

"Who?"

"Peggy."

Ruthie pursed her lips but didn't say anything.

"Peggy Nettleton. My secretary. She just left here. I think she hired you. I want to know why."

Ruthie looked as though I'd answered a question instead of asked one. "You follow her here, Marsh?"

I nodded.

"She thought someone was. I imagine it'll ease her mind when I tell her it was you. *If* I tell her."

"I'd appreciate it if you wouldn't."

"I imagine you would."

Ruthie stood up, took her cup and mine into the kitchen, and came back with refills. After I thanked her she returned to the kitchen again. This time she came back empty-handed. "Thought I had some biscuits but I don't," she said. She was stalling for time and I knew why.

Ruthie sat down in the chair again and looked back at the picture of her husband and his fish. "I learned most of what I know from Harry, Marsh. About business; about more important things than business."

"Me too."

"When he met me I was a hotheaded ex–barrel racer who'd seen more than anyone should have in Korea and had become semialcoholic and semipromiscuous as a result. He settled me down and straightened me out and he did it without raising his voice or his fist either one. I did what he wanted because he was the first real man I'd ever run across, the first who had thought enough about life to decide what was important and what wasn't, to use his brain more often than his dong. When he died I spent a long time wishing I'd died too; wishing I'd been the one down there in that ditch with a bullet through my brain, instead of him. I went back to my old ways there for a while, Marsh. I don't know if you knew that."

I shook my head.

Ruthie looked away from the picture and at me. "I tried to keep it from you because I love you, Marsh Tanner. You're the son Harry and I never had. Oh, I know you don't want to hear that sentimental swill, but it's true all the same and you damned well know it. Hell, when Harry was alive I spent more time asking him about you than about anything else in life, including his frigging fishing trips. God, I hate the taste of fish. And the poor dumb bastard never knew it."

I didn't say anything because I couldn't. Ruthie swiped at eyes that had somehow become soggy, then grinned. "Sorry if I embarrassed you, sugar bear, but hell. You embarrass too damned easy. Always have. Well, shit." She wiped her eyes again. "I'm leaking worse than a suckling sow. What I'm trying to say is, Marsh, I'd tell you almost anything in the world you want to know. My age. My bra size. How much estrogen I gobble of a morning. But you know that with that goddamned Harry hanging on the wall over there, looking at me with that shit-eating grin of his, well you know I can't tell you one single thing about why your little Peggy came by to see me this morning."

"But this is different," I protested. "She's my secretary. Hell, she may be my best friend. I—"

"You *know* what I got to do, Marsh; now don't pretend you don't. You *know* that I got to keep my mouth as zippered as a prelate's pecker or else those years with Harry don't mean owl manure and I got to turn in my license and spend the rest of my days letting Caldwell slobber all over my body at the noon hour in between the times I go out and spend money on things I don't need just to take up the slack till something comes along and kills me."

"Is she in danger? Just tell me that."

Ruthie just sat there, purposely bereft of any emotion beyond a vague, undifferentiated sorrow, her fingernails pressing tiny, curving cuts in the dead flesh of her high brown boots.

5

I drifted through the deposition in the Grantland case without doing me or my client any harm. Grantland's lawyer was a corporate type, not a litigator, and his idea of subtlety was the occasional insertion of a double negative into his questions. My client's counsel objected to the form of the inquiry so frequently I began to think the deposition was going to stretch into two days even though no one in the room wanted it to. But the corporate type finally wrapped it up at three-thirty without getting to the most important point, which was that a portion of the information I'd acquired in my investigation had been obtained through the use of electronic eavesdropping equipment in a manner at least arguably proscribed by Sections 631 and 632 of the California Penal Code. Which meant that the evidence wasn't admissible in any judicial proceeding, and that I was subject to a $2,500 fine and imprisonment for up to a year in the county jail if they could prove the violation. I'd been prepared to take the Fifth Amendment if the issue came up, but I was saved by an attorney's incompetence, and not for the first time. Now I had to hope that my client's lawyer could get the case settled so I wouldn't have to go through the whole thing again at trial.

When I got back to the office Peggy was there, and we exchanged a few careful comments about the telephone call of the night before. But she clearly didn't want to go into it, and was embarrassed by whatever it was she thought I'd concluded about her situation. Neither of us mentioned Ruthie Spring, so I assumed Ruthie had honored my request not to mention my intrusion of the morning. We dropped the subject, whatever the subject was, skipped through the day with as little contact with each other as possible, and went our separate ways as soon as the clock struck five.

My way took me out to dinner with a woman I'd dated on and off for the past six months, a widow whose husband had left her wealthy, childless, and determined to the point of frenzy to squeeze more out of life than a prim and proper marriage had heretofore provided. She had a passion for nightlife that offered a dab of danger along with the rest of the bill of fare. One night we'd collected a set of hostile stares at a series of black nightclubs in the Fillmore District, and this evening we provoked much the same reaction at a series of gay hangouts along Folsom Street.

When we got back to her place on Pacific Avenue, she invited me up for a nightcap. Normally that meant that before the evening had ended she would drag me through yet another testing ground of sorts, trying to make me a prototype when I was only a Model T. Janice was convinced that every man knew more than she did about sex, and could teach her volumes on the subject. Unfortunately, I'd long since run through my tiny bag of tricks. When I declined her invitation she pouted and protested, but I left anyway, after removing her hand from inside my shirt.

When I stopped for a drink at my normal North Beach haunt, I was feeling so chipper and unburdened I knew it was time Janice and I parted company, amicably but permanently. From the look on her face when I'd left her, she'd reached the same conclusion.

Rufus, the bartender, greeted me with a grunt. "You get lucky in the lottery or something, Tanner?"

"Why do you ask?"

"You're smiling. Last time you smiled like that you'd just copped a big fee for busting up an insurance scam."

I shook my head. "The best things in life are free, Rufus."

"Bullshit. The best things in life are for sale at Gump's and Neiman's. You and me, we put up with the crap from K Mart. The usual?"

"Sure."

Rufus gave me a double Scotch and I swiveled on my stool and surveyed my surroundings. Solitary people, mostly, single, alone but not lonely, not wealthy or attractive or desperate enough to compete in the city's more illustrious body bars, not so dissatisfied with their lot or their lives that they aspired to anything beyond the fuzzy, funny glow that the right amount of liquor provided them four nights a week. I was a member of the group myself, and had been for years. I counted several of the patrons as friends even though I'd never seen them outside the confines of the bar.

Rufus drifted back to my station. "I just remembered why you're smiling."

"Why is that?"

"Some lady called here for you a while back."

"Who?"

I expected him to name my date. "Patty, I think. No. Peggy. That was it."

"What did she say?"

"She said she needed you to come over to her place."

Rufus rolled his eyes in an extravagant leer, but my grip on the highball glass tightened. "She said it just that way? That she *needed* me?"

"Her words exactly. Got her begging for it, right? No wonder you been grinning like you just hit the Pick Six."

I pushed a bill at Rufus and slid off my stool and ignored his lusty taunts as I hurried toward the door. Two minutes later I was in my car, and five minutes after that I was winding my way out to the Marina District once again, breaking speed limits along the way. If Peggy needed me, it wasn't for anything resembling romance.

Parking was the usual maddening struggle, but I finally

34

outdueled a Porsche for a slot on Fillmore a couple of blocks south of my destination. The guy in the Porsche made an obscene gesture. By the time I got to Peggy's building I was running as fast as I could run.

I buzzed her buzzer, panting, looking and listening for signs of violence even though the front stoop was not the likely place for such signs to be. My mouth was dry, my chest tight from exertion and concern. After a lengthy silence, Peggy's voice crackled in the intercom. When I told her who it was she clicked me inside without another word.

Peggy's apartment was on the third floor. Because the elevator had been languid and infirm for years, she always used the stairs. I followed suit, and was breathing hard again by the time I reached the second flight.

The stairwell was dark, the nearest light globe a burned-out shell, the shaft as dark and musty as a gym shoe. When I stopped for another lungful of stolid air I heard scraping sounds from below, the vestibule or the adjacent garage. I waited till they stopped. Because they seemed tame enough to leave behind, I started up the final flight.

Halfway up, my foot kicked something lying on the step and sent it clattering to the landing below. My next step squashed something soft that gave way with a pop. I stopped and knelt to one knee and discovered a score of objects that lay scattered in my path like a volcanic spray of stones.

Upon closer inspection, the dark lumps turned out to be cans and jars and bottles and bags, foodstuffs littering the stairway as though someone had dropped their groceries or been the victim of a flimsy bag. The soft mound I'd stepped on was a sack of flour. My shoe was flocked from the powdery explosion and so were two stair treads and a banister support.

I looked for a moment longer, and spotted a woman's shoe and a paper sack, torn and emptied of its booty. I tried to remember whether the shoe was one I'd previously seen on Peggy. When I couldn't I tiptoed through the litter and made my way to apartment 32.

The door was ajar and I went inside. The living room was as dark as the stairwell, the only light a yellow stain that spread from the streetlamp beyond the windows. A quick glance revealed no sign of a disturbance: the apartment seemed as precise and handsome as its tenant. But Peggy was nowhere in sight. I turned toward the bedroom and had taken two steps when I heard a sound that made me stop and look back toward the windows once again.

Peggy was in the living room after all, stretched out on her couch in much the same position I'd seen her in at my office the day before. A dark shadow draped her torso in a sinister implication, and a shadow draped my heart as well.

"Marsh?" The word was blunted to a groan by her forearm.

I knelt beside her. "What is it, Peggy? What happened?"

She said something slurred and indistinct. I told her I couldn't hear her and she lifted the arm that lay across her nose and mouth. Because I was looking for it I immediately saw the damage she'd been trying to disguise.

Her cheek and lip were puffed and bruised, the purpled growths an outrageous graffito on that sharply sculpted face. Her forearm was scraped raw; a flat patch of blood had streaked her face as she hid it with her arm. Her blouse was ripped at the shoulder, revealing the parabolic stripe of a bra strap; her skirt was soiled and wrinkled. Her breath crackled as though her lungs were crumpled cellophane.

I swore from behind a jaw that had clenched to the point of pain, then blurted a question formed from my first fear. "Were you raped?"

When she didn't respond I was certain I was right. I made a fist and slammed my thigh. Breath sizzled through my teeth.

36

But Peggy shook her head. "He just pushed me down," she murmured.

"That's all? He just pushed you?"

She nodded.

"Where?"

"The stairs."

"How long ago?"

"An hour, maybe. It took me a while to crawl up here. I might have passed out for a minute; I'm not sure. It hurt pretty bad."

"Where?"

"My ankle mostly. And ribs."

I looked at her ankle but couldn't see it. When I reached for the pillow that was covering it I discovered the pillow was a cat. Her name was Marilyn. I'd met her before. We didn't like each other.

I brushed Marilyn and her protests off the ankle and felt its contours. It was fat and warm, like Marilyn. When I pressed just slightly, Peggy groaned. When I touched her ribs she did the same.

"I didn't think he was that way" was what I thought she said as my fingers roamed her foot.

My fingers stopped. "So you know who it was," I said with quick excitement. *"You know who did it."*

She shook her head.

"But you just said—"

"I know who, sort of, but I don't know his name. I—" She gasped and flinched and then fell silent.

"Where does it hurt?"

"My ankle. It's starting to throb." She laughed tightly. "You aren't trying to fix it with a hammer, are you?"

She'd made a joke through her pain, referring to the time I'd tried to change the toilet seat in my apartment by knocking off the rusted fastening bolts with a hammer. In the process I'd shattered the entire porcelain bowl, loosing a flood that damaged a carpet and a piano in the apartment below. The landlord was not nearly as amused as Peggy was when I told her about it.

"I'll call a doctor," I said. "But I don't understand about the guy. Who was it? Someone in the building?"

I wasn't sure she heard me. She began to talk in throaty, puzzled tones, as though she was the victim of a curse and not a felon. "I was *so sure* he wasn't violent. That's the thing that upsets me. I thought I could *handle* it, you know, but he didn't even listen. Or give me a chance to explain. He just swore at me and said what he says and pushed me down the stairs. I don't know how I could have been so *wrong* about him."

"About who?"

"The guy on the phone."

"*What* guy on the phone?"

"The one who's been calling me. I thought he was just a phone freak. Some poor little pervert who got off on talking dirty to women. A little smarter than most, maybe; a little more pathetic, maybe. But essentially harmless. I guess he's more than that, though, isn't he? He tried to kill me, Marsh, and all this time I thought I'd been doing exactly what he wanted me to do."

6

I had a thousand questions, but there were things to do before I asked them. "I'm going to call a doctor," I said, and started to stand up. "Then I'm going to call the police."

Peggy put out a hand to stop me, wincing in the process. "No, Marsh. Please. I'll be all right. I just need some rest."

"Your ankle isn't all right. It's the size of a grapefruit."

"It's just a sprain. I'll put some ice on it. It'll be fine."

"You might have internal injuries, Peggy. From the way you move I'd say you cracked a rib. At a minimum."

Her smile was forced. "If anything cracked it was the stairway. I really came down hard. Right on my . . . What's the word for tailbone?"

"Coccyx. And the stairway's fine. I just came from there."

She inhaled deeply, grimaced, then looked at me. "You could do one thing for me if you would."

"What's that?"

"Pick up the groceries I spilled. There's a straw basket in the kitchen, on top of the refrigerator. Maybe you could fit them all in there."

"Okay."

"I hate to ask, but I'm afraid someone might fall over them. Are you sure you don't mind?"

I patted her shoulder. "I'll pick up everything but the flour."

"Why not the flour?" Her puzzled glance ultimately took in my shoe. "What on earth happened?"

"I stepped on the bag. It went up like a land mine. I deserve a Purple Heart."

"Is your shoe ruined?"

"Naw. But I have an uncontrollable urge to start singing *April Love*. White bucks? Pat Boone? Get it?"

Peggy giggled, but not comfortably. I told her I'd be back in a minute, then found the basket and returned to the stairway and policed the area.

The bag of flour and a jar of Smucker's jam were the only casualties of the fall, and I left them for the janitor. The rest of it I put in the basket and took back to the kitchen, along with Peggy's shoe. Then I grabbed a pencil and a sheet of paper from the table by the telephone and took the elevator to the lobby and taped a warning sign on the stairway door.

Peggy didn't stir or speak as I reentered the apartment so I assumed she had fallen asleep. I tiptoed into the living room and eased into the chair opposite the couch.

My eyes adjusted to the darkened room, which was attractive and comfortable but not quite cozy. The couch and chairs were contemporary, upholstered in plaid and framed in oak. The carpet was a beige tweed. The wallpaper bore abstract swirls and slashes in brown and gold and white. The paintings and photographs—chiefly impressionist reproductions except for a giant daffodil painted by her daughter in what Peggy called her "Georgia O'Keeffe phase"—were grouped tangentially in a square in the center of one wall. The effect was subtly dramatic, but in contrast to Ruthie's place there were no cute mementoes, no family heirlooms, no vacation snapshots, and for the first time I wondered if there was something in her past that Peggy was determined to conceal.

As I was congratulating myself for not disturbing her, Peggy muttered, "I'm awake. You can turn a light on if you want."

"That's okay. This is fine. How are you feeling?"

"Better. At least I'm not nauseous anymore."

"Did you bump your head when you fell?"

"I think so."

"Nausea sometimes indicates a concussion."

"Not with me it doesn't. I get nauseous whenever I'm upside down."

"How's the ankle?"

"It still hurts a little."

Which meant it hurt a lot. "Can you move it?"

"A little."

"I'll get some ice."

I went back to the kitchen and took a tray of ice cubes out of the freezing compartment, emptied it onto a dish towel, and gathered the corners of the towel and wrapped them with a twist tie I took off the wrapper to a loaf of bread. Then I put the whole thing in a plastic freezer bag and took it into the living room and draped it over Peggy's ankle, which seemed swollen even more than when I'd first seen it, and was turning the color of plums.

Peggy thanked me. I asked if she needed anything else. She shook her head. I asked if she felt like talking about it yet. She shook her head again. I asked if she wanted me to call a doctor or take her to the hospital. This time she smiled wearily before telling me no. I told her to relax and try to sleep, then returned to my chair, leaned back, and closed my eyes.

The room was cool, the air a subtle scrim of gold, the sounds from the street outside muffled and occasional. I tilted my watch toward a depleted beam of light. It was almost eleven. I was tired despite the jolt of adrenaline that was a response to my concern for Peggy and my anger at whoever had assaulted her.

I stretched out my legs and slumped in the chair and spent several minutes trying to imagine what might have led to the attack, but finally gave up. Peggy would tell me, and then I would find the guy and have Charley Sleet arrest him and then it would be over. Simple. Nothing to be upset about. Nothing to lose sleep over.

"Marsh? Are you there?"

Her cry was urgent, frightened. I started, shook my

head, looked around the room, then hurried to her side and took her hand. "How are you doing? Is something the matter?"

Peggy rubbed her eyes and shook her head. "Whew. I'm sorry I yelled like that. I didn't know where I was. It felt like I was drowning, or something. I guess I must have slept for a minute. I'm just so *exhausted* all of a sudden."

"You had a shock to the system. It's trying to recover. It'll take some time. You should try to sleep some more."

"You know what I'd like first?"

"What?"

"A cup of hot chocolate."

"Okay. What do I do? I'm not much of a cook as you may remember from that time I tried to bake you a cake and your electric knife wouldn't cut it."

Peggy smiled. "You sure you don't mind?"

"Don't keep asking that. When I mind I'll tell you."

"No, you won't. You'll sulk."

I shrugged. "So what's the recipe for hot chocolate?"

"Well, I've got a mix in the cupboard to the left of the stove. There's coffee and tea in there, too; the hot chocolate's way in the back. Just add two tablespoons, I think it is, to each cup of warm milk. If you want some, then use two cups. Or you can make yourself some coffee. Or a drink. There's some Scotch in that hutch."

I shook my head. "I'm fine. What do I heat the milk in?"

"You can use the little saucepan hanging over the stove."

"Okay. One hot chocolate, coming right up."

Peggy raised her brow. "And a marshmallow on top? They're on the next shelf up."

"How about a dollop of brandy? Might help you sleep."

Peggy shook her head. "Just the marshmallow. Thanks, Marsh. You're too good to me."

I slugged her lightly on the shoulder, then went to the kitchen and found the hot chocolate mix and put four heaping tablespoons into the saucepan, then looked in the refrigerator. "You're out of milk," I yelled.

"I know. There should be some with the groceries you picked up on the stairs."

I looked through the various items I'd retrieved. "No milk here, either."

"Could you have missed it?"

"I don't think so."

"My God. It must have fallen all the way to the ground floor. Francisco will be furious."

I went back to the living room. "Who's Francisco?"

"The building superintendent. He's a fiend for cleanliness, which normally I appreciate, but I'll hear about messing up his precious staircase for a month."

I looked at my watch again. "It's eleven o'clock. Any chance he'll still be up?"

She shook her head. "He's a morning person. Up at four thirty or some ungodly hour. Why?"

"I thought I'd go down and ask him if he saw anyone hanging around the building earlier this evening."

"Oh." Peggy looked away from me, at the sparkle in the ceiling that tried to mimic private stars. "I'd almost forgotten why you were here." She closed her eyes. "I really don't want to go into it right now, Marsh. I'm sorry, but it's too . . . I'm sorry."

Her voice trailed off into an uncharacteristic whine. "One more question," I said. "Then I'll leave you alone."

"What's the question?"

"When you fell you must have made a lot of noise. Your coccyx, plus the soup cans banging down the stairs. Did anyone come see what was going on?"

She didn't hesitate. "Not that I saw. I think that stairwell's pretty soundproofed. I doubt that anyone noticed. Why?"

"That person might have seen the guy who shoved you."

"Oh." She swiveled on the couch and lay back down

43

and covered her face with her arm again, blocking out memory and me.

I surrendered. "Okay, Peggy. I'll talk to the superintendent tomorrow. And then I'll talk to you. In the meantime, why don't you go back to sleep?"

"I'll try. There's no need for you to stay, Marsh. I'm fine now. I just . . . got scared there for a while. I was afraid he might come back. But he won't. Not tonight. He plays bridge on Thursday nights."

I suppressed a surging urge to throw something. "How the hell do you *know* all this?"

"He told me."

"When?"

"On the phone."

"Tonight?"

"No."

"Then when?"

"I don't know. A couple of weeks ago, I guess."

"Damnit, Peggy. I don't get it. What the sam hell's going on?"

Peggy sighed again, this time without wincing. "It's nothing. I'll tell you all about it tomorrow. It's not very . . . I just want to go to sleep now. Please, Marsh?"

"But you're sure the guy who attacked you was the guy on the phone?"

"Yes."

"Why? What did he say when he shoved you?"

"He said what he always says."

"Which is what?"

" 'Think of me.' That's what he always says when he hangs up. 'Think of me.' And that's what he said tonight."

"Did he say your name?"

"No."

"Was he armed?"

"I don't think so. He just pushed me."

"Did he come down the stairs after you, to see if you were hurt? Or dead?"

She paused. "I don't remember. I guess I passed out."

"What was he wearing?"

"Marsh? Please? I don't—"

"Just a few more questions," I persisted. "You might not remember some of this in the morning. What was he wearing?"

"I don't really know. I barely saw him. A bulky sweater, I think. A ski mask. A stocking cap pulled low. Levi's. That's about it."

"Anything else? Smells? Sounds? Did you rip any part of his clothing, or scratch him or anything like that?"

"No. There was a smell. He wore some kind of aftershave, I think; I have no idea what kind. But it all happened so fast I didn't have time to do anything but scream. I didn't even have time to grab the banister to keep from falling. I just did a back flip down the steps. The judges gave me a nine point nine, degree of difficulty two point eight."

I smiled against my irritation and patted her hand. "You seem to know a lot about this guy. In the morning I'm going to know a lot about him too. Right?"

"Right."

"Go to sleep. You want me to carry you to your bed?"

"No. I'm fine here. You go home now, Marsh. Really."

"If you're not going to use the bed then I am. I'll see you in the morning. How do you like your eggs?"

"Marsh."

"Peggy."

She smiled. "Scrambled."

"Okay. How do you do that, anyway?"

She laughed and told me.

7

I slept fitfully, tossing and turning on a bed of tangled troubles and unfamiliar scents. Although the sheets were satin, the bedspread ruffled, the bedposts walnut, the headboard padded in soft brown leather, I didn't enjoy a minute of it. A mysterious figure kept crashing through my dreams, hooded, silent, skeletal, emerging from the far shadows of sleep to threaten havoc and assault. By five A.M. I was as rested as I was going to get, so I got dressed and went into the living room and joined Marilyn as she stood watch over Peggy until sunshine crept over the building across the street and eased through the blinds and licked at her eyelids until they opened.

She blinked and scratched her nose and looked around the room until she saw me. "Good morning."

"Good morning."

"How long have you been up?"

"A while."

"What have you been doing?"

"Watching Marilyn watch you."

She covered her face with her hands. "I must look like a harpy."

"From the expression on Marilyn's face I'd say you looked more like a Little Friskie."

"I don't feel frisky. I feel like I've been run over by a truck."

"Souvenir of your fall. I recommend a hot bath."

She nodded. "That would be wonderful. If I can make it to the tub."

I got up and went to the couch and looked down at her. "We'll go one step at a time. First, sit. Then, stand. Then we'll worry about traveling cross-country."

She threw off the blanket I'd draped over her and swiveled into a sitting position.

"When you stand up, put your left arm over my shoulder and I'll put my right arm around your waist. Don't put any weight on your ankle till you're sure you have your balance. Then gradually test how much it can take. My guess is not much."

I reached out a hand and Peggy grasped it with both of hers and I tugged her to her foot. When she was reasonably steady I moved to her side and we maneuvered into a fraternal embrace while Peggy touched her injured foot to the floor. "Ouch," she said. "You were right. It feels like someone's got it in a vise."

"Are you dizzy?"

"No. But I have a terrific headache."

"Let's head for the bathroom. I'll pretend I'm your crutch, and you can kind of hop along."

"Cassidy?"

"Funny."

We managed to get there without toppling over, though the jarring jolts of her hops made Peggy grunt each step of the way. When we reached the bathroom I opened the door, kicked the throw rug out of the way, lowered the lid to the toilet, and helped Peggy skip her way into the room and lower herself onto the blue plastic disk.

"So far, so good," I said.

Peggy was looking down. "How long will my ankle look like it's dying?"

"Several days. The color goes before the swelling, usually."

"I guess it's sweat socks for a while."

"Galoshes. Can you make it on your own from here or do you need help getting out of your clothes?"

I paired my question with a leer, but Peggy considered it seriously. "I'm wearing a full slip, of all things. It goes off over my head. I'm afraid I'll fall trying to get the damned thing off." She reached out a hand. "Help me."

I pulled her up. She balanced on one foot and I held one of her hands to steady her. With her free hand she unbuckled her belt, then tugged her slip up from beneath her skirt. When she'd finished she sat back down again, the slip a silvery cummerbund around her waist. Then she unbuttoned her blouse and took it off and tossed it at something behind me. "Hold me while I get rid of this thing," she ordered.

I put my hands on her hips while she wrestled the frilly satin above her bosom and then over her head. Her midriff was tan and taut, her bra two translucent scoops, her breasts fat and freckled at the top, as if sprinkled with cinnamon.

When she caught me admiring them she threw the slip at me full in the face. "I think I can handle it from here," she said, looking at me with her head cocked, amused more than angered by my thrall.

"Rats," I said.

"Sorry."

"I don't suppose you need me to scrub your back."

"I don't think so. One thing might lead to another, and I haven't brushed my teeth."

"Speaking of which, you don't happen to have a spare toothbrush handy, do you?"

"Afraid not."

"I thought all you swinging singles kept such conveniences around."

"No." Peggy's look darkened so considerably I guessed I tromped on a poorly buried memory. "Could you get me my robe?" The request was terse and clinical. "It's on the hook behind the bedroom closet door."

I went to the bedroom and found her robe—silk, white, floor-length, with a single red rose embroidered at its lapel—and took it to her. "Anything else?"

She shook her head. "I don't think so. Oh. Maybe you can turn on the water. As hot as you can stand."

"Okay."

"And I use those bath oil beads over there."

I looked where she was pointing and plucked two pink balls that looked like plastic marbles out of an imitation crystal canister and dropped them into the steamy tub.

"And my towel. On the shelf up there."

"Washcloth?"

"No."

"Soap?"

"No."

"Rubber duck?"

That finally revived her grin. She punched me on the arm, much harder than I'd punched her. "Will you get out of here?"

"Your wish is my command. The eggs will be scrambled when you're done."

"You don't have to do that."

"I know. But then you didn't have to let me help you off with your slip."

She reached for a sponge and threw it at me. I ducked, stuck out my tongue, and retreated. "And don't forget to add milk to the eggs before you pour them in the pan," she instructed, as I let Marilyn through the door before I closed it.

I went to the kitchen, put on the water for coffee, found some baking soda and cleaned my teeth with it and my index finger, then found the instant coffee, eggs, frying pan, mixing bowl, and started in on breakfast.

I puttered with the staples for ten minutes, trying not to make a mistake that would poison or inflame us. By the time there was coffee in my cup and the eggs were wrecked and ready for the pan I was feeling cocky and cute, giddy from a lack of sleep and from the slightly risqué byplay with Peggy in the bathroom.

With the flair of Julia Child, I added a dash of this and a pinch of that to the soupy slime of eggs. Then I remembered Peggy's caution and looked in the refrigerator for the milk, then remembered she was out. I was about to dump my concoction into the pan all the same, just to see what would happen if I fried it up as is, when Peggy called me from the bathroom. I put down the mixing bowl and hurried to the rear of the apartment.

The door was still closed. I tapped and she told me to come in. I was greeted by a cloud of steam and a meandering cat and the sight of Peggy standing in the center of her bathroom wrapped in a towel from her cleavage to her knees, her hair dripping like molasses onto her bare shoulders and her ankle dangling six inches above the floor like an ungainly grackle that was daring its first flight.

Her arms were crossed over her breasts and her face was as pink as her towel. "This is embarrassing," she said, not meeting my eye.

"Why? You look good in terry cloth."

"I don't mean that. I mean I have to stand on the edge of the tub to reach those damned things and I can't stand on the edge of the tub because of my silly ankle."

She was pointing to a shelf high above the basin. On it were several items—a bag of hair curlers, a can of air freshener, a still-wrapped bar of soap, a box of Kleenex—plus the item she wanted me to get. I hopped onto the tub, reached up and got the little blue box, then hopped back down and handed it to her.

She thanked me. "On top of all the rest I just got my period. This will not go down as one of my favorite days."

I lingered.

"Well? If you think I'm going to let you stay while I do *this,* you're insane."

"We don't have any milk. Remember? It went to join the janitor."

"What?"

"Milk. For the eggs."

"Oh."

"I'm going to improvise."

"Oh."

"If it doesn't work I'll go out for lox and bagels."

"Fine. Good-bye, Marsh."

"Or doughnuts, if you prefer. I like the powdered sugar ones. About half a dozen."

"Good-bye, Marsh."

"Or maybe croissants, if you're that type."

"Marsh. I mean it."

" 'Bye."

I returned to the kitchen and inspected the mixing bowl. The ingredients I'd added didn't seem to be blending all that well with the eggs. I stirred but didn't improve the situation, so I stirred some more, then opened the freezer and took out the quart of strawberry ice cream and added a teaspoon's worth of that as well. It still looked funny.

As I was debating what to do next I heard a knock on the door. When I was halfway to it I remembered why I was where I was and went back to get a rolling pin.

8

The woman at the door was small, stout, electrically alert,
a bundle of nervous energy in braided brown hair, a work-
shirt and Levi's faded to a matching azure, and a pair of
unlaced hiking boots that suggested her legs ended in
ragged stumps. Her vivid eyes hopped when I opened the
door. Her face narrowed as she speculated on my purpose,
and the measuring cup she had extended like a sacrament
was slowly lowered behind a thigh. "You're not Peggy,"
she intoned absurdly, her voice fit for someone twice her
size.

"No."

"Is she here?"

"She's getting dressed. She'll be out in a minute if you
want to come in and wait."

She hesitated. "I didn't mean to interrupt," she said
finally, glancing behind me for a hint of what was going
or had gone on. Finding nothing illuminating, she looked
up at me again. "You're him, aren't you?"

I shrugged. "I guess that depends on who him is."

"Tanner. The detective."

"Then I'm him. How'd you know?"

"She told me once you looked like a fighter who'd never
gotten hit. That was close, but not quite right. I'd say
you've been hit three or four times, but not hard enough
to put you down for the count."

She was grinning now, engagingly, and I laughed with
her. "I've been down and I've been out and whatever it is
you've decided is the reason I'm here at this hour of the

morning is most probably wrong. You must be Karen. The friend from upstairs."

"Right. Karen Whittle."

I stuck out a hand. "Nice to meet you."

She transferred the measuring cup and gave my hand a brisk pump. "Likewise, I'm sure," she replied, still not entirely at ease despite the banter. "I just came by for some margarine. I'm all out, and I've got a six-year-old up there parked in front of a pancake that will apparently remain inedible until something polyunsaturated is smeared all over it." She glanced up at me again. "You care if I just raid the fridge and disappear?"

"Help yourself."

I stood aside and let her into the apartment. She brushed past me and in the process glanced surreptitiously toward the living room. When she saw signs of bedding on the couch she seemed disappointed.

After that moralistic hesitation, she made straight for the kitchen, opened the refrigerator, and helped herself to two heaping scrapes of margarine from a yellow plastic tub. "I better get back before the batter turns to stone," she said after she replaced the tub. "Nice to meet you, Mr. Detective. Peggy thinks you're a pretty wonderful guy. I wish I had time to stick around and see if she could possibly be right."

"She says nice things about you, too," I said. "Of course she also says nice things about Imelda Marcos."

"That's probably why we're friends," Karen said. "I don't say nice things about anyone. See you, Tanner."

"See you, Whittle."

She walked to the door, opened it, then turned back toward me. "Nothing's wrong, is there? With Peggy?"

"Why do you ask?"

"I don't know," she said above a shrug. "She's been different lately."

"Different how?"

She frowned. "Nervous. Snappy. Worried. I don't know, she's just not the same person she was six months ago. Is she all right? What I mean is, are you here romantically or professionally?"

I didn't answer that particular question because I wasn't sure quite how to. "She had some trouble last night," I said instead, "but she's all right now. Do you have any idea what's been bothering her?"

Her eyes narrowed. "So you've noticed it too?"

I nodded. "The other day she fell asleep at the office. Normally she'd only lie down on the job if someone shot her."

Karen Whittle nodded. "I know what you mean. She's been exhausted for weeks. I've asked her about it but she won't talk to me. I thought maybe it had something to do with Allison, her daughter, but that's just a guess. And she talked about some phone calls a while back, obscene things, I assume, but she hasn't mentioned them for a while. So I don't know. But if you're here to find out and I can help you in any way, I hope you'll let me know. Peggy's real special to me."

I looked at her and made a quick decision to enlist an ally. "Someone shoved Peggy down the stairs last night."

Her eyes ballooned and she glanced toward the living room again, and then behind her, toward the hallway. "What stairs? *These* stairs?"

"Right. At about ten o'clock."

"But I saw her at the grocery store about then. My God. It must have happened right after. Is she hurt?"

"Twisted ankle. Sore ribs. She'll survive."

"But who? And why?"

"I don't know," I admitted. "In a few minutes I'm going to work real hard at finding out. I don't think she knows everything but she knows more about it than she's told me so far and I'm going to dig like hell for it. But if you learn something before I do I'd appreciate it if you'd let me know. It could help save her life. To be melodramatic about it."

Karen Whittle looked at me closely. "You're not being melodramatic; you're being serious."

I nodded. "Afraid so."

"Unbelievable. And it happened right here." She hesitated, then glanced quickly at her watch. "I've got to get back. Lily, that's my daughter, will be wild. You tell Peggy I'm here whenever she wants me. She should know that already, but you remind her, okay?"

I told her I would. "And maybe you can keep your eyes open for anything unusual around the building," I added. "Strangers, that kind of thing."

Karen Whittle nodded solemnly. "Oh, I keep my eyes open for that kind of thing all the time, Tanner. It's what I do best in the world, and I've been doing it for years."

She began to walk away before I could ask her what that meant. Then she turned back once again. "I'm going to say something that's probably insulting, but I'm going to say it anyway."

"Okay."

"Peggy's pretty vulnerable these days, Detective. What I want to say is that a wonderful guy wouldn't take advantage of that."

This time she was gone for good. I retreated to the kitchen, her admonition stuck like a thistle on the sleeve of my threadbare conscience.

I replaced the rolling pin on its hook and considered the state of the eggs. Unappetizing was a charitable description. I was still debating how to salvage them when Peggy shuffled up behind me and put a hand on my waist and looked over my shoulder. "I thought I heard you talking to someone," she said, her voice thick and drowsy, her breasts pressing as lightly as a breeze against my back.

"Your neighbor came by," I said. "Karen."

"Oh. What did she want?"

"To borrow some margarine."

Peggy laughed. "It serves us right, I guess."

"What?"

"I ran into her at the store last night. We started talking, the way we do. And I must have forgotten the milk and she forgot the margarine. Thank God for Karen,"

Peggy added after a pause. "She's the only one who keeps me sane. Besides you and Marilyn, of course."

"She seems kind of . . . intense," I said.

"She's had to be," Peggy said soberly. "She's had a rough time."

"Rough how?"

"Oh, the usual. A divorce. Messy, protracted, painful. A custody fight which she won, but ever since she's been afraid her ex is going to try to steal Lily away from her. Apparently he's tried it more than once. Last year some guy Karen thinks was working for her husband tried to lure Lily into a car as she was coming home from kindergarten, so Karen took Lily out of school and is teaching her herself. At home. She got permission from the state and everything. It's a tremendous burden, a tremendous responsibility. I really admire her for doing it." Peggy paused. "I've always wondered how I would react if I had to deal with a problem like that, having to sacrifice so much for someone else. I don't think I'd react very nobly, I'm afraid. I mean, when my father got sick I could have taken him in and cared for him myself even though he . . ." She blinked. "But I let him go to that home and, well, I haven't liked myself as much since then, you know?"

Peggy's voice gave way, leaving each of us alone with our altruistic inadequacies. Finally she patted me on the rump and moved to my side, though even that small maneuver hurt her. "Well, I'd better get dressed," she said as she adjusted her balance to protect her foot.

"Why?"

"I'm going to go to work."

"Oh, no you're not. Not with that ankle."

"It's better, Marsh. Really. I got in here, didn't I?"

"It may be better but it's not good enough for you to fight your way down Montgomery Street and up the stairs to the office. Anyway, at the rate you're moving, by the time you get there it'll be time to go home."

"You could give me a ride."

"I could but I won't."

"But—"

"I'll lock you out if you show up."

"Then I'll go up and spend the day with Art."

"Hah. It would serve you right."

Arthur Constable was the tax lawyer who had the suite of offices down from mine. He was a dandy and a prude and he fancied himself worthy of the trappings of a feudal lord just because he made more money than all the rest of us put together.

Peggy pinched the bulge of flesh that lodged above my belt and muttered something I couldn't catch, an angry something that seemed to vent the majority of her frustration. "Okay," she surrendered a moment later. "I'll stay home."

"Good."

"Can I at least go up and talk to Karen?"

"Yep."

"Can I—" She stopped so abruptly I turned to look at her. She was gazing at the counter top and what was on it. "What on earth is *that*?"

"Eggs. Pre-scrambled."

"I mean *that*?" She pointed to the mixing bowl.

"Cinnamon," I said.

"And that?"

"Pepper."

"And that?"

"Honey."

"Honey?"

"Honey."

"What else did you dump in there?"

"Strawberry ice cream and chocolate chips."

"You must be kidding."

"Only about the chips."

"Will you do me a favor?"

"Sure."

"Pour it down the drain. Please. Before I get sick."

"What's the matter?"

"*Look* at it. If you tried to cook that mess I couldn't get it out of the pan with a chisel. Please. Just do it. I'll go call Karen."

"Do you need help?"

"Nope. I've got this hopping thing down pat. I'll probably be made an honorary rabbit."

Peggy bounced out of the kitchen and I did as she asked, then rinsed out the mixing bowl and put it in the dishwasher, then went into the living room and waited for Peggy to hang up the phone. "So what do we eat?"

"Toast and juice," she said. "Or I've got some of those frozen waffles if you'd rather. You didn't add anything exotic to the coffee, did you?"

I shook my head.

"It's hard to believe you've survived to such a ripe age, Marsh, given the rather enormous gap in your knowledge of cuisine, haute or otherwise."

"Hey, I never cook breakfast for myself. I always eat at Zorba's."

"*Now* you tell me." Peggy laughed and gave me a shove, then instructed me how to put together a nonrepulsive meal. "I don't know if I can stand it without milk in my coffee, though," Peggy said when I had the toast in the toaster.

"Why don't I run up to your friend Karen's and borrow some. Tit for tat, as it were."

Peggy grinned. "Of course. Take that with you." She pointed to a large glass tumbler on the counter. "Get enough for you, too, if you want some cereal or something. It's apartment forty-one."

I grabbed the tumbler and took the stairs to the next floor up. When I knocked, the door seemed different than Peggy's, heavier, denser, a more formidable barrier. Moments later a shadow flickered behind the peephole in the center, and a high, thin voice asked me what I wanted. I told it I was from Peggy Nettleton and I was there to beg for milk.

As I held up the tumbler for inspection as proof of my mission, a deadbolt slid back and a chain rattled loose and two other safety devices clanked and scraped behind the door. Then it opened slowly and a young face peered at me from around its edge. "Hi," it said.

"Hi. Are you Lily?"

"Yes."

"I'm Marsh. I met your mom down at Peggy's place a little while ago. Is she here?"

"She's in the bathroom." The girl emerged enough for me to see that she was as bright and cheering as a daisy, blond, delicate, a blossom dressed in white flannel pajamas and fuzzy yellow slippers. Her cheeks were soft and dimpled; her blue eyes gleamed like stones in a stream bed. She seemed eager for me to join her, as though I was bringing her a treat.

When I was inside the apartment she closed the door and refixed the various security devices. When we faced each other it was with a matching shyness. I was about to ask about the milk when I heard footsteps behind me.

"Lily, have you seen my . . . good *God*. What on earth have you done? I've *told* you and *told* you never to let anyone in here. I . . ."

I turned in time to see a furious Karen Whittle glance desperately toward the wall beside the door. What she saw was a pistol—a snub-nosed .38 it looked like—dangling by its trigger guard from a nail within easy reach of Karen if not of Lily.

I stepped back against the door, trying to be less threatening. Since I wasn't sure she knew who I was yet, I hurried to speak out. "Take it easy, Mrs. Whittle. I'm Marsh Tanner. We just talked; down at Peggy's."

It was enough to stop her from arming herself but not enough to keep the bulge of alarm out of her eyes. "How did you get in here?" she demanded.

I glanced at the young girl and smiled. "I broke down the door."

"He said he was from Peggy," Lily blurted, almost in tears. "He said he wanted to borrow some milk. He had a glass and everything." The plea was unspoken, but what

59

it begged for was forgiveness or at least a suspended sentence.

"I don't care *what* he said, young lady!" her mother shouted. "People can say *anything*. You are not to let *anyone* in here. Do you understand? *No one. Ever.*"

"But Mom—"

"No. I don't want to hear it. Now go to your room and write your spelling list. I'll deal with you later."

I leaned against the wall to let poor Lily past. "It wasn't her fault," I said as the crestfallen girl slunk by, eyes downcast, shoulders slumped, the blossom now wilted and forlorn.

"Don't tell me how to raise my child," Karen Whittle ordered fiercely. "I don't have to take that from you. I don't have to take that from *anyone.*"

"Sorry," I said, since anything else would have probably propelled her back to the gun on the wall.

"You don't know. You have *no idea* what I—" She shook her head, suddenly and violently, as though to dissolve her thought in a milder solution. "Why are you here?" she asked finally, suddenly another person, the one I'd met at Peggy's.

I held up the tumbler. "To borrow some milk. For Peggy's morning coffee. So you won't have to pay her back for the margarine. Barter, and all that."

"Oh." Her swell of ire was still subsiding. "You want a full glass?"

"Half, if you've got it."

"I'll see."

She took the tumbler and disappeared around the corner. I took a couple of steps in her wake, then stopped beside the gun. It was real and loaded and disturbing. Its grip was chipped and cracked, as if it had been used to pistol-whip someone.

Two more steps brought me within sight of the living room. It was more like *Romper Room* than *House Beautiful*, with two desks, a blackboard and bookshelves, an art easel and similar accoutrements, all clustered in a circle at the center of the room. There were cutout animals taped to the windows, and lumps of modeling clay on a table in the corner. I had an urge to dip my hands in fingerpaint and smear every surface in the place, then carve a sailboat out of soap. But when I heard Karen Whittle returning I hurried back to the entryway.

She rounded the corner at a rush and thrust the half-full glass at me, almost spilling it in her haste. She asked if I needed anything else but there was never a question that was less sincere. When I shook my head she said she had to go to the store later, and would be happy to get Peggy some milk and anything else she needed if she'd call and tell her what. I promised to tell Peggy. Then I apologized for causing trouble for her daughter.

"It's all right," she said resignedly. "I'm sure I over-reacted. It's just that I thought I saw Tom parked on the street out front yesterday, and I've been hyper ever since."

"Tom's your ex-husband?"

She nodded. "He's made a try for Lily four different times. If he ever gets her I'll go crazy. I'll do anything to keep that from happening. *Anything.*"

Our glances met at the revolver hanging on the alabaster wall. When we realized the implication we were slightly stunned. She arched her back and gave me a level stare. "You know nothing of my situation, Mr. Tanner."

"I know that, Mrs. Whittle."

She nodded, accepting my admission. "Tell Peggy I'll call her. Will you be with her all day?"

"No. But someone will."

"Good."

"Say good-bye to Lily for me," I said, then waited while Karen Whittle undid the locks and let me out the heavy door.

When I got back to the apartment, Peggy was lying on the couch. I poured us each a cup of coffee, added milk to hers, and joined her. "Are you hungry for something else?" I asked.

"I'm fine."

"And you got a good night's sleep?"

She nodded. "How about you?"

"Fine," I lied. "And your ankle doesn't hurt as much?"

"No. I told you."

"So that means there's no reason why we can't have a nice long talk about what the hell's been bothering you for the last few weeks, right?"

Peggy's smile shrank. "Do we have to?"

"We do."

"But it's so—"

"Someone tried to frighten you, Peggy. Maybe even kill you. Surely you know me well enough to know that I'm not leaving this apartment until I learn everything you know about the guy who did it."

Peggy gave me a rueful smile. "I'm not worried about what you'll learn about him. I'm worried about what you're going to learn about *me.*"

9

"It has something to do with telephone calls, doesn't it?"
I began, trying to blend sympathy with insistence, trying,
most of all, to get Peggy talking long enough to come up
with something I could *do*.

She lowered her head, eyes downcast, fingers fiddling
with the lapel of her housecoat, wrinkling the rose. Her
bloated, blotchy ankle was extended toward the far end of
the couch, where Marilyn curled beside it like a heating
pad that purred.

"What is it, an obscene caller? Some guy harassing you
on the phone?"

"I guess so," she said, still lax and uninterested.

"You mean that's not it?"

"No, I . . . it's as close as anything, I guess." Peggy's
voice still indicated ambivalence and complexity, which
seemed a strange reaction if the problem was as basic as
I'd supposed.

"How long ago did it start?"

"About two months. Maybe three by now."

"How often does he call?"

"Every night, almost. He's only missed nine nights, I
think."

"Jesus. No wonder you're a mess." I was sorry I'd put
it like that, but Peggy didn't seem to notice.

"And of course now it doesn't matter whether he calls
or not," she was saying, "since I *expect* a call every night,
I *expect* to be upset, I *expect* to lie awake all night, waiting
for . . . just waiting." She paused, defeated and resigned.

"Sometimes when he calls it's a relief," she went on, her tone now low and wondrous.

I started to ask another question but Peggy interrupted. I had made her look at it again, whatever it was, and she was suddenly determined to tell me exactly what she saw. "I don't *know* anything anymore, Marsh. This thing has thrown me for a loop." Her eyes searched for an understanding she seemed dubious that I would give. "When you're a woman and you live by yourself it's very important that you develop the feeling that you can handle anything and everything that comes along, you know? It's absurd, of course. There are all *kinds* of things out there that I can't handle, from muggers to vacuum salesmen to gold-chain gigolos, but I've got to believe I *can* handle them, otherwise I'd never go out of the house. Well, this . . . this *guy* has totally destroyed my confidence. He's made me feel vulnerable, to all sorts of things. I'm having trouble handling that, is all. I'll snap out of it."

"You'll snap out of it a lot quicker if I can find him and shut him down," I snapped.

"Maybe." She was uninterested again.

"So he calls almost every night," I prompted. "But he didn't call last night."

"No."

"I'd say that's a pretty good indication he was the one who pushed you down."

"I suppose so." She didn't seem impressed by my deduction, seemed to already regard the inference as banal. I began to worry that she was suffering from shock or severe depression, so much so that she would neglect to protect herself, would possibly even court disaster in the hope of forcing the issue to its end, one way or another.

"What time does he call?" I asked.

"Usually about midnight. Sometimes not till one or two."

Her voice was singsong, a robot's rondo. I didn't know what to do about it so I just kept asking questions. "Do you know his name?"

"He told me to call him John."

"Last name?"

She shook her head. "I've no idea."

"Does he know *your* name?"

"Yes. That's the . . . yes."

"What else were you going to say?"

"That's the thing that scares me." Her whisper was symptomatic of her fright. "He knows so *much.*"

"How did he find out your name? Did you tell him?"

Finally she was animated. "*No.* He just *knew.* I don't know how, but he knew."

"Did he know the first time he called, or did he find out later?"

"He knew from the first. My name was the first thing he said to me, almost."

"Did he get nasty on the first call?"

"Yes. Sort of. He's not nasty, exactly. I mean, he is, but . . ."

"We'll go into that later. Did you try just hanging up on him?"

"Of course. I tried everything I could think of."

"What happened after you hung up?"

"He called right back and told me what he would do to me if I ever did anything like that again. It was . . . horrible. He was graphic, and sick, and he made me believe he was quite capable of doing exactly what he said he would do. So I didn't hang up anymore."

"And you tried to change your number, didn't you? But it didn't work."

Peggy's mouth dropped open, as though in that instant she considered me a pair with her assailant. "How did you know?"

"You told me, remember? You asked me in the office how someone could learn your new number so fast."

"Oh." She was dazed again, by events that had raced beyond her reach. "It took him *two days,* Marsh. Just two days to learn the new one. How is that possible?"

"Well, he could work for the phone company."

She shook her head immediately. The thought had obviously occurred to her already and she had rejected it. So I asked her why.

"He's so, so . . . arrogant. So self-confident. I can't see him working for someone else, being a part of a big bureaucracy like the phone company. Besides, they must have pretty close checks on access to unlisted numbers."

I shrugged. "I wouldn't overestimate their concern if I were you."

Peggy stayed silent. As she shifted position again her housecoat fell open, exposing portions of her breast and belly. Her underclothes were blue, the color of an empty sky. "How old do you think he is?" I asked.

She frowned. "I've tried to figure that out, but it's hard. In between, I'd say. Not a teenager; not an octogenarian. The problem is, I can't learn much about him because he gets furious if I ask a question. I have to answer all of *his*, but he doesn't have to answer any of mine."

Peggy began to cry in sniffles and snorts, a child whose best friend had just cheated at jacks. "You make it sound like a game," I said.

She nodded and dislodged a tear. "It's like when you're a kid, and one of you gets to be master and the other has to be slave. And then you switch roles, and then you switch back. Only with John it's never time to switch. It's always the same, night after night. I think it's going to drive me crazy, Marsh. I really do."

She broke down momentarily, her voice raw with the beginnings of hysteria. I went to her side and knelt until I could put my arm around her. She inclined her head against my shoulder. "I'm sorry this is so difficult," I said as her convulsions subsided. "But you've got to go through it so I can try to help. Okay? I'll make it as short as possible."

She sniffed and nodded. "But don't you have things to do? Isn't there somewhere you have to be today?"

"Later," I said. "Now, what about the voice? Does he have an accent?"

"No."

"Any kind of background noise?"

"No. Never. I've listened, but nothing."

"Is the phone hum always the same? As though he calls from the same place every time?"

She thought about it. "No. Sometimes it's different. Sometimes it even seems like long distance. That hiss, you know?"

"Does his voice remind you of anyone at all?"

Peggy managed an incongruous grin. "It reminds me of the minister at the church we went to when I was little. He made me feel like the basest sinner who ever lived. John makes me feel the same way." She looked at me. "No, Marsh. It's not Reverend Sowers. He's dead. A suicide. Preachers do that quite often, I've since discovered."

It wasn't a subject she should dwell on. "Do you think he's disguising his voice?"

"It's possible. He's very dramatic at times, very mesmerizing. Evangelical, almost. He could be acting, I suppose. Playing a role. He's a little bit like Burt Lancaster in that—what was it?—*Elmer Gantry*."

"Do you think he's religious? A lot of fundamentalists are pretty warped on sex."

She shook her head. "He never says anything that's specifically religious."

"Nothing about sin or salvation?"

"No. Not exactly."

"How about your daughter? Isn't her boyfriend an actor?"

She hesitated. "Derrick? Yes, but I'm sure it's not him."

"Why?"

"Well, what would he want to terrorize *me* for?"

"I don't know, but there was some trouble there, wasn't there? Something about money?"

She shook her head several times. "I'm sure it's not Derrick. He's a conceited rake, unfeeling, possibly even brutal, but he's not sick like this. And he's aces with women. Allison knows of several affairs he's had since they've been together. No. Definitely not Derrick."

She didn't sound nearly as certain as she wanted me to believe, so I scrawled Derrick's name on my invisible list of things to do and hurried ahead with my questions before Peggy made me stop. Interrogation is like gambling—when you're on a roll you go with it. Also like gambling, often you go too far.

"Does he ever refer to anyone else? Other women he calls, or friends, or me, even?"

She shook her head. "No one. It's as if I'm the only person in the world."

"So you don't know if he's married."

"No, but I'd guess he's not. From the kinds of questions he asks I'd say he's not married and has never had a serious relationship with a woman."

"How much does he know about you?"

"Too much," Peggy blurted quickly.

"Does he know where you live?"

"Yes."

"Work?"

"Yes. At least he knows I go downtown, and he knows the bus I take."

"Do you think he follows you around?"

"I don't know. I didn't think so at first, but lately I've had the feeling someone's been following me. It's probably paranoia, but . . ." She shrugged. "You know what they say—just because you're paranoid doesn't mean someone isn't out to get you. Yesterday I was certain someone was watching me, but I couldn't pick him out."

I didn't tell her that she was right, and that the person who was watching her was me. "Until he shoved you down the stairs did he make any other approach to you? Other than the calls?"

"No. Nothing."

"Not even a pinch on the bus?"

She shook her head and breathed deeply. "Can we stop now, Marsh? Please?"

"Let's go back to the phone number. Who did you give the new one to?"

"Well, there was you."

"Who else?"

"Allison, of course. And Karen upstairs. And my boyfriend."

"Which one?"

"Stan."

"Still going with him?"

"No. He dumped me."

I hadn't known that. The information was oddly cheering. "Was he angry with you? Did you have a fight?"

"No, what he was was in love with some girl he met on a rock-climbing trip. Apparently what they experienced on top of some stony promontory reeked with a symbolism that could not be denied."

Peggy's jealous slur momentarily erased her discomfiture. "So he wouldn't come under the definition of a jilted suitor," I said.

"Not even slightly."

"Who else got the number?"

"I don't know. I think that's about it. I just changed it three weeks ago."

"No other girlfriends?"

"Just Karen. Girlfriends are hard to come by these days. Most of the women I know seem to want a fellow-feminist more than a friend; a documented outrage more than a good laugh. Either that or they're determined to tell me something personal about themselves that I'd just as soon not know. At one point I knew of four different men—men I'd never met before—who were premature ejaculators, all because their lovers felt their lives would be enhanced if they told me that. Ah, well, I've been quite a turkey myself of late. To have a friend you have to be one, and I haven't been able to manage that since . . . this." She gestured absently toward the telephone, which in that instant gave off the vibrations of a weapon as ominous as the one on Karen Whittle's wall.

"Okay," I said. "I guess that brings us to the last item."

"Which is?"

"What does this guy talk about when he calls?"

She sent me a twisted smirk. "You know damned well what he talks about," she said. "He talks about sex."

10

"I think we have to go into it, Peggy," I began carefully.

"I don't want to."

"I know you don't, but what he's said might tell us who he is."

Her eyes glistened once again, as though my words had burnished them. "Don't you think I've thought of that? Don't you think I've gone over it and over it until I'm so full of self-loathing I almost gag?" She choked back a sob, and the effort made her bruised ribs protest.

"You're not a man, Peggy. Something he said might mean something to me that it wouldn't to you."

She scowled at me, intense and intent. If I was going to be of help I was going to have to hurt her and she was going to have to let me do it. The mutual knowledge made us adversaries. "You're serious about this, aren't you, Marsh?" she said softly.

I nodded.

"Why? Why bother with it?"

I tried to make it light because the truth seemed at that moment distracting and unhelpful. "Because you're the only secretary I've ever had who's been able to keep my ficus alive."

Peggy's smile was dry, as incongruous as a cactus flower. "There's one thing you ought to know, Marsh."

"What?"

"If we go into this, if I tell you everything that's gone on between me and this . . . this creep, it's going to change the way you think about me."

"No, it won't."

Her expression was soaked in melancholy. "Oh, but it will. If I tell you what you want to know, you may never want to see me again."

"Not possible," I said, because I believed it, or because I wanted to believe it, or because I hoped it was true.

"No, Marsh. We're going to disappoint each other before this is over. Believe me. I've done things with John that nice girls don't do, and you're going to find that hard to fit into the picture you have of what you think I am."

"I thought you'd never seen him."

"I haven't. But he ordered me to talk about certain things and I did. Eventually. After I was convinced he would hurt me if I didn't, and after he convinced me that he had an uncanny ability to know when I was lying and when I wasn't, and after I realized . . ."

"What?"

"Nothing. The point is, I gave in to him, Marsh. Don't you see? I let him rape me, in a way."

"No, you didn't. You—"

"Whatever he wanted to know, I told him," she interrupted, her words heated and precise. "And I told the truth, because in the end there didn't seem to be all that much reason not to." She paused for breath. "And you know something?" She flung the question like a gauntlet.

"What?"

"What I just started to tell you was that it got to the point, once in a while, where I *liked* it. I *enjoyed* some of our talks. Can you believe that? And accept it?"

What she saw on my face made her doubt it.

"I was a very proper girl, Marsh," she went on, in a hurry to make me understand. "And for the most part I've been a very proper woman. I mean, they're not going to canonize me or anything, but I've pretty much lived by the old rules, and when I've broken them I've lived with a lot of guilt. But basically I've believed there are things you don't do, and things you don't say, even though every fiber of your being might cry out for you to do or say them.

With the result that I sit here alone most nights, just me and my nineteenth-century morality and my twentieth-century guilt. Then this *guy* comes along, and throws out all the rules, turns me inside out, makes it not only okay but *obligatory* that I think and talk about forbidden things, and in the process he provided some kind of crazy therapy for me. As the weeks went by I moved from this horrible fear and loathing to the point where I found myself trying my best to be truthful to him, and in the effort to do so I found myself thinking about things that had troubled me since adolescence. He's told me a lot about myself, Marsh. Or rather I've told *myself* a lot about myself since he started asking all his questions. Even though I know it has to stop, even though I know it's ruining my life, still there's one sense in which I'm grateful for—"

I forced myself to break her faulty idyll. "He tried to kill you, Peggy."

She blinked. "I know, and I don't understand it. The only thing I can think of is, I must have made him angry somehow. Maybe he thought I was lying about something I said, or maybe he thought I was trying to trap him." Her eyes widened and her breath quickened. "*I* know what it was. I did something yesterday, and this is his way of telling me he knows all about it, and that I'd better not do it again."

"What did you do?"

"I . . . after I fell asleep at the office I realized that this thing has worn me out. I'm exhausted, and it's doing things to my body and my mind, and it's not fair to you or to the other people in my life. I decided I had to try to put a stop to it, so I saw someone I thought could help."

"Who?"

She brushed away my question. "It doesn't matter. What matters is, he must have been following me yesterday morning. He must have felt threatened by what I'd done, and pushing me down the stairs was a warning. A warning not to ask for help. God. I'll bet he knows *you're here.* I'll bet he's even *more* upset with me. What if he—"

I put my hand on Peggy's shoulder to brake her surging panic. She trembled beneath my fingers, the engines within her taxed to the point of breakdown. For the first time I fully appreciated the degree of pressure she'd been under, and I began to consider how to convince her to check into a hospital, for rest at a minimum, for psychiatric help at best.

"Don't worry about this guy," I told her, trying to be soothing, to be more reassuring than I felt. "I'll be around for a while longer, and I'll arrange for a substitute if I have to go out, so there'll be someone with you all day. He won't be able to get at you again, Peggy. No chance."

Peggy's motors unwound a bit, but still were far from idle. She frowned and shook her head. "You can't stay here any longer, Marsh; you've got a meeting in an hour. Anyway, I'll be okay, now that I know what he's trying to do. I just wasn't prepared last night. He took me by surprise."

I'd forgotten about the meeting, but the appointment sparked an idea. "I'm going to call Ruthie Spring," I said. "You remember her, don't you?"

Peggy cocked her head. "I remember," she said warily.

"Ruthie and I owe each other so many favors we've stopped keeping track. If she's free, I'm sure she'll be glad to come over and stay till I get back."

"No. I can't ask her to do that."

"You're not asking her to do anything."

I reached for the phone and called Ruthie. Luckily, she was in. Even more luckily, she was a quick study. After I asked if she could come stay with Peggy, she asked me if Peggy was on an extension. When I said she wasn't, Ruthie asked if Peggy knew that I knew about her visit to Ruthie's office the day before. I told her no, and that we'd talk about it later, then told her I'd wait till she arrived, then be back to relieve her at six at the latest. I also told her to bring her gun.

Peggy was watching me intently as I replaced the receiver. I thought she was going to accuse me of tailing her to Ruthie's, but that's not what was on her mind. "Do you ever look around and ask yourself how on earth you could let life toy with you like this? How you could let yourself get trapped in something that turns out to be so completely and totally disastrous?"

"Frequently," I admitted. "But you didn't *let* anything happen, Peggy. You didn't have any choice. The guy picked you out and set out to ensnare you, like the spider and the fly. He convinced you he was capable of violence if you didn't go along, and what happened last night shows you were right to be convinced. You shouldn't feel guilty about the situation, Peggy. You're the victim, not the perpetrator."

As I paused for breath I wondered how much of my statement I actually believed, and whether I would believe more or less of it as events progressed.

"But I do feel guilty," Peggy said.

"So do I," I admitted.

"Why on earth do *you* feel guilty?"

"Because I'm supposed to be an expert on trouble, on putting a stop to it or keeping it from happening in the first place. And here a whole big batch of it has hatched right under my nose while I've been stumbling around like a big dumb ox, overlooking all the signs."

Peggy patted my knee. "Don't, Marsh. It's not your fault. I tried my best to keep it from you."

"Why?"

"I was embarrassed to ask for help. And I was afraid I couldn't pay your fee."

"What the hell made you think there would *be* a fucking fee?"

As I regretted my outburst, Peggy recoiled from my verbal slap, then closed her eyes and bit her lip. "The last time I felt this dumb was when I was in high school," she murmured finally. "And I was *real* dumb in high school, believe me."

We exchanged apologetic smiles. Time wandered through the room, oblivious to our woes. The shadows fleeing from the rising sun were passing through as well, dark strangers on eerie business of their own. I was more enervated than I should have been, more reluctant than my task demanded. "What does the spider say when he calls you up?" I asked when I thought Peggy was ready to confront both me and her dilemma once again.

"Who?"

"The spider. The guy on the phone."

"Sex. I told you."

"I mean specifically."

"Specifically, he asks questions."

"What kind of questions?"

"Oh, about what I think, what I like and don't like, what I do and don't do."

"And all these questions are about sex?"

"Just about. But then from one point of view everything in the world is about sex, isn't it?" Peggy gave me another empty laugh. She had slipped back into a spell, the one she assumed whenever we talked about the calls.

"Does he ever talk about what *he* does or likes or wants to do?"

"Not often. It's as though he wants to learn about women, Marsh. About what makes them tick. He's always asking if 'most women' do this or 'all women' do that. I think he's been very unsuccessful with relationships in the past and he thinks I can tell him how to change his luck. It's like I'm a teacher and he's my pupil. Sexology 101." Peggy lowered her eyes. "And I'm such a dedicated teacher I've told him things I've never told another soul in my whole entire life."

For the second time that morning I was angry with Peggy—angry at her flip remark, angry that she was not as incensed as she should have been at what the spider was doing to her, angry, deep down, that in a short time the spider had reached a degree of intimacy with Peggy that I had not achieved in all the years I'd known her.

It was perverse and egotistical, my reaction, akin to the unfeeling assumption men frequently exhibit that women who are raped have somehow brought it on themselves. I wasn't proud of myself, but I wasn't able to be proud of Peggy, either.

"I need specifics," I said roughly. "How did he start out? What did he ask you first?"

Peggy shook her head, but it was a rejection of her predicament more than a refusal to engage my question. "Just personal things," she murmured. "Age. Marital status. Children. The first call wasn't so bad, except when I told him I was going to hang up. That was the first time he frightened me."

"What did he say?"

"He threatened to do various things to me, most of them having to do with disfigurement. He mentioned acid, for example. And I don't mean LSD. Burns. Blindness. I have this terrible fear of burns. I always have had, since I was little. It's almost as if he knew that."

"Could he be a scientist? A chemist who uses acid in his work? Does he use a lot of jargon?"

She shook her head. "Not really. No more than normal."

"Okay. What else? The first time."

"That was it."

"What was it?"

"The first time. He wanted to know all about the first time I had sex. How old I was, where we did it, who the guy was, how it felt, whether I wanted it to happen or was forced to do it, whether I had an orgasm, what we did in foreplay, whether we took precautions or assumed the risk of pregnancy. It was a real case study on a one-night stand. He's probably writing it up for *Penthouse.*"

"And you told him what he wanted to know?"

There was still a stain of anger in my voice, and a stain of something else as well. Peggy heard it and was insulted by the implication that she had not resisted. "Not at first I didn't," she protested. "Not till after I hung up and he called back and threatened me. And not even then until he kept pressing me for details, demanding more and more, until all of a sudden it seemed easier to tell him what he wanted. . . . I was sixteen when I first had sex, Marsh. Almost thirty years ago. And I remember it as if it were yesterday. Amazing, isn't it? He had a birthmark on his thigh. It looked just like a football. He was very embarrassed about it. Much more embarrassed about that than about what he was doing to me in the back seat of that rattletrap car."

Life is awesome at times, revealing, shocking, tantalizing in its sly suggestion that there is much more to it than we know, that the past has splashed us far more thoroughly than we suspect. Peggy was awed by her life at the moment, amazed at memory, surprised at significance. The possibility occurred to me that her reactions to the spider and his calls were so complex and deep-seated I could inflict psychological harm by probing for the details, that my questions, if at all, should be asked by someone trained to cushion psychic blows. But when I looked at Peggy's purpled ankle I resolved to press ahead.

"Does he ask for specific names? Of your first lover, for example?"

"Yes. Always."

"Has he ever indicated he knows any of the people you mention?"

"No."

"Okay. What else happened the first time?"

She frowned to remember. "I think that's all. Then the next night he started asking me what I like in men. General stuff at first—short or tall, fat or thin, dark or blond, hairy or smooth. Then the sexual stuff. Size of penis was a big subject. We got down to some fairly precise measurements. Is there a calculus that covers phallic displacement, Marsh? At one point I felt my mathematics was inadequate to the discussion."

Once again her effort to lighten the weight of the event agitated me unreasonably. I was reacting personally, not professionally—my relationship with Peggy had so dislodged my normal reactions I could no longer trust my instincts. Which meant that from then on I was going to have to double-check the decisions I reached and the actions I took. Peggy deserved my best, but if I wasn't careful I would come closer to giving her my worst.

As she answered my questions Peggy had progressively relaxed, now seemed eager to make me understand the exact dynamic between her and the man I called the spider. I crossed my legs and closed my eyes and leaned back and let her talk.

"And of course he wanted to know all about my marriage," she went on, "why I'd married Jim, what it was about him that first attracted me, whether clothes were important, or his car, or how much money he had. What we did when we dated. What we talked about. Whether he always asked me out or whether I asked him sometimes. Whether I was honest when he asked me questions or whether I just said what I thought he wanted to hear. And, of course, whether we had engaged in premarital sex.

"That was clearly important to him. He wanted to know how long it took us to reach that point, whether I resisted his advances or whether I wished he would make love to me before he actually did, how long after we started dating we first had intercourse, whether I really wanted to or gave in because Jim insisted, whether we planned the first time we actually did it or whether it just happened, whether I was drunk at the time, where we were, how it felt, whether we used birth control or were just lucky, whether we did it on every date after the first time or whether we tried not to for a while, whether we felt good about it or guilty that we'd committed a sin, whether it was the way I had always believed it would be or whether it was disappointing. He was very concerned about whether sex was a big part of my marriage, whether I told Jim the things I liked for him to do or just let him please himself, whether I ever got bored with it, and why.

"And then I mentioned that I'd had an extramarital

affair, so we went all through that, too. Who my lover was, whether he was married, too, where we went, how we covered our tracks, what I got out of the affair that I hadn't gotten out of marriage, whether the impulse to cheat was sexual or something more, whether Jim knew, whether I was sure he didn't, whether it would have made any difference if he had, whether having an affair necessarily meant the marriage was doomed, whether I felt like a sinner while it was going on, whether the affair had given me everything I thought it would, whether I would do it again knowing what I know now."

Peggy paused for breath, still entranced by recollection. I was about to break in but she began to speak again, this time more urgently. "I have to admit, Marsh, that those kinds of questions were interesting to me, or rather my answers were. As I said, it was therapeutic in a perverse sort of way, an ordering of all these jumbled thoughts and feelings I'd been carrying around for years, sort of like finally finishing a puzzle I'd neglected for too long. And he really and truly seemed interested in my answers, more interested than anyone else had ever been in what I had to say on the subject of human relationships. It sounds crazy, I suppose, but I'd even find myself wishing I could meet the guy, have a drink with him some night and continue the discussion face to face, exchanging impressions of reality or whatever. But then something would ruin it. I'd forget the rules and ask him a question about himself and he'd scream and order me never to do it again. Or he'd ask me something vulgar, like if I'd ever let a man fuck me in the ass."

The crudity was calculated, a belated attempt to provoke my disgust, to drive me away from the subject so that Peggy's duet with the spider would remain a private rite, its parameters known only to the two participants. But I couldn't leave it, not without some lead, not without someplace to go when I left Peggy behind with Ruthie Spring.

"Do you think he's married?" I asked.

"No."

"Do you think he's a virgin?"

"Possibly."

"A priest?"

"No. No, of course not. Why do you think that?"

"He sounds like a bit of a moralist."

"He is, I guess. But he can't possibly be a priest."

"But he's educated?"

"Yes."

"Any idea what he does for a living?"

"No."

"Any idea where he lives?"

"No."

"Any indication he has a sexual fetish of some kind?"

"Why?"

"Because this town caters to every whim. If he's into bondage, say, I can find out what establishments feature that particular service and maybe get a line on him in one of them. My police pal Charley Sleet is a veritable *Baedeker* of San Francisco perversion palaces."

I was suddenly prattling, feeling crazy myself, semi-detached from my senses. Peggy was shaking her head while observing me closely. "He's interested in all of it, Marsh, but not one thing more than another. He asked me once if I'd ever had a lesbian relationship, but I don't get any hint that he's gay himself. And we've touched on every perversion in the book, at least as much of the book as I know about, but I have no idea which if any of them he's actually committed himself."

"Do you think he's terrorized other women like this, or do you think you're the first?"

"I think I'm the first."

"Why?"

"I don't know. I just think so."

"It sounds as if you're *proud* to be the first."

Her smile betrayed a wound. "It's happening already, Marsh. See? I told you it would."

I had no answer for her, at least not one that encompassed what seemed to be the truth.

"I've had enough for now, Marsh. Please? I don't want to do this anymore."

By that time I didn't either.

11

Our itchy silence was only interrupted when Ruthie rang the bell from down below. I buzzed her inside and went out in the hall to wait for her. She emerged from the stairwell moments later, as irritable as a cowgirl just thrown from her horse.

For one of the few times in memory she didn't smile when she saw me. "What the hell happened, Marsh?" she asked, her voice a rasp of concern. "It wasn't rape, was it?"

I shook my head. "He shoved her down the stairs."

"Shit. Is she hurt bad?"

"Her ankle's sprained and her ribs hurt, but I think she's all right. She won't let me call the doctor. Or the cops."

Ruthie's angry eyes were comets in the dark hallway. "She know who did it?"

"She says it was the spider."

"Who the hell is that?"

"The guy who's been hassling her on the phone every night," I explained. "That's what I call him: the spider. She told you about all that, right?"

Ruthie nodded. "I *hate* the bastards who don't have the guts to ask for it like a man. But she didn't tell me he was tracking her, Marsh. She didn't tell me the son of a bitch was liable to try some barnyard stuff. If she had I wouldn't have let her out of my sight."

Ruthie's fury warmed the hallway. I put my arm around her to cool her down. "You couldn't have known, because Peggy didn't know. She had him pegged for a talker and it turns out he's something else. That's why she's so frightened. That's one problem. The other is, the guy has obviously brainwashed her. I'm not real sure she wants him caught." I looked at Ruthie closely. "She tells me she doesn't have any idea who it is. Did she tell you anything different?"

If Ruthie knew more than I did she disguised it behind a firm denial. "Nope. I tried to get at it every way I could think of, but if she knows the guy's name she's still sitting on it."

"If she did know his name there's no reason not to tell you, is there?"

Ruthie shrugged. "Maybe she's just got a Texas hunch. Maybe she doesn't want to rope him without being positive her loop's around the right neck. You got any ideas, Marsh?"

I took my arm from Ruthie's shoulders and leaned back against the wall. "The only thing I can think of is maybe an old boyfriend. She's gone out with some doughnut holes from time to time. Maybe one of them didn't like the brushoff she gave him."

"Maybe," Ruthie said dubiously. "Hard to believe she'd run with anyone *that* loco, though. From what she told me about the telephone talk, this spider guy would make a corkscrew look like a stiff dick."

I looked at my watch. "The first thing is to make sure he can't get at her again. I can be back here at six, maybe a little earlier. Can you stick around till then?"

Ruthie nodded. "No sweat. All night if you want. I got a date but I can break it. Do old Caldwell good to keep it holstered another night. Let the old mercury rise a little higher in the tube, if you know what I mean."

"That's all right, Ruthie," I said. "I can handle it tonight, and the weekend, too. But tomorrow and Friday you might have to come over for a while, if you can."

"Whatever's right, sugar bear."

Ruthie's tone was careful and calculating, and I wasn't

sure why. When I asked if she'd brought a weapon, Ruthie patted the hand-tooled purse she always carried, the one made with saddle leather and trimmed in silver conchas, the one that weighed a ton even before she dropped her pearl-handled .44 into it. "I'd like to get something a little more aggressive working for us, Marsh," she said. "Don't like to sit back and give these perverted jaspers another free shot."

"What do you have in mind?"

"I'd like to check out the son-in-law. From what Peggy tells me he's a tad provoked with her. Then there's those boyfriends you mentioned. If you're staying here with Peggy then I might just look one of them up this evening, to see how he stacks up. Plus there's the folks in this building. If one of her neighbors had a mind to, he could scare the girl pretty damned easily, and keep track of her, too."

I glanced involuntarily down the hall, then nodded. "I'd like for us to team up on this, Ruthie. Divide the duties, and hit it as hard as we can. I'm going to try to clear the decks today so I can free up as much time as I can."

"I've already done the same. And I'd be happy to have you as a sidekick, Marsh. Hell, we'd be just like Roy and Dale. That is, if that little filly in there goes along with the idea."

"I don't think she'll object. The guy got to her, Ruthie. I've never seen her frightened before. Of anything."

Ruthie's lips thinned. "And remember this. She was damned frightened even before he decided to get physical with her. When she came to see me yesterday she was already half wild. She know you trailed her to my office, by the way?"

I shook my head. "Maybe we can forget it happened."

Ruthie only smiled. "You like her a lot, don't you, Marsh? Got a big old mushy spot in your ticker for Miss Peggy."

I shrugged. "I guess I do, Ruthie. Maybe more than I realized."

"Just don't let that soft spot spread to your brain, sugar bear. Can land you in a cesspool full of trouble if it does."

I smiled. "I was just thinking that myself. So if you see me softening up, you just kick me in the butt."

"Oh, I'll kick your ass, don't think I won't. Kick you somewheres else, too, if that's what it takes. Give you gonads the size of Gibraltar."

I held up my hands in mock surrender, then looked at my watch again. "I've just got time to hunt up the building manager and ask if he saw anyone suspicious around here yesterday, then I've got to be off. Maybe you can get Peggy talking, see if something pops out that we can use. Otherwise, I'll be back at six or so and we can plan our next step."

I started for the door but Ruthie held fast. "You spend the night here, Marsh?"

I admitted I had.

"You plan on spending it here again?"

"I guess so."

"You sleeping with her, Marsh? You dropping your bucket down her well?"

I started to say something a trifle nasty but Ruthie cut me off. "Not that it's any of my business, usually, who you bed with, but when I got John Henry on me I always like to know the variables, and sex is the trickiest little old variable I've ever come across. I got me a two-inch scar below my left tit because during my deputy days I didn't know one of my esteemed colleagues was sweet on a prisoner we were transporting to the county lockup and he give her the chance to cut us both before she was through. Love slows down the reaction time is what I'm saying, Marsh, know what I mean?"

"I'm not sleeping with her, Ruthie. And I never have."

Ruthie nodded twice. "That's good enough for me." Then she smiled a sly stripe. " 'Course the odds of you mounting her before all this flushes out are pretty damned good. Nothing like the scent of danger to activate the old artillery. Man I dated before I met Harry used to need me to shave him with a straight razor before he could get it up. Might keep it in mind, just in case that's a kink you'd like to keep out of your rope."

"Thanks for the warning. I think."

Ruthie laughed. "Unless I miss my mark, that warning's going to be about as useless as a condom on a canary. Well, you best get on your way, Marsh. I'll ride herd on little Peggy till you make it back to the corral."

I ducked back in the apartment just long enough to get my jacket and say good-bye to Peggy, then trotted down the stairs to the ground floor. Someone had cleaned away the traces of Peggy's fall, all except the lingering smell of raspberry preserves and the cloying scent of a pine cleanser. I opened the door to the lobby to see if the superintendent was in sight. Since he wasn't, I opened the door opposite the one to the lobby.

The garage was low-ceilinged and even darker than the stairwell. It smelled of oils and solvents and generated claustrophobia. The cars were dark hulks of uncertain function hiding behind thick supporting timbers. Still, it was cleaner than such places usually are and provided that most coveted of luxuries—a place to park.

I crossed the slippery floor until I reached a row of doors along the far wall. The one to my left was labeled STORAGE, the next LAUNDRY, the next FURNACE/INCINERATOR. The one I knocked on was on the far right, the one marked SUPERINTENDENT.

The door opened immediately. The man who looked up at me was short and wiry and suggested the harnessed energy of a coiled spring. He wore brown work clothes that were clean and pressed and black brogans that bore a shine more common to jump boots. His black hair and eyes and his caramel skin forecast his ancestry, and his bearing forecast his pride in it. "You are not a tenant," he announced before I could say anything.

"I'm a friend of a tenant," I said quickly. "Ms. Nettleton. In thirty-two. She's my secretary. My name's Tanner." I stuck out a hand.

He was still suspicious but he gave my hand a vibrant shake. "I am Francisco Mendosa. Is there a complaint? Miss Nettleton has not told me of a problem. I cannot repair what I do not know is broken."

He seemed genuinely concerned about the condition of the building and the welfare of the tenants, which made him as rare in the city as a cheap drink. "It's nothing like that," I said. "I'm here about Ms. Nettleton's accident last night."

His eyes narrowed. "What kind of accident?"

"She fell down the stairs."

"Ah. The groceries."

I nodded. "They were hers. I tried to clean up as best I could, but . . ."

His mouth puckered with disgust. "The flour was mixed with the jam. It made a purple glue. I used a putty knife, and a cleanser, and even then . . ." He shrugged helplessly.

"She hurt herself when she fell," I continued, "and—"

"It is not my fault the stairs are dark," Mendosa interrupted. "The owners allow only forty watts. It is not enough. I have told them many times. Mrs. Clinton is seventy-four. She has fallen twice. One day she will be badly hurt. I will advise her to see my son. He is a lawyer. He will make them pay for their neglect."

"What's your son's name?"

His eyes narrowed. "Why do you want to know?"

"I used to be a lawyer myself. I thought I might know him."

"His name is Raoul Mendosa. His office is in the Embarcadero Two. He does mostly immigration work. Since July he is a partner in his firm."

I nodded. "I don't know him personally, but I know of him. He has a fine reputation."

It was true; he did. Mendosa preened at my compliment. I let him enjoy the moment before I got back to business. "Peggy—Ms. Nettleton—didn't slip on the stairs, Mr. Mendosa. Someone pushed her."

His mouth curled. "Who would do such a thing? Mr. Tomkins?"

I filed away the name. "She doesn't know. Whoever did it surprised her and she didn't get a good look at him."

He sighed. "Muggers. They are everywhere. But this is the first time inside the building. I will check the doors. I will also notify the owners, as well as the other tenants. Many things can be improved. The lights. The locks. The elevator. I do my best with what I have, but I cannot be everywhere."

Mendosa's voice vanished into the silent contemplation of the landlord's universal negligence. I asked him not to speak with anyone about Peggy's fall for a few days, until I talked with him again.

"Why not?" he asked. "The tenants should know that security has been broken, so they can take precautions."

"The man who did it may have been interested only in Ms. Nettleton. He may not be a threat to anyone else."

Mendosa frowned. "Are you a policeman?"

"Private detective."

"And you are going to find the man?"

"If I can."

"And you believe I can help you in this?"

"You can if you saw any strangers in the building yesterday. Particularly yesterday evening."

His eyes drifted from my face and stared at the dark wall at my back. "I saw no one," he said after a moment.

"Were there any delivery men or service people? Anyone out of the ordinary you let in the building?"

He thought for another clump of seconds. At my back the furnace made unsettling noises. "No. No deliveries; no repairs. I do the repairs myself, better than the so-called experts."

I reached in my pocket and took out my wallet and gave Mendosa a business card. "If you think of anything at all that might help, I'd appreciate it if you would give me a call."

He took the card, rubbed it with his fingertips, then put

it in his breast pocket. "Raoul's card is engraved," he observed with a blend of pleasure and amazement. "I will help you if I can."

"Don't try to do anything yourself if you see someone hanging around. Just call me. And maybe get a license number if he drives away."

"I will if it is possible to do so."

I told him about Ruthie staying with Peggy for the rest of the day, and about Peggy's bad ankle, and then I started to leave. But I turned back before he closed the door. "How many apartments are there in the building?" I asked.

"Sixteen," he said. "Four each floor."

"How many men are there between the ages of thirty and fifty?"

He wiped his face with his hand. "Men? There are not that many men. Most are old women, because the rents are cheaper than in most Marina buildings. The rents are cheap because the owners spend so little for maintenance. They believe I can do magic with nothing to work with. They are wrong. I have told them many times, but nothing changes. The boiler will be next. It will not last another winter."

"The men," I reminded.

"Mr. Farley. Twenty-two."

"Married?"

"Yes."

"How old?"

"Fifty. Maybe less."

"What does he do for a living?"

"He is a tailor. He has a shop on Chestnut."

"How long has he lived here?"

"Longer than me."

"Anyone else?"

Mendosa squinted.

"What about this Tomkins you mentioned? Why did you think he might have hurt Ms. Nettleton?"

"Of course. Mr. Tomkins. Twenty-three."

"Married?"

"No."

"Age?"

"Forty. Perhaps more."

"Job?"

He shrugged. "He is in and out at all hours. He dresses like a *pachuco*, with the high collar, the open shirt, the chains, the boots."

"How long has he lived here?"

"A year."

"Has he ever said anything to you about Ms. Nettleton?"

"He has said he would like to commit an obscenity with her." Mendosa twisted with embarrassment, failed to meet my eye.

"When was this?"

He shrugged. "Maybe two months ago."

"Did he ever mention any other women in the building?"

"Miss Whittle."

"Anyone else?"

"Miss Smith."

"Who's she?"

"Forty-four."

"Job?"

"Some say she is a whore."

"Who says?"

"Mr. Tomkins."

"Was he joking?"

"He was too angry to be joking."

"What else did he say about her?"

"He said that she and Miss Nettleton were two of a kind."

12

I got to the office by eleven and puttered about in a semi-attentive effort to take care of the odds and ends that were dangling from various current files in an attempt to clear my schedule of everything but Peggy. As I was filling out a time sheet on a pending missing persons case, the lawyer for the Arundel Corporation called to tell me the jury had found in favor of his client after deliberating only twenty minutes, not even stringing it out long enough to collect a free lunch. After hanging up I hurried to the cabinet, extracted the file, and calculated my bill for services rendered, then put a note on Peggy's desk for her to get that statement in the mail first thing. Which led me to wonder when Peggy would be coming back to work. Which led me to consider safety precautions.

I'm in and out of the office all day, leaving Peggy alone much of the time she's on duty. It wasn't as bad as it might have been, since the office is on the second floor and the street-level door is unmarked and opens inconspicuously onto an alley. Not many people show up who don't know where they're going, so safety hadn't previously been a concern. But if Peggy was being stalked by someone determined to do her harm, either I had to make some arrangement for her protection or convince her to stay home until the spider was caught and put away. Since I didn't think I could accomplish the latter, and since I didn't think she'd stand for anything as overt as a bodyguard, I tried to think of something in between. As I was toying with increasingly absurd possibilities, I heard someone walking down the hall. Which gave me an idea good enough to make me put away the Arundel file and walk down the hall myself.

The name on the door at the far end was chiseled into a plank of solid oak, then gilded with a swipe of gold. The door itself was wrapped in a seamless leather swatch held taut by a rectangle of brass tacks with heads as shiny as tiny suns. The stereo speakers cut into the ceiling next to the canister light played a sublime motet that calmed me down and suggested my problems weren't so bad they couldn't be cured by whatever was on the other side of that distinguished door. The trip down the hall from my office, in other words, was professionally and aesthetically uphill.

Arthur Constable was a tax lawyer who limited his practice to people who really needed one, people who bought stock in H&R Block rather than took their returns there. I didn't know Constable well, partly because he was often out of town setting up limited partnerships in places like Braddock or the Bahamas, partly because our paths seldom crossed in the normal course of things, but largely because his penchant for personal display was a bit too aggressive for my taste. He was as thin as wire, about six feet tall, his footsteps so dainty that I could always identify them when they passed my door. Which was why I had followed him to his office to ask if I could share in his secretary's peculiar skills.

A couple of years ago, Constable had begun collecting modern art, as an investment of course, something to do with all those dollars he raked in from clients who could deduct his fee and thus didn't care how much he charged. Soon, Constable's art collection had overrun his condominium, and he housed the overflow in his law office.

The result was both peculiar and disconcerting. Constable's collection was limited to sculpture in decidedly human form, à la George Segal, and thus his office teemed with amazingly lifelike personages, constructed from plaster or plastic or putty, accomplishing everything from knitting to urination. To me the effect was of a fairly unruly mob, but Constable evidently loved it. To guard it all, Constable had fired the secretary who used to work on her tan on the roof on sunny days, and hired a young man who possessed a combination of skills unique in the annals of secretaryhood—a 250-pound former linebacker who offered Constable an equal measure of brawn and short-hand speed.

When I pushed my way into Constable's office, his beefy secretary was the first object I saw, dwarfing the similarly unbelievable figures at his back. The sign on the desk claimed his name was Richard Husky, and his desk was exactly across my path, so I could get at neither Constable nor the artwork without bypassing Richard's formidable presence. The biceps that bulged below his sleeves and the chest that deformed his shirt announced that the passage would not be easy.

I thought he recognized me but I wasn't sure. His eyes remained friendly, at least, and as I approached the desk his huge hands stopped performing amazingly intricate feats on a digital calculator. "My name is Tanner," I said. "I have an office down the hall."

He nodded. "I know." His voice was surprisingly gentle for such a giant.

I gestured toward the broad expanse of desk he sat behind, which was a teak slab atop four plexiglass supports that were so transparent the wood seemed to float in the air like a caliph's carpet. "Do you have a gun in there by any chance?" I asked.

"What?" A blood vessel appeared above his temple.

"Do you have a gun in the desk drawer? Or somewhere nearby?"

He hesitated, discomfited by the questions. "Yes."

"Do you know how to use it?"

"Yes," he repeated.

"Do you mind if I ask your boss if I can lease you and your weapon for a while? It's no big deal. You probably won't even have to leave your desk."

He thought about it, then shrugged his massive shoulders. "Whatever."

I gestured toward the door that lay beyond the sculpture court that lay beyond the desk. "He in?"

Richard nodded. "If you'll wait a moment, I'll see if he's free. He's been trying to reach Brazil, but the connection's bad."

He stood up. I gestured to the sign on his desk, the one etched in brushed aluminum. "Is your name really Husky?"

He shook his head and smiled. "Arthur thought it fit the scene. For what he pays me he can call me anything he wants. My real name has eleven consonants."

I had always assumed Richard was gay. Now I thought perhaps he was just good-natured. He left his desk and threaded his way between a kinetic figure with a plexiglass abdomen that revealed a colorful collection of entrails, and a tangled mound that was in fact two plastic people coupling, and disappeared behind the floor-to-ceiling door. I looked over the crowd he left behind, and decided they all looked much more human than I did.

The door reopened as I was running my hand along the spear of a big brown bushman, and Richard motioned for me to enter. As I passed him I sniffed a sweet cologne, and noticed a small pistol in a holster at his belt. The more I saw of Richard, the better I liked my plan.

Arthur Constable was dressed more for a formal dinner than a day at the office. His suit was black silk, his tie thin and silver-threaded, his cuffs French and linked with polished coins. His hair was prematurely white, to match the silver in his accessories. His eyes were blue, his skin ruddy, his mustache trim and sophisticated.

Constable and his desk were on a platform that raised them both a foot off the floor, so that when I accepted his invitation and sat down, his professionally pleasant smile was distinctly on a plane more elevated than my own. "I'm Marsh Tanner," I said again. "I'm a private investigator. I work down the hall."

Constable bowed his head. "Of course. It's nice to see you again."

"This is quite an office," I said, taking in the couch, coffee table, lamp and easy chair, drapes and chandelier. "I probably should apologize for lowering the property values in the neighborhood."

Constable waved away my lowliness. "To each his own, Mr. Tanner. On the whole I find the building quite satisfactory."

"Me, too," I replied, then wondered how to begin, since my errand suddenly seemed absurd. "I've got a bit of a problem at the office," I said finally. "I thought maybe you could help me out."

Constable raised his brow. "How would I do that? Is it a tax question of some sort?" His tone implied that taxes were surely the least of my worries.

I shook my head. "It's my secretary. Some guy has been harassing her on the phone for weeks. Last night he assaulted her as well, trying to hurt her or scare her, or maybe even kill her."

Constable frowned, and one of his small hands made a small fist. "How terrible. Is she all right?"

"Yes. Luckily."

"Are you certain?"

"Yes. About her physical condition, at least."

"Where did this happen? Here? In the building?"

I shook my head. "At her apartment."

"Have the police been called?"

"No."

"Why not?"

"She doesn't want them. But that's not the problem. The problem is, I'm sure she'll insist on coming back to work tomorrow, and I'm worried about what could happen if I have to leave and she's in the office alone."

Constable unwound his fist and folded his hands in front of him. "I see. And do you have an idea that I could be of service?"

I nodded. "I thought I could notify your secretary when

Peggy would be alone, and he could open the door to the hallway and I could leave the door to my office open as well, and then he could tell if anyone tried any rough stuff down the hall. And charge to the rescue. I don't imagine anyone who likes to pick on women would decide to go up against him."

Constable was silent for a minute. "It's not at all a foolproof system, Mr. Tanner."

"No," I agreed. "But I don't think she'll put up with a bodyguard. A security guard at the front door might do it, except I can't afford to hire one."

Constable's face brightened. "I have an idea for an improvement. Do you care to hear it?"

"Sure."

He leaned back in his chair and stared at the ceiling, which was a swirl of rococo. "I have recently had a new sound system installed in my office." He gestured toward a black stack of components rising against four feet of wall space to his right. The speakers were the size of refrigerators, the components included two video monitors and a compact disc player. "The system broadcasts to this office, the reception area, the hallway outside, even to my private bathroom." Constable glanced at a narrow door to his left. "The audio man who installed it is a young genius. He was recommended to me by Bill Graham himself."

Since I wasn't sure what he was driving at I didn't say anything.

"The audio engineer's name is Manchester. My idea is, he could install a simple transmitter near your secretary's work station, and connect it to a simple speaker at Richard's desk, so that he would be certain to hear all relevant sounds, not just those loud enough to travel around the corner and down the hall and through my door. The installation would be temporary, of course, removable when this nasty business is cleared up."

"It's a good plan," I admitted. "Except that Richard might hear some things I don't want him to hear. Things my clients would want to remain confidential."

"It could have a switch at your secretary's end, so the system is activated only when she's alone or there's a sign of trouble. And deactivated if you're engaged in matters of a private nature."

When I didn't react, Constable hurried on. "My system is state of the art, which means Mr. Manchester charged me a small fortune for it. I'm sure if I asked he'd install a simple intercom arrangement for next to nothing. If you're interested I would be happy to get in touch with him immediately."

I dislike being indebted to others, in either the monetary or the moral sense, so I hate to have other people do me the favors that create such imbalances. But I couldn't deny that Constable's suggestion was substantially more certain to protect Peggy than my own neanderthal approach, and as the seconds ticked by and Constable eyed me from his perch on high I could think of no real reason to refuse his offer.

"Okay," I said, with a reservation born of years of misfires arising out of just these situations. "But I pay all charges, plus I pay Richard a hundred bucks a week to keep his ears open, and a couple hundred more if anything comes up that requires him to run to the rescue."

"That seems satisfactory," Constable acknowledged. "I'll try to reach Mr. Manchester right away."

I looked at my watch. "I have a meeting, but I'll be back in the office by four. Maybe you could call me then."

"Of course."

"I appreciate your help."

"I'm happy to do it. I can certainly understand your concern."

"I'd better go ask Richard if he's willing to help me out."

Constable shook his head. "There's no need. I'll mention it to him when he finishes his current project. I'm sure he'll be thrilled to have something more . . . demanding to do than fill out tax forms while he watches over my funny little family."

Constable tittered a deprecating laugh, and I thanked him once again, then went back to the office, locked up, and headed for my appointment.

My destination was the twenty-fourth floor of the Transamerica Building. The meeting was with a lawyer in one of the larger firms in town, a hundred attorneys give or take a dozen, practice strictly commercial and insurance defense. I'd never done any previous work for either the lawyer or his firm, so we measured each other warily as I was ushered into his tasteful, conservative digs by his secretary, who looked nothing at all like Richard Husky.

The lawyer's name was Mason Yockey. He was about my age, which would have made him either a senior-junior or a junior-senior partner, at an approximate salary of two hundred and fifty thousand per, not including bonuses. But however much Mason Yockey was paid, the look on his face suggested he wasn't paid enough.

Yockey was beefy, of average height, handsome in a rotund sort of way, the way tank cars and beer cans are handsome, but he was not robust. He looked on the brink of an exhausted collapse, and he looked as if he might welcome it when it came.

He waved me to a chair, thanked me for coming, tugged his tie knot another inch away from his throat, and sat down behind a desk awash in paper. "I got your name from Andy Potter," he said to open the conversation. "He had a lot of nice things to say about you."

"Andy and I go back a long time."

Yockey nodded. "You used to practice law, I believe."

"Yep."

"Why'd you quit?"

"I got tired of feeling the way you look."

I grinned to show it was nothing personal. Yockey seemed neither amused nor insulted, seemed beyond any emotion more electric than ennui. "Yeah," he managed finally. "It's been a bad day. Hell, it's been a bad year. Which I guess is why you're here. I'm hoping to take a bit of the load off."

"How?"

His gaze lumbered away from mine and landed on the two-foot stack of files on the floor beside his desk. He looked at the stack and then at me, as though it was a problem child and I was the counselor who was going to put out the fire that burned between them. "The defendant in all those cases and about a hundred more just like them is Lind Pharmaceuticals. Ever hear of them?"

"I think so," I said, not quite remembering where.

"Well, they're not as big as Lilly or Merck or those type, but they do a big business in some specific areas. They've got the most effective arthritis medication on the market, and a decent hypertension suppressant, and some more esoteric stuff that does well, too. They grossed about three hundred million last year. If it wasn't for the fucking litigation they're drowning in, they'd have had a big year."

"What kind of litigation?"

"Ever hear of the Dalkon Shield?" Yockey looked at me carefully.

"Sure."

"Well, about ten years ago Lind made one of those intrauterine devices too. Not nearly as popular as the Shield, but unfortunately it had the same side effects, or so about two hundred plaintiffs claim."

"You mean infections, infertility, spontaneous abortions, wires through fetuses' jaws, and like that?"

Yockey seemed to shudder. "Yeah. All that stuff. Christ." He paused to regain his breath and his perspective. "Anyway, my job is to come up with a defense to all these claims and I guess one of them is going to have to be one that the courts have thrown out in most jurisdictions but has been admitted in Oregon and a few others."

"What defense is that?"

"Basically it's a promiscuity thing. If we can show a plaintiff has had multiple sex partners over the past few years—a promiscuous lifestyle in other words—we can argue that any uterine infection or other reproductive problem resulted from a venereal disease of some sort and not from the use of our device."

"What do you mean by promiscuous lifestyle?"

"Sex with multiple partners, like I said."

"How many is multiple?"

"I don't know. Five. Ten."

"How about two?"

"Two?" Yockey rubbed his head. "Sure. I guess. Two or more. Hell, those hayseeds on the jury will buy anything if you present it right. Two. Multiple. Like I said."

When I didn't respond, Yockey continued. "So basically that's the job. We give you a list of plaintiffs in this area and you locate witnesses who can testify that they screwed any greasy dick that came their way and I try to convince a judge that kind of garbage is relevant so we won't be tossed out on our ass when we offer the evidence in court. We'll pay your rate, plus expenses, plus a premium of a thousand dollars per plaintiff that you give us a successful defense for. What do you say?"

"You really want to know?"

Yockey fidgeted. "Sure. That's what you're here for."

I smiled. "I was going to say you ought to be ashamed of yourself. But from the look of you I'd say you already are."

13

My glittering self-righteousness lasted about a block and a half. By the time I turned into the alley I work in I was feeling sorry for Mason Yockey and ashamed of my own hypocrisy. My house is all glass and has been for years. I don't throw that many stones, and when I do they somehow turn into boomerangs and I usually regret it.

When I got to the second floor there was a young man on a stepladder right outside my office, stapling a wire along the shadow molding in the hallway. An untethered length dangled down beside my doorjamb, swaying to and fro, like a lead I'd never followed but should have.

The man on the ladder was half my age, with a tangled cape of henna hair that fell below his shoulders, cords faded to the color of ice, and bare feet. When he saw me coming he hopped off the ladder and waited for me. The smile on his face revealed a lot of gum. "You Mr. Tanner?"

"Yep."

"I was hoping you'd show up."

"You need to get inside." I gestured toward the door.

"Right. Arthur told me what you need. I got a little micro mike right here, small enough not to attract attention but sensitive enough to pick up anything above a burp. Take me about ten minutes to hook her up, then I'm gone. Amp and speaker's already installed, right behind Richard's desk. Stuck it onto one of those human sculpture things. A few of them talk already, so it'll just seem like one more if it starts broadcasting when someone's around. Got a headset option for him, too, in case you don't want everyone in the waiting area hearing what's going on down here."

"Sounds good," I said. "How much am I going to owe you for all this?"

"Installation's free. Gear will run you about a hundred."

"That sounds too cheap. And I want to pay you for your time."

"The time's on me," he objected. "And the Japs dump this stuff over here for next to nothing, for sure below cost. This is pretty basic, what with the wires and all; outmoded, really. Everything I use is a fucking loss leader, anyway, which is why I can underbid the big boys when I want. A buck goes a long way in electronics these days. And it'll stay that way unless they do something stupid with the yen. My name's Manchester, by the way."

He stuck out a hand and we shared a brisk shake. He was one of those kids you see around from time to time, competent, intelligent, totally immersed in passion—music, chess, mathematics, computers—apparently as happy as hogs in mud, as Ruthie Spring would say. I'd always envied such a focus, and I envied young Manchester right then.

I unlocked the office and let the kid finish up his job. He put the microphone behind the ficus and fastened the on-off button in the kneehole in Peggy's desk. When he was done he suggested we check it out.

I went down to Constable's office and stood beside Richard as the kid made various noises in my office with what sounded like a harmonica. The speaker broadcast every reedy tone in a surprisingly rich facsimile. When he'd finished with a riff I looked at Richard. "This arrangement okay with you?"

He grinned. "Anything Mr. Constable wants is okay with me. He tells me to chase a pack of Libyans with my hands tied behind my back, I just take off running."

I smiled. "I don't think there'll be more than one," I

said. "But he might be a little nuts. The main thing is to keep my secretary from getting hurt. You just scare him off. Don't try to apprehend him."

Richard folded his arms and looked like he was carrying firewood. "You really think he'll make a try for her right here in the building?"

"I don't know what I think at this point. Maybe by tomorrow I will. Did Constable tell you I'm paying you a bonus for this?"

He shook his head.

"Well, it's worth a hundred a week to me not to worry when I leave Peggy alone. And if you have to play Superman, there's a few hundred more in it for you, depending on my bank balance."

"You don't have to do that. Hell, it's worth it for the excitement." Richard looked behind him at the thicket of modern art. "Watching over Arthur's family all day isn't exactly as stimulating as watching Riggins come at you off-tackle and wondering how you're going to knock him down."

Despite his disclaimer, I wanted to be certain Richard kept on his toes, so I told him I'd pay the first week in advance. When I reached for my wallet he waved me away. "I like to earn my money, Mr. Tanner. Next week will be fine."

We chatted for another minute, then I went on my way, which was back to the office to tell young Manchester his system was working fine and to thank him for his effort.

He told me there was nothing to it, just some old stuff he'd been wanting to get rid of anyway, and he had a deal on some video disc players if I was interested. Better than cost. When I told him I'd pass, he gathered up his tools and started to leave. But when he reached the door he stopped and looked back at me with a half smile on his lips. I thought he was going to ask why I wanted the microphone installed, but he had something different in mind.

"Been cheaper to use the one you already had," he said, still smiling, still watching me closely.

I didn't know what he was talking about and I told him so.

He nodded thoughtfully, as though I'd confirmed a suspicion, then beckoned for me to follow him out into the hallway. When we got there he closed the office door and leaned back against it. "I hate to tell you, Mr. Tanner, but your place is already bugged."

I tried to conceal my surprise. "Are you sure?"

He nodded. "No doubt about it. And this isn't some Stone Age junk like I hooked up, either. This is state of the art. Little transmitter about the size of a pea, will broadcast anything audible in that room a distance of half a mile."

"Any idea where it transmits to?"

Manchester shrugged. "*I* sure don't have any way to track it. The spy guys have tracing gear that could do it, but that's not my line of work. None of my business what's going on here, Mr. Tanner, but if I was you I'd pry the little bastard out of there and drown it."

"Where is it?"

"You know that print behind your secretary's desk? The Cézanne?"

I nodded.

"Look in the upper right corner of the frame. Little quarter-inch hole drilled in there among the curlicues, the bug's stuck right inside, snug as an egg in a nest. Perfect position, which is why I was checking it out as a possible mount for my own device. That baby cost five hundred bucks, easy, Mr. Tanner. Pick up a pin dropping and send it three thousand feet. Wish I had one of my own, just to see what makes it tick."

"Any idea who might do that kind of work? Planting it, I mean?"

He looked at the letters on my office door. "Hell, man. I thought that was the kind of stuff *you* guys did."

I thanked Manchester for his help and went back in the

office and got out my Swiss army knife and pried the little bug out of the picture frame. It weighed nothing and was entirely unremarkable, except for its totalitarian implications. I was wondering who might have wanted to eavesdrop on me when I realized that the target was clearly Peggy, the bugger undoubtedly the spider.

I tossed the insidious little nugget up in the air and caught it, then opened the drawer of my desk and took out a bottle of vitamin E capsules that had been in there since the last time I swore to do something about my health. I dropped the bug in with the oblong cure-alls, then replaced the bottle in the desk, locked up the office, and drove to the Marina, stopping along the way to pick up my shaving kit from my apartment, seething all the while at the stealthy invasion of my privacy. By the time I got to Peggy's I knew a little more about what she had been going through since the spider put her in his sights, and had empathized enough with the past targets of my own eavesdropping efforts to resolve not to do that anymore.

When I buzzed at the street door Ruthie let me in. The smells of jam and cleanser still loitered in the stairwell, though less densely. When I got to the third floor Ruthie was waiting for me in Peggy's doorway. "You got back early," she said as I joined her.

"The meeting didn't turn into a job after all."

I was too embarrassed to tell Ruthie about the bug. When I looked past her into the apartment I could see the couch was empty except for the forsaken afghan and the equally forsaken Marilyn. "Where's Peggy?" I asked.

"Napping."

"How's she doing?"

"Physically, she's choice to prime. The ribs are almost a hundred percent and she can walk on the ankle if she's careful and doesn't tip. Says she's going to work in the morning. You should probably try to stop her but you probably won't be able to."

I nodded. "She's almost as independent as you are."

Ruthie looked at me. "Almost," she muttered enigmatically.

Because of the way she said it I looked at her. "What does that mean?"

She bit her lip and shrugged. "Nothing, I reckon. We had a little spat, is all. She didn't like me fussing over her, I guess, and I can't blame her since I'd feel the same way if we were vice and versa. And she liked it even less when I started asking questions about this dude on the telephone. Sometimes I ain't real tactful, I suppose. Probably because I come from a long line of Texas assholes. And there's no asshole in the *world* as big as a Texas asshole. 'Course being an asshole will get you a long way in the detective business. Or just about any damned business these days."

Ruthie's jaw swelled in an angry bulge. I didn't want to do anything to fan the flames, but I had to ask her what Peggy had to say about the spider.

Ruthie pushed herself away from the doorjamb. "Come on inside, Marsh. I'll see if she's still bedded down, then we can palaver in the front room. I got a cup of coffee turning tepid on the windowsill."

Ruthie went to the bedroom door and peeked inside, then went to the couch and sat down. I joined her in the living room, taking the chair I'd occupied the night before, depositing my kit on the coffee table.

Ruthie sipped her coffee and made a face. "Too late in the day for this swill. Want me to make some fresh?"

I shook my head. "Keeps me awake."

"Hell, Marsh. You should be glad there's something in the world that does."

I let Ruthie prattle away about all the reasons there are not to fall asleep in the middle of your life, because I knew she was doing it mostly to gather her thoughts. After a couple of minutes she wound down, and when she was ready to talk about what I wanted to talk about she crossed a leg and looked at me. "Seems to me this thing's a little like the Patty Hearst business," she said.

"How do you mean?"

"The guy on the phone is fucking little Peggy over, and for some reason she's helping him do it. What I mean is, I'm not real sure she wants it to stop."

I'd had the same impression and for reasons that had more to do with me than Peggy I had tried to suppress it. Now I tried to rebut Ruthie. "I don't think she liked getting shoved down the stairs."

"No, but I think she kind of likes it when he talks trash to her. Now, Marsh. Don't give me that look. You know it's true and you know we're not going to get this gopher out of her garden unless we know exactly what the variables are. Correct?"

"Correct."

"So why do you suppose she let this John guy whittle on her like that?"

I shrugged. "We all have some unresolved sexual desires, Ruthie. Maybe Peggy's working through something from her past."

"Sounds kind of pointy-headed to me."

"Maybe. But even if she wanted to stop it I'm not sure she could. At this point I'm not as interested in why Peggy's doing what she's doing as I am in getting hold of the guy and putting him out of commission."

Ruthie didn't say anything.

"Do you think she knows who he is but isn't saying?"

Ruthie shook her head.

"Did you come up with any new candidates when you talked to her today?"

"I worked her as much as I could, Marsh, but she wasn't ready to chew on it. Wouldn't tell me anything at all about the guy. About precious little else, neither. We sort of discovered we don't like each other right at the moment, is what it comes down to. Not that it'll affect the way I do my job."

I decided to let that pass until I could think of what to do about it. "How about the men in her life? Any of them look like a candidate?"

"Not real good, but there's a couple worth eyeballing. The son-in-law, or whatever he is. A boyfriend named Hess. Maybe some others." Ruthie looked at her watch. "I might just pay Mr. Hess a visit tonight, if you're here for the duration."

"I can stay, but there's someone in the building that's worth looking into. Why don't I see if he's in, then you can take off when I get back."

"Suits me," Ruthie said. "Who is it?"

"Name is Tomkins. Apparently he tried to hit on Peggy and she wouldn't play. The janitor says Tomkins was pretty hot about it."

"Yeah, well, she gets that look on her, Marsh. That 'you're not as good as I am so how dare you speak to me that way' look. Tossed it at me a few times today. Tends to get under your saddle blanket, let me tell you."

I grinned. "How come you're so upset, Ruthie?"

"Ah, shit. I just get pissed off when women like your little Peggy in there do what she's doing. She's a *victim*, goddamnit. Why the hell doesn't she act like one?"

...ted to Ruthie upstairs.... giving him diminished... for the
bedside...loved... watering the side of too ...ordeal
der plate ... The ... off his body was as... his soul too
bitter... it... his... ind toys.
soften ... in... ... ... as L...
...y ... ...y ... ...
...ound the... as... that
all I had... this... was... well ...
s hand. I left the apartment to the thro...

14

I left Ruthie in the living room and took the stairs to the lobby. The bank of tenants' mailboxes was just inside the front door, four ranks of four doors of vented brass. A Judson Tomkins had printed his name in childish block letters on a white rectangle taped to the door to box 23. I went back to the stairwell and climbed one flight.

The only sounds in the hallway were my sharp knocks on the door and the wooden rattle they produced. I kept at it for more than a minute, then checked my watch. It was just after five. If he worked nearby he could be returning any minute. If he worked downtown it was hard to tell. Not many people made it out of the financial district without at least one stop along the way, whether at a strip joint like Pandora's or a singles stop like Perry's or a hardcore drinkers' hangout like the ones I frequent.

I was halfway back to the stairwell when I saw him coming. When someone tells a tale you automatically imagine faces to match the deeds described. Sometimes the actual participants fulfill your expectations; other times the disparity is so dramatic you begin to doubt the story's truth. Based on Francisco Mendosa's account of their conversations, Judson Tomkins fell in the former category.

His head was large and blockish, his body overlarded, his eyes fleshy slits of shallow suspicion. His nose bore a drinker's mottled glow, his lips bulged in pulpy, overripe dimensions, his cheeks were sprayed with a two-day growth of reddish beard. The cuffs of his plaid shirt hung almost to his fingertips, giving him a primate's aspect. His black slacks were knit, so snug the side pockets flared like displaced ears. The heels on his boots were as high as ink bottles, and made him seem top-heavy.

Tomkins looked me over warily as I approached, decided I was neither friend nor foe, and prepared to shoulder past me in the narrow passage. When I held my ground he had to stop. "What the fuck, Jack," he grumbled. "This ain't a one-way street." His teeth were stained and irregularly aligned, like rotting fenceposts.

"I've been looking for you, Tomkins."

That brought a wary scowl and a blustering pose. We were chest-to-chest. I could smell his beery breath and hear the soggy murmur of his lungs. He wanted to shove me out of his way or worse, but he was afraid I might be someone it would be a mistake to anger, which made Tomkins one of those men who live on the edge of law and ethics, whose lives and livelihoods make them vulnerable to both de jure and de facto enforcement authorities, who have frequent need to look behind them.

While Tomkins idled in uncertainty, I stood and watched and waited. "What are you, another cop?" he asked finally. "I thought I'd seen them all by now."

"Why would you think that?"

"Because you look like one and act like one and if it looks like a turd and acts like a turd then I figure it's going to smell a lot like shit. For your information, that school beef is a crock. Hell, I was just on my way to work. I never got off the fucking sidewalk. I never touched the little—"

Tomkins broke off his protest because what he said was more revealing than he intended. "Did you take a fall for it, Tomkins?" I asked mildly. "Or are you out on bail?"

Instead of answering, Tomkins began to swell with confidence. "You ain't no cop. A cop would already know that shit. A cop would be here to remind me of every last detail of that fucking trumped-up rap. So since you're not a cop there's no reason in the world I got to talk to you, right? Hell, I don't got to talk to you even if you *are* a cop."

"Why don't I take a guess, Tomkins?" I continued mildly. "Why don't I guess that you're on probation or parole. Why don't I guess that you're about to have your probation revoked because you got caught hanging around a schoolyard. Why don't I guess that you took a fall on a sex charge. Indecent exposure, maybe? To a schoolkid? You're a registered sex offender, right, Tomkins?"

"You punk. You don't know crap."

"Why don't I guess that a lot of people don't know that about you, Tomkins. Maybe the manager of this building? Your boss at work? The boys at the bar? A girlfriend? So do we talk or do I spread the word about your checkered past?"

Tomkins seemed to be trying to disappear, to hide behind his buttons. "What the hell do you want?" he asked with half the voice that had cursed me moments earlier.

"Let's go to your place," I said. "I'll ask you some questions. If you answer them, I'll leave."

"What kind of questions?"

I looked up and down the hall. "Inside, Tomkins. Not here."

He cursed again, but shouldered past me and fumbled at the door to his apartment, then finally went inside. A manila envelope lay on the floor just inside the door, and he kicked it out of his way as he stomped into the room. I followed him in, and was immediately awash in a sordid confirmation of my suspicions.

It was a smaller place than Peggy's, a studio apartment with a small kitchenette and a smaller bath and a single room that encompassed all the rest. The bed occupied most of the floor space, the grimy bedclothes worn and faded, as though someone had lain ill in them for weeks, and finally expired. The smell of the room was sour, a fetid blend of sweaty clothing and spoiling food and mildewed furnishings. I made my breaths as shallow as I could.

With a twist and a kick, Tomkins sent the bed up into the wall, so there was room to get to the couch beneath the window. He'd acted so quickly I wondered what there was about the bed that could possibly be more revealing than the seamy panoply that surrounded it.

The apartment was a pervert's paradise, all four walls a tattered collage of flesh—hundreds of nudie pictures torn from various skin magazines, from the slick, proud boasts of *Penthouse* and *Playboy* to the sad, flat hopelessness of the less prominent publications. Women alone, women with men, women with women, women with phallic substitutes both electric and not. Color, black and white, and grainy washes that fell somehow in between. A few were Polaroids, amateur poses of amateur women snapped by Tomkins himself or maybe even gifts conferred on him by the hapless subjects.

The raw material from which the display had been constructed littered the floor, magazines and books by the hundreds, most of them shredded and torn as though their innards had been ripped away by starving beasts. I was already revolted before I noticed the crowning touch—on the ceiling above the place where the bed had been was a giant color enlargement of the Madonna and her naked child.

"This going to take long?" Tomkins asked as he took off his jacket and tossed it toward a metal folding chair. "I got things to do."

"I can guess," I said, still looking at the pictures.

Tomkins chuckled. "Like 'em?"

"Not particularly."

"Yeah, that's what they all say. But they all keep lookin'. Just like you."

As I shifted my stare, Tomkins scraped some magazines off the couch and gestured to it. "If you're through looking you can sit down. Or maybe you want to see my videos. I got some videos you can't believe. There's one my navy buddy sent from Panama that'll make you shoot your gun in five minutes, guaran-fucking-teed. I tell you, man, the thing I love about women is, they'll do god-damned *anything* for bread."

"Sit down, Tomkins. Let's get this over with."

Tomkins finished with whatever he was doing and looked at me with a smile that tried and failed to belie the room. "You want a beer?"

"No, thanks."

"Care if I have one?"

"Go ahead."

He went to the kitchen nook and opened the tiny refrigerator and took out a can of Coors. Half of it was gone by the time he took a seat across from me. "So what's the deal?" he asked, folksy, friendly, licking suds off his lower lip, as if to parody the slavery sadist his room suggested. I took one more look at the women who surrounded us. They made me feel as doomed as a gladiator, my gender a crime that I was guilty of, my punishment a unanimous thumbs down.

"A woman in this building's being harassed by someone, Tomkins," I began. "Sexually harassed."

"Yeah? Who?"

"Never mind that now. I'm here because someone suggested you made a good suspect."

"What asshole said *that*?"

I ignored him. "You been making phone calls, Tomkins? You like to do more than look at sexy pictures?"

Tomkins frowned absently. "Calls? What calls? You from the fucking *phone* company, or what?"

"I mean, have you been telephoning women, threatening to harm them if they don't stay on the line, asking them about their sex life? Is that part of your thing, Tomkins? Along with your interest in erotic art?"

His smile turned thin and cunning. "Shit. I don't do stuff like that. But hell, maybe now I'll start. The broads, man, they *love* it when you're evil."

After another pull at his beer his grin became sloppy and taunting, a consequence of the beers and the lifelong disintegration of his mind and my own false step. I tried to match him with Peggy's description of the spider who'd ensnared her, the man who so enticingly combined guile and charm with psychological terror, and I couldn't do it. Surely Judson Tomkins was not a man to whom Peggy Nettleton would confess anything at all.

"If it is you making the calls, I'm advising you to stop," I said halfheartedly, then waved toward the contents of the room. "One look at this place and the cops will haul you in for questioning on every sex crime committed from Oxnard to Ukiah. I can have a police detective over here in fifteen minutes. You'll be on a list you won't get off of even if you become a monk."

Tomkins swore again. "I'm already on a lot of lists, Jack. One more won't make no never mind."

"I hear you got a bad time from Miss Smith up in forty-four."

Tomkins sneered. "That whore? What about her?"

"What'd you do when she turned you down, Tomkins? Threaten to knock her around?"

"Turn me down? Hell, I wouldn't give her the satisfaction. She's a walking, talking condom, man. I wouldn't touch her unless she was dipped in bleach."

"How about Peggy Nettleton?"

"Miss High and Mighty? What about her?"

"You hit on her, too; right?"

"So what if I did? I was just fooling around. So I made some crack about her tits. Hell, at her age she should be glad I noticed."

"You try to pay her back for telling you to get lost? You shove her down the stairs last night, Tomkins?"

He wrinkled his lips and sniffed. "I don't know nothing about it."

I gave him my roughest, toughest look. "That better be true. Because if I find out it's not, I'm the one that'll be doing the pushing."

"Yeah? You and what army?"

I glanced at Tomkins' gallery again, and stood up and

115

glared down at him. "You want to try me right now? Here in front of your girlfriends?"

He leaned away from my challenge. "You prick. So I like a little T and A. So what? That makes me like every sap in the world who watches the jigglers on TV. You probably like the little boys, right? Along with the rest of the fags in this town. Hell, you're probably one of those Man-Boy Love Society creeps. 'Sex before eight or by then it's too late.' Huh? *Those* guys are the perverts. Me, I'm just the boy next door."

I'd had my fill of Judson Tomkins, but I tried one more tack. "This apartment isn't cheap, Tomkins. How do you afford to live here?"

"Hey. I pay the rent. What's it to you anyhow?"

"You deal in porn? You sell those pictures to your buddies?"

He started to squirm. "Naw. This is a private collection, is all."

"Then what do you do for a living?"

"I got a job."

"Where?"

"A bookstore. I'm a fucking intellectual. What of it?"

"What bookstore?"

"Place on Turk."

"I bet I know that place. The Pink Palace, right?"

"Yeah. So?"

"So you buy this stuff at discount."

"Yeah. Wholesale's the only way to fly."

"You into the production end? You got a photo studio somewhere? Or maybe you bring them here."

He shook his head. "Who'd want to work with those cunts? They're ball-busting bitches. All of them." Tomkins looked at his wall of skin. His look was pained and despairing, as though the naked bodies were flesh of his flesh and blood of his blood, offspring who had deserted the family for a life subsumed in corruption. "Will you get the fuck out of here?" he said finally, his voice suddenly a quiet and effective plea.

I walked to the door. When I turned back I caught Tomkins eyeing the brown envelope that lay on the floor beside me, the one he'd kicked out of his way when we'd come in, the one an appropriate size to contain the latest addition to his gallery. "Leave the women in this building alone, Tomkins," I ordered harshly. "Understand? If you don't the only pictures you'll be looking at are the ones in the San Quentin *News*."

15

When I got back to Peggy's, Ruthie had her coat on and was ready to leave. "I'll mosey on out of here, Marsh," she said, without her usual humor. "Going to stop by and have a chat with one of the boyfriends, then go home and wait for Caldwell to come over and join me in some unnatural acts."

"What's the boyfriend's name?"

"Owen Hess. He's the one who threatened her. Lives out on Diamond Heights. I'll pay him a social call, see if he still has a stone in his hoof over little Peggy, then talk to you tomorrow. I can be back here by nine if you want."

"Good. That'll give me a chance to hunt up the daughter in the morning."

"What about the guy in the building?"

"He's definitely a deviant, but from Peggy's description the phone thing seems too sophisticated for him. He's warped enough to keep an eye on, though. Pornography is like dope and Oreos—the more you get the more you want."

"Anything else you want me to do, Marsh?"

I shook my head. "Peggy still asleep?"

"Yep."

Ruthie's tone still had an edge to it. "Don't be too hard on her, Ruthie," I said. "She's scared and she's trying to hide it by being brassy or bossy or whatever. Not everyone's as tough as you are, you know."

"Ah, hell, Marsh. I'm just a loco ole woman who's just a tad jealous of that filly in there, you know?"

"Jealous of what?"

Ruthie shrugged. "Of how she looks, what she knows, who she is." Ruthie gave me a crooked grin. "Hell, maybe I'm just jealous of who she works for."

We exchanged glances that condensed a lot of history, then Ruthie waved abruptly and vanished through the door. I went to the living room and awaited Sleeping Beauty.

She emerged an hour later, shuffling through the bedroom door. She yawned, then rubbed her eyes and looked at me. "Hi," she said.

"Hi."

"What time is it?"

"Six-thirty."

"God. I slept three hours."

"Good."

"You always seem to be watching me wake up."

Peggy looked around the room. "Where's Ruthie?"

"Home."

She sighed. "We had a fight, kind of."

"I know."

"It was my fault. I acted . . . prissy. She asked me a lot of questions and was angry when I wasn't as responsive as she wanted me to be. But . . . I don't know, Marsh; I haven't worked all this out yet, you know? I'm not sure *what* I think about it all, and Ruthie couldn't seem to accept that. She just keeps hinting *she'd* never let herself get caught in a situation like this."

"Ruthie's hard to handle sometimes. But she doesn't hold a grudge."

Peggy rubbed her eyes again, then crossed her arms and shivered. "You're both being so *good* to me. I'm so guilty I can hardly stand it."

"If I was being good I would have brought back something for us to eat."

She smiled lazily. "Did you learn anything today?"

"About the spider?"

She frowned. "Who? Oh. The spider. It's funny, but I don't think of him that way. Yes."

"I'm not sure if I learned anything or not. Do you know a man named Tomkins?"

She frowned.

"Lives down in twenty-three. Looks like a character from central casting, star of *The Man Who Raped LA.*"

Peggy's slack features immediately congealed. "Him."

"Didn't you have some trouble with Tomkins?"

She wrinkled with distaste. "Not really. He asked me out once. I turned him down. He responded with a vulgar comment about my breasts. Since then he has some snide remark to make whenever I run into him. He's definitely unpleasant, but I don't think he's more than that."

"Ever been inside his apartment?"

"No. Why?"

"Do yourself a favor and don't."

"Why?"

"He collects porno pictures. Has them all over the walls. And I do mean *all* over. I felt like Gulliver in Gomorrah."

"Somehow I'm not surprised."

"Which means he has a problem with sex. Which means he could be our man."

Peggy sighed sleepily once again. "*Everyone* has a problem with sex."

My impulse was to deny it, since that's not an admission I've been schooled to make about myself, but I only shrugged.

"I think you're going to have to narrow the field," Peggy added, then moved away from the bedroom doorway and into the kitchen, shuffling along in robe and slippers, treating her ankle gingerly. She opened the refrigerator, fumbled with some utensils, and joined me in the living room accompanied by a glass of chocolate milk. "I see Karen went to the store for you," I said.

She nodded and took a sip that left a mustache on her lip. I was disappointed when she licked it off.

"I can't narrow the field without your help," I said as Peggy slipped into the now-familiar daze that made her eyes solid, blinkless orbs, impermeable to the encroaching world. When she didn't respond I repeated the statement.

"I know, I know," she said, still unhinged, still ambivalent.

I opened my mouth to prod her once again, then decided against it. I was tired, too, and I was out of approaches that would make either of us feel better.

A minute later Peggy stopped chewing a nail. "Have you had anything to eat?"

"No."

"I'll fix you something."

"We could go out, if your ankle's better."

"No. Let me cook. How about pasta? I've got some pesto sauce frozen, and some noodles. Pasta and a salad. I've got some green beans, I think. What else do you want?"

"Nothing. That'll be fine."

"Coffee?"

"No."

"A drink?"

"Sure."

"Wine?"

"Scotch. But I can get it."

"Sit still. My ankle's fine. You've been waiting on me long enough. Now it's my turn. After dinner I'll even listen to your confession. You've heard mine, now surely you have something to get off your chest. Something you're embarrassed about. Something you've never told a soul."

"Only about six thousand things."

"No maybes. Before the night's over we're going to be even in the embarrassment department."

She went off to the kitchen again, limping but not seriously. The *Chronicle* was on the couch so I leafed through it. The Giants were still looking for a place to play. The Warriors were finally starting to win some games. The Niners were still trying to explain their early-season collapse, the mayor was still trying to explain the police department, and George Will was still trying to explain Ronald Reagan.

Peggy brought me my drink and a glass of wine for herself and sat down on the couch. "It'll be about half an hour."

"Fine."

"You want some cheese or something?"

"No, thanks."

"You want to talk some more, don't you?"

"Right."

"You won't let me get out of it, will you?"

"Nope."

"Can I go to work tomorrow?"

"Yep."

"Really? Somehow I thought you'd object."

"I've made some arrangements." I told her about the speaker system that ran from her desk to Constable's office.

"You did all that? Just for me?"

"It wasn't all that much. Constable knows this kid who hooked it up practically for free."

"Why?"

"I don't know. Who cares? If he hadn't done it you wouldn't be going to the office tomorrow."

"Oh, yes I would."

"Oh, no you wouldn't."

We smiled and sipped our drinks and salivated to the scents of boiling starch. I thought about telling Peggy about the bug Manchester had found in the office, but I decided that was something she didn't need to deal with yet. "What about your husband?" I asked after a liquid moment.

The question startled her. "Jim? What about him?"

"Any chance he's behind all this?"

She frowned. "That never occurred to me."

"Why not?"

"I don't know. I guess because I've repressed those days so completely they seem never to have happened."

"Could he be pursuing some belated vendetta against you?"

"Why?"

"You tell me. Maybe because of that affair you mentioned."

She thought about it. "I don't think so. No. We didn't know each other well enough to hate that much."

"You haven't had any mysterious phone calls, letters, other hints that he might be trying to get back in your life?"

"No. Nothing like that."

"You haven't seen him around?"

She shook her head.

"So much for him. What about the old boyfriend? Ruthie's on her way to see him."

"*Which* old boyfriend?"

"Hess."

"Oh." She shook her head again. "I'd like to see *that* confrontation."

"That was something more than apathy, right?"

Her lip stiffened. "He threatened to kill me, so I suppose you'd say it was."

I decided not to go into that any further until I heard from Ruthie. "So he's one candidate," I said. "How about other guys? What about the patent lawyer?"

"No. That parting was amicable. We were both pretending to be people we're not just to keep the other interested, and we finally decided to stop. When we did we discovered we were bored."

"You sure that's it?"

"He sent me a birthday present, and he's just gotten engaged to his secretary."

"Okay. Who else? The pharmacist?"

"He moved to Hawaii."

"Wasn't there a professor or something?"

"A flight instructor."

"The sky diver. Right. What about him?"

"He died. His ultralight crashed, somehow."

My face reddened. "You didn't tell me that."

"No. I didn't." She looked away and wiped her eyes. "He was a nice guy. We had fun." She sniffed. "I've got to check the noodles."

"Do you toss them at the ceiling to tell when they're done?"

Peggy acknowledged neither my explicit question nor my implicit apology.

By the time I'd finished my drink she called me in to dinner. We ate in a polite silence, the classics of KKHI in the background, our increasingly imperfect relationship a blemish on every instant.

When we finished dinner I helped with the dishes and we returned to the living room. Peggy picked up the entertainment section of the paper. "*Midnight Cowboy*'s on tonight. Want to watch it?"

"Too sad. That's the saddest movie ever made."

She looked back at the paper. "How about *Annie Hall*?"

"I've seen it."

"So have I."

"Whatever you want."

"I want to watch it."

"It's your house."

"Thanks for pointing that out," Peggy growled. We watched the film.

Movies are never quite as good as you expect them to be, and on the second viewing they're never quite as good as you thought they were. But *Annie Hall* was good enough to shield us from each other, and we got to ten o'clock without having to face either our problem or our stunted responses to it.

As Channel 2 slipped out of the movie and into the news, Peggy made some signs of sleep. "I'm exhausted again," she said. "I don't see how that's possible."

"Sleep's a good form of avoidance."

"Or therapy."

"Or withdrawal."

Peggy sighed. "Since I need all of those and then some, I think I'll go to bed."

She went into the bedroom without another word. I stayed where I was, tired of forcing the issue, tired of contemplating the frequence and variety of sexual psychopathy, tired of the distasteful ebb and flow of my attitude toward Peggy and of hers toward me.

I get mad when I get frustrated, always have, presumably always will, and right then I was mad at Peggy. Because the object of my ire was blameless, guilty only of being beyond my help, it was not an admirable ire. Which made me a louse. Which made me angry. Which ignited the cycle once again. It occurred to me that between Ruthie and me, Peggy's two saviors were inflicting more punishment than the villain from whom we were supposedly protecting her.

As I was about to stretch out on the couch, Peggy called me from the bedroom.

I went to the doorway. "Need something?"

She was in bed, covers pulled to her chin, the only light the empty fluorescent glow that inserted itself through the half-open bathroom door.

"I just wanted to tell you that I feel much better. So you don't have to stay."

"But I am."

"Why?"

"Because whatever's going on is still going on."

"But he can't get at me here."

"Sure he can."

"You could give me your gun."

"No, I couldn't."

"Why not?"

"I don't have it with me."

"Oh."

Peggy raised a knee, and the covers made a mountain. She smiled a hazy smile. "Are you sure you want to stay?"

"Yes."

"Then in that case maybe you ought to sleep with me."

16

I was sure she didn't mean it the way it sounded, but that didn't stop my nerves from performing gymnastics at the prospect of the alternate entendre. Peggy and I looked at each other, to read reactions, interpolate interpretations, assemble enough instruction to keep from making a big mistake. "The couch is fine," I said finally, my words contradicting the thickening of a nether organ.

"No. Here."

She confirmed her invitation by tossing back the covers at her side, exposing a tempting wedge of bone-white satin. Her grin was wide and unnatural. "Come on. Strip to your shorts. This is a down comforter, so you'll be plenty warm. Hurry up."

"Just a minute."

I went into the living room and retrieved my shaving kit, then hurried to the bathroom and brushed my teeth, washed my face and hands, and removed a major portion of my clothes. As nervous as a movie groom, I started back to Peggy's bed. Unfortunately, before I made it through the bathroom door I saw my reflection in a full-length mirror. The figure I cut in boxer shorts and socks acted like a dip in an icy pool. I was a character from Jacques Tati, peaked and pathetic, predestined to provoke a laugh. I shook my head, closed my eyes, removed my socks, made a wish, and scampered into the far side of the bed as fast as my pale white legs would carry me.

When I finally came to a stop I was quivering and panting, unsure of myself and my situation, my rewards and responsibilities. "It'll warm up," Peggy said across my shakes. "Just hold still a minute."

She flipped the comforter over most of me, but it didn't help—I was still trembling like a cat poised before a robin. "It's not *that* bad, Marsh." Peggy poked me in the ribs.

"Easy for you to say."

"If it's so unbearable, here. Come over next to me. I've warmed that spot up." Peggy slid a body-width to her left.

"I'll guts it out," I objected. "Stay where you are. I mean were."

I concentrated on warming up by concentrating on what was next to me, which as far as I could determine from a sidelong glance across the gray and moonlit shadings of the room was a naked female enveloped in a pink and diaphanous shroud that served not as insulator but as tantalizer, its lacy drape and shifting shadows calculated to make its contents elusive and irresistible. Impaled on the sharp scent of Obsession, I evolved from shivers to sweat.

"What do you usually sleep in?" Peggy asked as I basked in the heat of my cascading bloodstream.

"Pajamas."

"Flannel or polyester?"

"Polyester, I think."

"Hmmm."

"Sorry."

"I think I know what I'm getting you for Christmas. Long leg or short?"

"Long. How about you?"

"Nothing."

"Really?"

"Not even my rings. I can't stand anything touching me while I'm sleeping."

"You're not naked now."

"No. But I'm as close as I think I ought to get."

I had no idea what we were doing or where we were going, but I knew I was enjoying it more than the rerun of *Annie Hall.*

"Hold my hand," Peggy said suddenly.

A warm knuckle pressed against my flank. I enveloped it along with its neighbors. "Are you frightened?" I asked.

"Of you?"

Of me? "Of him. The spider."

"No, I just want to be cozy. It's been so damned long since I've been cozy. And I don't want to think about any of that tonight, so please don't mention him again."

We lay there for minutes longer, touching more of each other by the moment, exchanging the heat of our bodies as we warred with the heat of our imaginations, nestling into each other's affection as if we were orphaned waifs. "Marsh?"

"Hmmm?"

"What are you thinking?"

"I don't know."

"Come on. What?"

"I'll bet you could take a pretty good guess."

"The man on the phone?"

"No."

"Oh. Then you must be thinking about me."

"Actually I was thinking about Marilyn."

She poked me in the ribs. "You're not thinking about my cat, you're thinking about me."

"Maybe."

"What about me?"

"Guess."

"Sex?"

"Your paranormal powers are stunning."

She hesitated. "Should I apologize, Marsh?"

"Why?"

"I don't know. I'm teasing you, aren't I? Inviting you into bed this way?"

"Maybe. A little. A little less than a lot, actually."

"I didn't mean to."

"I know."

"I thought we could be . . . platonic."

"It's okay."

"And you could tell me your troubles. But you're not going to, are you?"

"I doubt it."

"Why not?"

"Because *my* troubles are on vacation. This week we're specializing in *your* troubles. If you want to go into them, I'm giving a volume discount."

I expected her to object to my evasion, but she let it pass. "What's the worst thing you've ever done to a woman?" she asked instead.

"I don't know. These days it seems to be quite an insult whenever I pay the check."

"No, really. Have you ever hit a woman?"

"No."

"Have you ever forced one to have sex when you knew she didn't want to?"

"I don't think so. But maybe that's a rationalization. In my day we assumed most of the resistance was pro forma, but I guess some of it must have been real. And I've poured a lot of women a lot of drinks in an effort to pickle their inhibitions. I suppose that's coercion, in a way."

"But what's the very worst thing, Marsh? Please. You learned a lot about me last night. I want to learn something about you. Something I didn't know before."

"I helped a girl get an abortion once."

"When?"

"College."

"How old were you?"

"Twenty."

"How old was she?"

"The same."

"Was she your girlfriend?"

"Yes."

"So it was your child?"

"Yes."

"How did you do it?"

"She made the arrangements; I just paid. I wasn't even along when she went to see the guy. He was kind of the school abortionist. Ex officio, of course. Probably had an endowed chair. He gave her a pill that induced a spontaneous emission of the fetus. Actually she was never sure she really was pregnant; she was only certain she was late. But if she was, that's very likely the only child I'll ever produce."

"You really believe they're children at that stage?"

"I believe they're something more than dust."

"So you're pro life."

"You mean against abortion."

"Same thing."

"Not literally. But no, I'm not against abortion. I just think we have to make sure abortion is something more resonant than a Big Mac."

"I wish I'd had an abortion sometimes," Peggy said softly. "Isn't that a terrible thing to say?"

"You mean Allison?"

She nodded. "I mean I love her, you know that, and I wouldn't want anything to happen to her now, but she ruined my marriage, coming along when she did, and I was so young and messed up I probably ruined *her* in ways I didn't realize. So sometimes I wish I'd canceled that first one, and tried again when I was a little more together."

"And sometimes I wish the opposite—that my college girl had had my baby."

"Where is she now?"

"I haven't the faintest idea."

"Life is weird, Marsh."

"And getting weirder. And now we're even in the embarrassment department."

"No we're not. Yours is over. Mine's still going on."

We fell silent, breathing shadows, inhaling darkness and perfume. After a while Peggy turned to her side and with her free hand trailed her fingers across my naked chest. "Do you think we'll actually do it after all these years?" she asked, her eyes wide, her voice disembodied, as though she read a script written in a language she didn't understand.

130

"Do what?" I said, my mind a captive of her fingers.

"Have sex, you dope."

"I don't know. Do you?"

"I don't know. I do know I feel very close to you right now."

"Good."

"And very sexy."

"Good."

"Do you?"

"Yes. To both."

"I swore we never would, you know."

"I know."

"Do you know why?"

"I think so."

"Then you know it's not that I didn't want to. That night you came to dinner on your birthday I toyed with the idea of decorating a box to look like a sponge cake and jumping out of it in my birthday suit, as sort of a special gift."

"That would have been nice. Since I wouldn't have had to exchange it or anything. So why didn't you?"

"I was afraid things would have gotten out of hand."

"I'm afraid you were right to be afraid."

"Of course part of me wanted things to get out of hand."

"Of course."

". . . Marsh?"

"Hmmm?"

"Do you feel a little like a teenager right now? Like the first time you were alone with a girl?"

"A little."

"It's odd, isn't it, how those feelings come back sometimes, no matter how old we are and how much we've seen and done since then. Some days I feel like I'm still only twelve years old, and all my wishes are going to be fulfilled. I sort of like it, you know? Feeling able to do anything I want with my life."

"You still can. Name something you want to do."

"Be a U.S. Senator."

"You're kidding."

"Now I don't. But I did. I wanted to be Margaret Chase Smith."

"Well, you could still . . ."

Peggy laughed. "You don't really believe that, do you? That everything in the world is still possible?"

"I guess not. I guess I want to but I can't."

"That's what growing up means, Marsh. It means you can't believe anything you can't see and grab hold of and put in your purse."

"That's a depressing thought."

"I know. God, don't I know . . . Marsh?"

"Hmmm?"

"What do you want to do right now?"

"Lick the polish off your toenails."

"Are you *serious*?"

"No."

"Thank God . . . Marsh?"

"Hmmm?"

"Would it be all right if I did this?"

"Sure."

"How about this?"

"Fine."

"Faster?"

"No, that's about right."

"You could do something if you want to."

"Okay. How about this?"

"Yes."

"This?"

"Yes, but not so hard. Wait. Let me get rid of that. Do you mind? Are you sure? Good. There. That's perfect. Just keep doing it just that way. . . . Marsh?"

"Hmmm?"

"Do you think this will change the way we are with each other?"

"Probably."

"For better or worse?"

"I don't know."

"Does that mean you want to stop?"

I said no, not unless she did, and we had fun with each other for several fevered minutes, until the face of Karen Whittle laid claim to the center of my mind and had the effrontery to remind me of her earlier admonition. As Peggy and I made a slipknot of our bodies, I considered the situation and my obligations in light of it. Five minutes later I decided to live up to what seemed like a reasonable definition of a wonderful guy.

As I pulled away from our embrace, I sensed that Peggy was relieved. I began an awkward apology, but Peggy told me not to mind, that it was all right, that she understood. "It wasn't working, anyway," she added, and turned my heart from cake to stone.

17

I was asleep when the phone rang, but I don't think Peggy was. At least she didn't sound sleepy when she snapped on the light, reached for the receiver, mumbled a garbled greeting, listened, then propped her pillow against the headboard and leaned against it with a resigned sigh and said, "Hello, John."

It took me a few seconds to realize what was going on. When I finally put it together I scrambled out of bed and hurried into the living room and curled up beside the second phone, pulling the abandoned afghan over my nakedness as I listened for sounds from the bedroom. When I heard the low drone of Peggy's voice I eased the receiver off its cradle and put it to my ear.

"Are you badly hurt, Margaret?" His voice was low, soothing, neutral. Not mad, not threatening, not obsessive, not easily distinguishable from a million other benignant voices.

"I'm all right." Peggy's own voice was a match for his, gentle, almost reverent. "I don't know why you did that to me, John," she went on, now a trifle plaintive.

The spider didn't answer for a moment. When he did the words wafted through the wire in a condescending lilt. "You need not understand, Margaret. You need merely obey."

"But I don't want it to happen again."

"Then you must do as I say, mustn't you?"

"But I *have* been."

"No, you haven't. You've been seeking aid. You've been trying to identify me."

"No, I—"

"*Do not lie!* You are *not* to lie to me. Haven't I made that clear? Don't you realize by now that I *know* the truth? That I am inside your body, inside your head, inside your soul? Don't you know that you can't be false to me, Margaret? About *anything*?"

Peggy's submission came in sirens of shallow breath. "I'm sorry, I . . ."

In the next instant his voice was a caressing puff. "They cannot help you, you know. You are beyond the help of anyone but me."

"I know."

"It is fruitless to tell others about our relationship. No one can understand it. Only you and I know its depths and contours. We are locked in a special embrace, Margaret. And we will remain together until we die. You know that, don't you?"

"Yes."

"You know there is no escape."

"Yes."

"You know that I am prepared to eliminate anything or anyone who comes between us."

"Yes."

"And to follow you to the end of the earth if you try to flee from me."

"Yes."

"So you will not defy me again, will you?"

"No."

"And you will tell those you have asked for help that you no longer need them."

"Yes."

"Is anyone with you now?"

"No."

"Are you certain?"

". . . There was someone here last night, but not to-night."

His voice hardened. "What would happen if I called this number?"

He read off the digits of my own telephone number, the one in my apartment.

Peggy's gasp was audible to both of her auditors. "I don't know what would happen," she said.

"There wouldn't be an answer, would there?"

"I don't know. How could I know that?"

The spider chuckled confidently. "Well, it doesn't matter. If he is there beside you, if he is listening, so be it. He will see how fruitless it would be to interfere. Fruitless, and perhaps dangerous. So I bid you welcome, Mr. Tanner. I hope you enjoy our session."

He allowed silence to build the moment. Although I was on the brink of an outburst I stayed mute, an impotent onlooker huddled beneath a colorful blanket that failed to remove my chill.

"Shall I tell you what we're going to talk about this evening, Margaret?" the spider continued after a moment.

"All right."

"We're going to talk about clothes." He tittered. "Does that surprise you?"

"I don't know. I guess so." Peggy's voice had a higher pitch, a thinner timber than the one I knew so well. She was even less than the teenager she had mentioned hours before, was now a naughty child, leery of punishment, anxious of fate.

"You have a nice wardrobe, Margaret. Lovely things."

"Thank you."

"What I'm wondering is, whom do you dress for?"

"I don't know what you mean."

"I mean when you cover your nakedness in the morning, whom do you want to impress? Whom do you want to *excite*?"

"No one. I just want to look nice."

"Come now."

"No. Really."

The spider's words were stern. "I see I must be specific.

When you go out shopping, and you see one dress with a high neckline and another with a low-cut bodice, why do you choose the latter garment?"

"But I don't, always."

"Not always, perhaps. But when you do, what are you thinking? 'How much of my bust shall I expose tonight? How much flesh will it take to excite them? How much trembling breast will make them want to touch me, feel me, kiss me, *defile me*?' Isn't *that* what's in your mind when you buy such clothing? Driving men crazy with desire?"

Peggy's voice became the spider's opposite, a timid whisper. "No. Nothing like that."

"You *lie*!"

"No. Not this time."

The spider's fury ebbed to a reasonable drone. "You know your purple dress? The knit sheath with white buttons and the white piping at the hem and neck?"

Peggy knew it and I did, too. "Yes."

"You must know what you look like when you wear that dress, Margaret. You do, don't you? You look at yourself in the *mirror*, don't you? Like all women?"

"Yes. Sometimes."

"Then you know that you look like a *strumpet*, Margaret. A woman whose flesh is for sale to the highest bidder. A woman who wants to be handled like a common rag, passed around from man to man until she is filthy beyond description."

"No. It's not like that. It's just a dress."

"Ha. I tried to persuade myself that you wore it for my personal pleasure, you know. I tried very hard. But too many others shared the experience, Margaret. Too many others sought to know the rest of you, just as you hoped they would."

"No, I—"

"Why else would you wear such things? You *know* men lust for women's breasts. You *know* they will be looking at yours, and wanting to do more than look. You *know* that, don't you?"

"I don't . . . some of them might. Not all."

"*All* men. *All* men, Margaret. *All normal men* want to suckle women's breasts. It's biological, genetic, a universal constant. Why do you deny it?"

"It's just *clothes*, John. Just a *dress.*"

"But they *make* dresses that don't display your bosom, do they not? They *make* dresses that camouflage your cleavage, that keep your charms a secret. And since that is the case, by choosing a design that *does* display them to the world you are confessing that you very badly *want* to display them. That is irrefutable, is it not?"

"No. I . . ."

"The question is why? Why do you expose yourself that way? Are you out to seduce a specific man? Or are you merely a vengeful harlot who seeks to frustrate men in every way she can? Which is it, Margaret?"

"It's nothing like that. I only want to look *nice.* I buy all *kinds* of dresses. Some with high necks, some with low. It's just fashion, is all. Variety. A different look. It has nothing to do with men."

"*No!* You're teasing us. Demeaning us. Forcing us to confront our private baseness. You want us to want you, and at the same time you want us to know we can never have you. You're *cruel*, Margaret. You and the others who do as you do. *Cruel and sadistic.*"

"I am not. *You* may react that way when you see a woman in a scooped neck, but that doesn't mean she *wants* you to react that way. Women can attract men without baring their breasts, John."

"But that's the *point*, isn't it? They don't *want* to attract. Not really. They only want to tease. In reality women *want* to be sex objects, because as such you have us where you want us, as helpless, craven fools. 'Eat your heart out.' That's the phrase, isn't it? *That's* what you want us to do, eat our hearts out *until we choke on the horrible refuse of our desire.*"

138

The spider's voice was raw and wounded. Peggy seemed startled by his outburst, and hesitated until he had time to recover his composure. When she went on it was in a comforting contralto. "You're wrong, John. If other women have teased you, I'm sorry. But I haven't. You know that."

"How about underclothes?" he demanded roughly.

"What?"

"Your *underwear.* What do you wear underneath? A garter?"

"No. Not usually."

"Then what?"

"Panty hose. A bra. A slip sometimes."

"Girdle?"

"No."

"Good. Panties?"

"If I'm not wearing panty hose."

"What kind of panties?"

"Various kinds. You don't want to know this, John."

"*Don't tell me what I want!* I *know* what I want. *Your* function is to *give* it to me. Or do we have to review what will happen if you don't?"

"No. No review. Please."

"Very well. Are your panties those little bikini types?"

"Yes. Some of them."

"Lace?"

"Some."

"Black?"

"A few."

"What other colors?"

"White. Yellow. Blue."

"Dark blue?"

"Light."

"Has anyone ever ripped them off you?"

"My panties?"

"Yes."

"No. Never."

"That's too bad. Do you wish they would?"

"No."

"Ha. You lie, but it doesn't matter. Your brassieres."

"What about them?"

"What size?"

"Thirty-six."

"What else?"

"What do you mean?"

"*Bra* size. There's more than a *number,* isn't there?"

"I don't . . . oh, the cup. I wear a C cup."

"Good. What color?"

"Black or white. Blue. And beige, sometimes."

"You mean flesh color."

"Yes."

"Strapless?"

"One or two."

"Those kind that force them up? So you look more voluptuous than you are? So there is more for men to see?"

"No. None of those."

"Padded?"

"No."

"Good. Do you have the kind with holes in them? So only the nipples peek through?"

"No. What do you think I am?"

"Oh, by now we both know what you *are*, Margaret. Would you buy one with holes if I asked you to?"

"I . . ."

"I might want you to start dressing up for me, you see. I might want you to wear enticing things, and tell me about them when I call. How they look. How they feel. Yes. I think I just might. I might even buy them for you, would you like that? If I bought some things and sent them to you? Then I would be the only one to know what gossamer garments are caressing your flesh. Then you'll be exactly the way I want you to be."

"Please don't do that, John. It would make me feel . . . It would change it all. I don't think I could do that, no matter what you do."

When he spoke again he seemed annoyed. "If you wear

a low-cut dress does it mean you're not wearing a bra?"

"Not always. There are low-cut bras."

"Do you wear *nothing* underneath sometimes?"

"No."

"You're lying."

"No."

"You're *lying*."

"In the fall, is all. Just when it's terribly hot. Just a few days a year."

"Do you feel sexier then? When you're wearing nothing underneath?"

"Only cooler."

"You lie again. Why? What's the *point*?"

"Okay. I feel sexier."

"Do you do anything about it?"

"No."

"You don't flirt? Or pick up a man? You don't seduce someone on hot nights, so they can make that void at your center go away? That void we talked about last week? Or do you merely masturbate? Relieve yourself with your own devices? Tell me which."

"None of those things. I just go home and try to cool off."

"I doubt that. I doubt it very much. That pilot you were seeing. One night when it was beastly hot I saw you put your hand in his pocket. And he placed his hand on your breast, right there in public, right there on Montgomery Street. You were like two farm animals, rutting in the sun. I was disgusted. I want you to know that. I was very disgusted with you. I was glad when he died. Oh, you didn't know I knew about that, did you? Yes, I was very pleased when he died, Margaret. It was the best thing for us."

Peggy was stunned to silence, and my mind kicked into a higher gear, one that explored the likelihood that the spider had killed Peggy's former lover, had tampered with his ultralight somehow, had gotten rid of an irritant that tainted his alabaster fantasy. I thought Peggy had begun to cry but I wasn't sure.

"I've decided I want something from you, Margaret," the spider said stiffly.

"I've already given you everything I have." Peggy's words were a murmur of collapse, but the spider was heedless of her misery.

"Oh, you can give much more. For example, I want some of your underthings. A bra. Panties. A slip. One of each. Ones you have worn but have not yet washed. In fact, I insist on it. I *want those things.*"

"No. Please."

"I want them and I will have them. Won't I? *Won't* I, Margaret?"

"Yes. If you want. Yes."

"You will put them in a small bag. Plastic. White. A kitchen trash bag. And you will leave them somewhere for me. But where? Let me think. It should be convenient, public, busy, so I will not be noticed yet can tell if you and your friends make the mistake of lying in wait for me. Let's see. I have it. The Transamerica Building. The little park in back. Leave the bag on the bench on the Washington Street side. At precisely five P.M. tomorrow. Just deposit the bag and leave. I'll take care of it from there. And don't bother having it watched. I will know if you have done so, and you will pay, and pay dearly, for your mistake. Do you understand your instructions?"

"Yes."

"And be sure they have not been washed. Be sure they still carry your scent. I want to smell your flesh, inhale your musk, feel exactly what you feel. I may even put them on, the panties, I mean. Women's underwear leaves such a sensual sensation. It's surprising more men don't wear them, isn't it?"

"I wouldn't know."

"Oh, you're such a priss. I'm not a pervert, Margaret. A transvestite or any of that. I'm just open to new experience. That's what all this is about, don't you agree? Experience? You know you enjoy it as much as I."

"No, I don't."

"Ha. If you must delude yourself you may. Or perhaps you are posturing for Mr. Tanner. Whichever, I don't mind. There is one last item, Margaret, and then we're finished for the night. We know you've seen a great many men naked, right?"

"Not many. A few."

"Ha. I'd call a dozen many, wouldn't you?"

"No."

"Semantics will not shield you from the truth, my dear. The fact is, you've had sex with at least ten men. Correct?"

"Yes."

"And performed fellatio with two."

"No, I haven't . . ."

"*Remember?* We already *discussed* this. *Fellatio*, I said. With two men. Right? *Isn't that right?*"

"Yes. I know you don't like it, John, but yes, that's right. Why do you keep talking about that if it upsets you so much?"

"I *talk* about it because I am shocked, and ashamed, and *amazed*, that you could allow such *filth* into your life. You *tell* me you didn't enjoy it, you *tell* me you only did it because your partner expected you to and you didn't want to anger him. You *tell* me that, but you are lying."

"No."

"*Stop* it. Just stop it. It is far too late to change what you are, Margaret. What you have let yourself become. What I need to know tonight is whether you *think* about them."

"What? The men?"

"No, the *organs*. Do you dream about penises? Do you find them attractive? When you sit home alone do you get an urge to see one? To fondle one? What do you call them, by the way? Dicks? Pricks? Peckers? What do you *call* them, Margaret?"

"Cocks."

"What? I couldn't hear you."

"Cocks. I call them cocks."

"Very well. Do you get those urges I described? Do you yearn for men's cocks, Margaret? That's what I need to know. *How do women feel about men's cocks?*"

Peggy paused for so long I thought she had dropped the phone. "How do you feel about them, John?" she said finally. "Isn't that what this is all about? How do you feel about yours?"

"*Bitch! Cunt! Never* ask me questions. I've told you a thousand times. *Never* ask me what I think again, or you *know* what will happen to you. You *know* what I will be forced to do. *Don't* you?"

"Yes."

"Oh, I'm too upset to continue. See what you've done? And we were progressing so nicely. You will pay for this, Margaret. You. Will. Pay. Think of me, Margaret. *Think of me!* And don't you *dare* forget my gift."

18

Peggy replaced the phone with the sound of a cage locking shut. I was left listening to a persistent, constant buzz that mocked my all-too-fickle heart. Though I was heated to a glow by what I had overheard, I gathered the afghan around my nakedness and went back to the bedroom, uncertain of what to do when I got there.

Peggy was still in bed, still propped against a pillow, still staring into hostile space. Her face was stricken and subdued, but when she sensed my presence she tried a smile.

"Are you all right?" I asked.

She managed a listless shrug. "Pathetic, huh?"

"Do you want anything? Coffee? A drink?"

She shook her head, then looked away from the unforgiving abstractions that swarmed around her. "You have such a hateful expression on your face," she said, so softly I almost escaped her indictment.

"He pissed me off. I wanted to strangle him. I still do."

"No. That may be part of it, but most of it is me. You're disgusted with me."

"No, I'm not. Don't be silly."

Her look was hyper-kind, the look of religious zealots and parents proclaiming affection for their offspring. "Oh, but you are. I told you this would happen. Two hours ago you said you loved me. Do you remember that?"

"Sure, I do."

"And now look at you. You can't *wait* to get out of here, can you? You're trying desperately to think how you can possibly avoid getting back in this bed."

"No, I . . ."

She bowed her head as though I'd cursed her. "*Leave.* Just leave."

"No. You're still in danger."

"I'd rather be in danger than in contempt."

Her implication drove me a further step away from her. I tried to camouflage my retreat with a rearranging of my blanket, but she knew it for what it was. "Please, Peggy. Don't do this."

"Just go, Marsh. Do us both a favor. Maybe someday we can have a big laugh about all of it, about how quickly we went from one extreme to the other, but not tonight. There's nothing I want to laugh about tonight, Marsh. There really isn't."

She rolled away from me, burrowing beneath the covers, curling as though I was poised to strike her. "I still want to help you, Peggy."

"But I don't want your help. I don't need the condemnation that comes with it."

"The guy is nuts. You can't tell *what* he'll do next. He probably doesn't even know himself."

"I know what he'll do," Peggy said from beneath the blanket. "He'll call and call, night after night. And I'll talk to him the way I did tonight, about whatever it is he wants me to talk about, and it won't be so bad, after a while. It won't be bad at all."

"He'll destroy you, Peggy. He'll chip away at your self-esteem until it's gone."

Peggy's laugh was a hopeless croak. "Self-esteem. What a quaint expression. Good night, Marsh. I can handle it from now on. I should never have gotten you involved."

"I want to *be* involved. Remember?"

"But now you don't."

The statement contained enough truth to make me veer from the subject. "You go back to sleep. I'll sleep on the couch. We can talk about it tomorrow."

"No. Please get *out* of here, before I have hysterics."

"It's three in the morning, Peggy. This isn't the time to be making decisions."

"I can't stand that *look* on your face, Marsh Tanner. I can't stand what you're accusing me of being. Because I'm *not* that. I'm really not. And I never have been, no matter what you think."

"I'm not accusing you of anything, Peggy. It's not your fault this creep's obsessed with you."

Her smile stretched wearily across her face, the journey spartan and unproductive. "Oh, Marsh. What I've always admired about you most was your honesty. Well, be honest with yourself now. Face up to what you really think about all this. Just please don't do it while you're still here in my apartment. Go home, Marsh. Just go home."

The covers heaved and twisted atop Peggy's muffled sobs. I stared at them until they had been immobile for several seconds, then went into the bathroom, put on my clothes, grabbed my shaving kit, and went out into the night.

Neither of us delayed my departure. As I crossed the street to get to my car a gray Ford almost ran me down. The driver looked at me savagely, as though he was Peggy's surrogate and I was a menace to him as well. I returned his epithet, then drove home at the pace of a snail.

My apartment was as cold as my reflection in Peggy's eyes, and was commandeered by the memory of my ignoble reaction to the spider's latest bite. Peggy had been right, I *had* been revolted by her telephone conversation, by what she'd told the spider, by how little resistance she'd offered to his demands, by the throb of intimacy that occasionally passed between them. The fact was both humbling and alarming—humbling because it made me less of a man than I envisioned, alarming because the long-term consequence of my behavior was Peggy's permanent exit from my life.

I tried to wash away the night with my usual method— a glass of Scotch and a deep sleep. Neither of them worked the way they were supposed to, so at five A.M. I got dressed again, stumbled down to my car, and drove east across the bay, over the Oakland hills, down the San Ramon Valley, through the Diablo Range and into the Central Valley.

I guess it's a psychic imprint from my rural youth that makes me do it, but whenever life turns particularly odious, whenever I need to escape my surroundings or the heavy baggage of my self, I head for the wide-open spaces. Amazingly, there still are some to be found, even in California.

As soon as I could I left the interstate and meandered to Modesto, where I stopped for an early lunch at a Mexican place that came close to serving the real thing, which meant the food was hot enough to burn away everything short of the incipient scalding of my palate. At one o'clock I called my office. There was no answer so I left a message for Peggy on the machine, reminding her how the speaker system worked, where the on-off button was, and who would come to her rescue in the event she needed saving. At the end of the message I apologized for everything I could think of to apologize for. It seemed a craven response to the evening's events, but it was all I was capable of at the moment.

After hanging up I headed farther east, cracking the window to invite the brisk dry wind to chasten me with an hour-long slap to the face. The agricultural miracles being staged around me gradually lulled me into a charmed amazement, and I drove all the way to Sonora before I decided I could turn back, that enough of the past few days lay like litter along the highway to let me live a little longer with what I had become, in both Peggy's eyes and my own.

The return trip offered fewer diversions, and as I drove through Tracy my mind began to rattle across my cobbled history with women. I've thought about it for years, and I'm still not sure why sooner or later it's always gone wrong. I've had scores of relationships, of varying degrees of intimacy. One of them reached a formal engagement

148

before it self-destructed, and a couple of others included serious speculations on the advisability of matrimony. But something always happened. The breakup was not always my doing by any means, at least not overtly, and the precipitant was often something trivial—a dispute over the merit of a movie, a broken date, a drink too many, a remark too thoughtless or too frank. But regardless of who or what initiated the break, deep down I was always relieved. Except maybe once.

In my younger years I used to feel that the women in my life were too different from me—active instead of sedentary, talkative instead of thoughtful, gregarious instead of private. But now the problem has become the opposite. Rather than my antithesis the women I know are far too much my like—independent, comfortable, penurious, wary of being hurt or, worse, of looking foolish, far too firmly convinced of life's imperfectibility to believe it will confer anything more robust than a semitolerable existence, an existence that is most efficiently managed as a sole proprietor rather than in a partnership, no matter how modern the terms of the agreement. From this perspective, bachelorhood was not only what I wanted, it was near nirvana.

Yet I still resisted, and for the past eight years my resistance found its focus in my secretary. Peggy suggested a more traditionally elegant possibility, an enduring association that was mutually mature, respectful, admiring. For almost a decade she had been the template for the woman who would, if I could only find her, be a mate for life despite the prattle of the diehard pessimists and the recently divorced. How then to explain the fact that twelve hours earlier my ideal woman and I had recoiled at the first sign of frailty in the other, at the first hint that the other was not precisely and completely what we imagined them to be. Despite our past and our ideals, we seemed to have surrendered our history without a fight.

As I waited at the Bay Bridge tollbooth, I wondered whether Peggy and I would ever see each other again on anything approaching our former terms. By the time I was across the bridge I knew that I needed the answer to be yes, and that I was willing to do almost anything to see that it was.

When I hit the city it was almost five. I assumed Peggy would be home, and hoped that Ruthie would be with her. Then I remembered the spider's demand of the night before—that Peggy deliver him a gift of her unmentionables. Irate once again, I almost turned for home and left their little gesture to play itself out without me. But the more I wrestled with the exchange, the more I realized that the circumstance offered the chance that in his haste to recover the silks he coveted the spider would expose himself to capture. I made a quick decision to act instead of brood, and ducked off the Embarcadero Freeway at Clay, drove to my usual lot, left the car behind, and set out on foot for the Transamerica Building.

The evening flood had already begun, the sidewalk gorged with office workers exhibiting their first flair of the day. I shouldered my way among them, till I could view the tiny redwood park where the spider would retrieve his spoils. There were several people sitting among the trees and fountains and blue-and-orange assemblages, but none seemed conceivably my nemesis. Indeed, all of those on the Washington Street side of the park were women, and thus more likely targets than accomplices.

Trying to anticipate the event, I took two turns around the block, but the result was not encouraging. There were too many entrances and exits to be confident of trapping him or of remaining undetected. Defeated, I crossed Washington and headed toward my office. But halfway up the stairs a second thought occurred to me, and I retreated to Washington Street, turned my back to the pyramid, and looked north.

My hunch had been correct—someone standing on the roof of the second building south from mine could easily see everything that transpired in the little park where Peggy was to leave three tokens of her ensnarement. I went back to the parking lot, fumbled in the trunk of my car until I found my binoculars, then hurried to the office again.

Peggy was sitting at her desk, a plastic bag placed precisely in front of her as though it were only lunchtime and that were only her lunch. She nodded at me as I entered, and I said hello. Our eyes sought anything but other eyes.

I sat in the waiting chair and crossed my legs. "Are you going to leave it for him?" I asked, gesturing at the shiny sack.

She nodded, her face as devoid of expression as I had ever seen it.

I looked at my watch. "How soon are you leaving?"

"Right now."

"Okay."

"Aren't you going to try to talk me out of it?"

"Would it do any good?"

"No."

"I didn't think so."

"I'm going home afterward."

"Fine."

"Nothing happened today that you need to know about."

"Good."

"I got your message on the machine."

"Good."

"It doesn't change anything."

"I suppose not."

She looked at her watch. "Well, I'm going."

"Do you want me to come with you?"

"No."

"Do you want me to come over tonight?"

"Definitely not."

"Okay. Well, have fun."

"There's nothing fun *about* this, you bastard."

Peggy snatched the bag off the desk and hurried out of the office. I waited till her footsteps had descended out of earshot, then went through the door and walked the other way, toward the exit at the very end of the hall, the one next to Arthur Constable's office.

As I passed Constable's door I glanced inside. Constable and Richard were standing behind Richard's desk, deep in an animated discussion. From the look of it, Richard had done something wrong. The crowd of sculptured people made the chastising a public spectacle.

I was about to go on my way when Constable looked up. When he recognized me he smiled and waved. I waved back. When he noticed the binoculars he frowned and mouthed in mime, asking whether there was a problem. I shook my head and went on my way.

I shoved open the heavy fire door and ran up the steps to the roof. It was windy, the breeze racing in to cool us off and bed us down. I walked to the edge of the building, my feet crunching into the graveled roofing that the sun had made as soft as fudge, and jumped from my building to the next, and then to the next one after that. When I got to the end of the block I looked down onto Washington Street and across to the park.

The view wasn't as good as I'd hoped—part of a tree cut off a corner of the park, and the distance made the faces on the rushing pedestrians miniature and virtually indistinguishable. I rubbed my eyes, checked various vantage points for the one offering the best perspective, and settled down to wait.

Peggy appeared in the next moment, her bag clutched tightly in her fist. She proceeded into the park without hesitation, went directly to a vacant bench, placed the plastic bag on the nearest corner, and turned and left, walking directly toward me for several steps before heading up Columbus toward her bus stop. Even from a distance I could see her look of brash defiance, a rebellion I deserved in common with the spider. I muttered a self-directed curse and sat down on a crate, staring at what passed for a public park, the cheap binoculars bifurcating the world into interlocking circles and pressing the people into oddly shaped mutations.

An hour later I was still waiting and the bag was still resting on the bench. No one had approached it, not even a thief. Fifteen minutes after that I gave up hope and left the roof.

The stairs took longer to descend than the reverse. The lights in Constable's office were out except for those that lit the permanent occupants. I hurried out of the building and trotted to the park, to make one last try from closer in. By the time I got there, the bench was empty.

I swore so bitterly two heads turned my way in pious disapproval. Their probity incensed me all the more. I looked this way and that, and this way once again. Miraculously, I saw the bag, squeezed into the grimy fist of what appeared to be a transient.

On the slim chance that it was the spider in disguise, I trotted ahead of the man, then turned and walked back toward him, giving me full view. Disguise was out of the question. So was anything that required my suspect to do anything more complex than breathe and scavenge. When he disappeared into an alley, I gave up.

Back in the office I tried to think of something sensible to do. Surprisingly, I managed to do just that. After toasting my perspicacity, I picked up the phone and called a cop.

19

Charley Sleet's the best cop in San Francisco, which means he's respected, feared, and steered clear of, leaving him both effective and incorruptible. It also means he's embarrassed as hell about the series of scandals that has rocked the department over the past two years—the sex parties, the sadistic drug raids, the petty harassment of department critics, the overzealous roust of a local sex queen—but he's not so embarrassed that it affects the way he does his job.

Charley has helped me out in several of my cases, and I've helped him in one or two of his. We play poker once in a while, or go to a ballgame or meet for a drink. But my idea of a nice evening is to stay at home, and ever since his wife died Charley's is to stay anywhere but—preferably at a greasy spoon in the Tenderloin, waiting for someone to come to him for help. So we don't see each other all that often anymore, but we enjoy it when we do.

When he came on the line I asked Charley if he had time for a drink. He said he had an appointment in the Moscone Center, then a bust going down in the Western Addition. He suggested we meet at the House of Shields in an hour, that is, if I was buying. I said it was his turn. He reminded me that I'd bet on the Niners against the Bears and hadn't made good my loss. I told him I could afford two rounds and after that he was on his own. He told me two rounds was all he had time for.

I was settled into a booth at the back when Charley crossed New Montgomery in front of the Palace Hotel, entered the bar, and momentarily eclipsed the light from the setting sun. When he saw me he waved, said something gruff and scatalogical to the tuxedoed bartender, got his usual double shot of Bushmills neat, and sauntered back to where I was sitting. The booth shrieked beneath his eighth of a ton, and the table between us tilted precariously when Charley rested a forearm along its edge. The stuffed moose above our heads seemed cheered by the arrival of a kindred spirit.

Charley toasted me silently, knocked back half his whiskey, and put the glass on the table within easy reach of his paw. "This business, or you got another wager on your mind? Like maybe you like Nebraska over Oklahoma."

"Business, mostly."

"Good. I was afraid you'd hit the skids so hard you were welshing on the twenty you owe me."

"What twenty? I thought I was only into you for the Bears game."

"Remember New Year's? You bet me someone would murder Dan White within a year after he got out of Soledad. I'll take it in cash or a gift certificate at the Tosca."

"Wait a minute. I think we've got a definitional problem here."

"You said murder. Suicide isn't murder."

"I said kill, not murder."

"Kill, my ass. Just for that I want cash."

"It'll have to be next month."

"I thought you had a client."

"I've got a case, not a client."

"What the hell is that supposed to mean?"

"It means I've got a client but I'm handling the case for free."

"Jesus. I keep thinking you'll wise up and you keep staying dumb. Do I know her?"

"Who said it's a her?"

"You always limit your charitable impulses to the fairer sex, Tanner. What's the scam?"

"This is confidential, Charley."

"You insult me again and it'll cost you more than a drink to take up my time." Charley looked at his watch. "Let's get to it, can we? I got a hooker primed to roll over on her pimp. She's meeting me at Laguna and Eddy at seven."

I took a deep breath. "It started with anonymous phone calls. Sex stuff, though not crude, particularly. With threats of harm if she didn't answer his questions, tell him everything he wanted to know, stay on the line as long as he wanted."

Charley was nodding his head before I finished. "We get a bunch of that these days. And they get even more of it over in Berkeley. Who we talking about, anyway?"

I shook my head. "It's kind of touchy. I'm not sure where I stand on this myself anymore, so I'm not sure how much I can tell you."

Charley shrugged. "Up to you. She file a complaint?"

"For what?"

"P.C. 653(m)—a misdemeanor to annoy by phone through the use of obscenities or threats of injury."

I shook my head. "No complaint, Charley. She doesn't know who it is. Or so she says."

"You sound like you don't believe her."

"I don't know what I believe," I said truthfully.

"This have anything to do with the Tomkins character you asked me to check on?"

"I don't know," I admitted. "What do you have on him?"

"He's a sex offender all right. On probation for P.C. 314 exposure. Only thing unusual about him is he comes from good stock. Family owns a big chunk of Cow Hollow, since back before the quake. So the little boy gets good lawyers, which means so far he's stayed out of the joint. But the DA's sure they've got him violated this time. Strong witness; multiple offense. They plan to send old Jud to Folsom on the first bus. If you've got him on a harassment number, the DA will be happy to hear from you. Can't hurt you to do him a favor, either."

"I can't prove anything yet, Charley. Tomkins lives in the building where the calls come in, but the woman says she doesn't recognize the voice."

"Well, if she doesn't know him that lets out a civil injunction, which is the other way they usually go. Get a court order telling the jerk to leave them alone. Problem with the injunction isn't getting it, though, it's enforcing it. Cops don't like to act on two-bit harassment calls, even though for the victim two years of two-bit harassment can add up to a million dollars' worth of grief. You sure she doesn't know the bastard?"

"She says not. That's all I know. Why?"

"Oh, sometimes they get real embarrassed by how involved they've gotten with the jerk. So they hold that part back. The name, I mean."

"That's possible in this case," I admitted. "She's certainly let herself get knotted up with the guy."

"Okay. So what do you want to know?"

"First, if she did file a criminal complaint, could the investigation be done in secret?"

"So the loon doesn't know she went to the law, you mean?"

I nodded.

"We try, but we're not real good at it. In these cases the guy usually watches his victim like a hawk, which means he'd probably get wise right away if we started checking it out. And I gotta tell you, Marsh, sometimes it jacks them up even more when they know we're after them. They get a rush from the chase."

"That's what I was afraid of."

Charley drained his drink and I motioned for two more. "Most of these creeps keep their distance, Marsh," he went on. "They keep close tabs on the women but they usually avoid personal confrontations. Worship from afar, and all that. Probably won't come to a hill of beans."

I shook my head. "This one got violent, Charley."

"When?"

"Two nights ago."

"What'd he do?"

"Shoved her down the stairs."

"Where?"

"Her apartment."

"She all right?"

"Twisted ankle and sore ribs."

"He say why he did it?"

"Not specifically. But she went to someone for help earlier that day, so it figures he knew that and was warning her to drop it."

"That someone you, old buddy?"

I shook my head.

Charley shrugged. "I've pulled a couple of these psy-rape cases myself. Talked with the shrinks a few times. Some of these bastards are total empties—see things that aren't there, obey secret commands and all that—but others seem pretty normal except for a fixation on one particular woman. Problem is, the proverbial magnificent obsession's not all that distinguishable from criminal harassment sometimes. Legally speaking, that is."

The waiter brought the second round of drinks. I paid him and pocketed the change.

"The profile says the guy has repressed sexual desires," Charley said after the waiter left, "probably the result of your basic strict upbringing. Probably preached at by his mama that sex was evil, and men who did it were devils, the whole repressive number. So the guy's born to be a zero with the broads, and his gonads shrivel to the size of BBs when he has to handle them one-on-one, so he moves to the phone bit. This lets him say what's on his mind, and what's on his mind can be pretty sick. He convinces himself that the victim really does love him in spite of what she says, and that his function in life is to make her realize it. Of course, underneath it all he despises her for her sexuality, and every time she does what he wants her to do he despises her even more, which is why you can't ever ignore the possibility of violence. What's he do, make weird demands on her?"

I nodded. "Telling him all kinds of details about her sex life is what most of it amounts to."

Charley looked at me through lidded eyes. "Victim feels guilty about the whole business a lot of the time, Marsh. Starts feeling sorry for the guy. Decides the whole situation must have been her fault, somehow; that she must have led him on. Gets to where she feels the only way everything'll be all right again is if she just keeps doing what he wants. Lots of times they don't want help from the outside, or say they don't. Lots of times they stop resisting the bastard and try like hell to help him achieve his fantasy. I know a couple of times we nailed the guy but the victim wouldn't testify against him on the criminal charge. One time they ended up getting married, for Christ's sake."

"The human animal is a wondrous thing."

"So I've observed. And it's amazing what some of these bastards can get people to do. Case in Wisconsin, the guy convinced a bunch of women to walk down the street half naked in order to cure some weird affliction he told them they had. Apparently they really believed if they showed the town their tits they'd be cured of what ailed them."

"So what would you do if you were a victim?"

Charley shrugged. "I got to tell you, Marsh, a lot of women just leave town. Figure that's the only way it's going to end."

"That's not an option here I don't think," I said, wondering if I spoke the truth, wondering if Peggy would all of a sudden just disappear.

Charley looked at his watch. "Time's awasting, Tanner," he chided. "How often does he call?"

"Every night."

"She know anything at all about him?"

"Just basically that he's educated and he's a loser with women."

"So is half the world, you and me included. What kind of evidence has she got?"

I thought about it. "Only her word, I guess. Plus I overheard one of the calls."

"She should start taping them. Every time he calls, get it on tape."

"Last time I checked, that was illegal."

"I didn't say she should tell the FBI she's doing it—just that she should. Second, she should make a diary of the calls—when, what he said, like that. Then she should try to get something specific out of him, something that might ID him."

"He hates it when she asks him questions."

"Yeah, well, he'll keep playing God till someone puts a stop to it. She have a trace put on her phone yet?"

"I don't think so."

"Might give it a try. The phone guys are pretty quick these days. If she keeps him on a couple of minutes they can usually track it down."

"I don't know if she'd go for that."

"What the hell? She want the guy out of her life, or not?"

"I don't know," I said without thinking, then felt traitorous doing so.

"So she's hot for him, huh?"

"Not exactly. But he has some hold on her. I'm not sure what it is. She's only prepared to go so far to catch him. It's as though there's some sort of rules to their game or something."

Charley hesitated, then gave me a mischievous grin. "Well, hell. If you're in on it, Tarzan, then maybe she could take a chance."

"On what?"

"Bait a trap. Lure the guy somewhere, offer him whatever she thinks will get him hottest, then you pounce on him like a pit bull when he shows up to collect his prize."

"I thought of that," I admitted. "But lots of things could go wrong."

"Yeah. And next time he jumps her she could go out

and stay out. Then you'd be stuck with that—what was her name?"

"Ramona."

"Right. The one who filed your cases under the client's first name."

"And typed my letters with the red ribbon because she thought it looked cute."

Charley laughed his volcanic laugh and leaned back against the booth, which provoked another anguished moan. "From what you've said and the way you've said it," he drawled, "I got to think we're talking about one of two people."

"Who?"

"Ruthie or Peggy. Which is it?"

I sighed and told him, but it didn't seem to help.

Charley went off to meet his hooker and I left Shields' and strolled over to Third Street and dined on the blue plate special at Max's Diner. I spent most of the mealtime considering Charley's suggestion that I devise a suitable charade that would lure the spider from his web to a place where I could nab him while at the same time insuring the survival of the bait.

The obvious lure was Peggy, the obvious ploy the offer of a sexual favor that could only be enjoyed in person, a favor irresistible even to someone whose amatory adventures were exclusively vicarious. Over coffee and dessert I imagined Peggy in a variety of seductive deployments, but by the time I paid the check I hadn't come up with anything more reliable than a B movie plot.

Similar stratagems wriggled through my mind on the way back to my car, until I reminded myself that for all intents and purposes I'd been ordered off the case. At least that seemed a corollary consequence of being ordered out of Peggy's apartment the night before, and if I honored her desire there was no need to plot erotic scenarios and I could go home and watch the week's installment of *Hill Street Blues*.

But the past both opens and closes the doors to future conduct, and I couldn't let it drop. Peggy was my secretary and something more than my friend. She had helped me over so many bumps in my own uneven life that I had to try to return the favor whether she wanted me to or not. At least that was both my resolution and my rationale as

I drove north on Sansome Street, and what made me stop off at the office instead of throwing in the towel.

The office was uninviting as it always is when I'm the only person in it. I sat down at Peggy's desk and spun her Rolodex until I found the card I wanted, which was right next to Peggy's own. After jotting the information in my notebook, I picked up the phone and dialed Peggy's number. My essay at harmony was delayed, however, because it wasn't Peggy who answered the phone, it was Ruthie Spring. I asked her how it was going.

"We're eating," she said, her words guarded, obviously overheard.

"I suppose I'm still persona non grata over there."

"Yeah. And I ain't all that grata either."

"She tell you what she did at the office today?"

"Nope."

"You want to know?"

"If it had something to do with the guy on the phone I do."

I told Ruthie about the bag of Peggy's underthings, about her promise to deliver it to the spider, about its deposit in the little corporate park, and about my fruitless vigil. When I'd finished, Ruthie scoffed and swore. "Going to take more than a game of capture the flag to snare this dude," she grumbled. "Hell, he probably just put you through some paces to see how gullible you are."

"You see the boyfriend Hess?" I asked, sidestepping further examination of my failed surveillance.

"Yep."

"And?"

"Just a minute. Let me close this door."

I heard muffled scraping sounds, and a brief muddle of voices, then Ruthie came back on the line. "I don't put him at the head of the parade, Marsh, but I could be wrong. He doesn't like the way she handled the kiss-off, that's for sure, and he had a few gutter words to say for your friend and mine, but I don't think he's wild enough to be doing more than fuming. Claims he hasn't seen her for six months. Claims to hope to never see her again. Claims that if she's in some sort of trouble it couldn't have happened to a more deserving gal."

"He threatened her, didn't he?"

"He admits to it. Even admits to belting her one time. Says it was just temper and booze. Says he only did it after she unloaded on him in one of their fights, made light of everything from his Mercedes to his taste in clothes, which means she probably had things to say about his performance in the hay as well. Says he's glad he's rid of her, says he spent over a grand on her while they were courting, taking her places and showing her things and buying her trinkets, and didn't get anything out of it he couldn't have gotten from a two-dollar whore."

"Nice guy."

"Yeah, he's a hothead. Probably a coker, too; he's got all the marks."

"What marks?"

"Too much money from too little effort and not a ghost of an idea how to spend it on anything worthwhile. People don't know shit these days, you know that, Marsh? Best thing most of them can think of to do with their spare time is go out and give fifty bucks to someone just because he claims to have come up with a new way to cook a chicken. *Dogs* got more imagination than that, for Christ's sake."

I laughed at Ruthie's truth. "You ask Hess where he was Tuesday night?"

"Yep. He was out on the town. Alone. Bar hopping down Union Street, hoping to fill his bed."

"He have any luck?"

"Nope. I gather he bunks alone more often than not, though he'd deny it if you asked him. He comes on pretty strong, but he comes on pretty rich, too, so I imagine he throws one every now and then."

"So we move on, is that your recommendation?"

"Yep. For now. He'll stay put if we want to look at him a little closer later on."

"Okay. I'll try to talk to the daughter tonight. You going to sleep at Peggy's?"

"Nope." Ruthie's voice tightened around the word.

"Why not?"

"She told me I wasn't welcome. And don't get any ideas about handling the job yourself, because I'm a hell of a lot more welcome than you are." Ruthie hesitated. "If I didn't know better I'd guess you bedded her last night, sugar bear. And then I'd guess that neither of you could live with what you thought it meant once the sun came up and the lights turned on."

"We didn't make love, but we came close."

"Sometimes close is worse than all the way."

"I guess this was one of those times. She tell you about the call?"

"A little."

"She tell you I listened in?"

"Yep."

"She tell you anything else?"

"Told me you got bent out of shape about the way she talked to him."

"What else?"

Ruthie ignored me. "We got to cut her some slack, Marsh, or we're going to lose her. What we got to remember is, she can have you and me and the Chinese army around here day and night, but the guy can still get at her anytime he wants. She knows that. It scares her, and the only thing she can think of to keep him out of her tent is to do what he wants when he wants her to. Not many women brave enough to do anything but in that situation. Men, either. And I can tell you this, Marsh Tanner. It's going to be hard to get much cooperation from our client if you keep edging up on her pussy every time you're alone together."

"It's more complicated than that, Ruthie."

"Maybe it is. And maybe you just hope it is so you can believe there's some high and mighty reason for you to be doing like you've been doing."

I'd spent most of the morning wrapping my mind around just the sort of accusations that Ruthie was engaging in, and I didn't want to deal with that part of the problem anymore. I pushed Ruthie away from my ethics and back to the case. "She tell you anything at all that's useful?"

"Not that I can see. She didn't have much to say, Marsh. I've had an easier time with a breeched calf."

"So when you heading home?"

"Soon as I finish the cheesecake."

"You think I should set up outside her apartment and keep watch tonight?"

"Just a second. Someone's at the door."

Ruthie left me with a dead line, then came back a minute later. "Damn neighbor woman wants to borrow some ice. Now where were we?"

"Do you think I should stake out her apartment tonight?"

"In this neighborhood you're liable to get arrested you stay in one place more than an hour."

"Well, maybe I'll chance it anyway. I'll talk to you after I see the daughter. Tell Peggy I said hello. Tell her to call me at home if she wants anything. Tell her—"

"You want her to know any more than that you got to tell her yourself. I'll be around if you need me, Marsh."

"Thanks, Ruthie. I hate to say it, but I think I made all this a lot worse than it was before I got involved."

"Hell, that's the PI's stock in trade. Harry used to say he'd had a good day if he hadn't gotten anybody killed."

21

I hadn't been sure where Peggy's daughter lived, hadn't even known what surname she went by, but the Rolodex had given me what I needed, on the card following Peggy's own: Allison Nettleton, 428 Delaware Street. The telephone number was listed as well. Both the number and address had been erased and amended several times, in testimony to Allison's peripatetic lifestyle, and the card was tattered and dingy as a result. From what Peggy had told me from time to time, Allison's life was tattered and dingy as well.

It was almost eight. I dialed Allison's number and got a busy signal. I dialed again five minutes later. Still busy. After downing a quick finger of Scotch, I drove out to Potrero Hill.

Allison's building was across from an auto parts warehouse and within earshot of the freeway. Because it was only a few feet up the hill it lacked a view and consequently hadn't been redeveloped out of existence. Even so, there was evidence of gentrification in the neighboring lots.

The stucco facade was stained and chipped, a window was broken and patched with black Visqueen, the garage door tilted beneath a fractured hinge, and a digit on the house number was missing. It was what passed for a low-rent district, which meant the place would be a steal at six hundred a month.

I rang the bell. Music drifted down from the second floor, a repetitive monotone that threatened to build to significance but never did. I pressed the buzzer and waited, and pressed again and waited even longer. The next time I kept pressing until the door popped open. When I went through it I entered a carpeted staircase that was narrow, dark, and purple.

No one appeared at the top of the stairs to ask me what I wanted, no one called out an inquiry or a greeting, no one did anything except produce a series of thudding sounds, as though someone on the second floor was using the building as a drum. Louder now, the music drilled toward the center of my brain and made me long for Mozart.

I climbed the stairs, which were spongy and infirm. When I got to the top I took my bearings. Although no one seemed interested in the fact, I was inside the apartment and not merely in an entryway.

The design was the reverse of the norm, with the living room at the back and bedrooms at the front. The place was unquestionably occupied, because from where I stood I could see down the hall and into a room that contained at least one pair of bare feet. They rose vertically off the floor, heels down, toes splayed, as if their owner was asleep or dead. I coughed but no one stepped forth to greet or challenge me.

In addition to the large room at the back I could see a portion of a kitchen and the corner of a bedroom, and could smell what I guessed was herbal tea and an additional aroma that I guessed was human sweat. As I walked toward the living room an orange object hurtled across the door opening, then disappeared as completely as if it had fallen down a well. The odd apparition was followed by two more percussive thuds that caused the floor to tremble and the light fixture to rattle like coins in a can. I walked to the doorway and looked inside.

The living room was virtually hollow, the dominant feature a polished floor shined to a golden glow. The walls were cobalt blue. The floor was barren but for a stereo tape player shoved against one wall and a futon sleeping mat rolled up and stored directly across from the stereo. Next to the mat was a pole light that sprouted several metal shades from which beamed lights that made the room seem psychedelic and me feel like twenty years had somehow disappeared.

The feet I'd seen from the top of the stairs belonged to a young man lying on the floor. His head was propped against the rolled-up mat. Eyes closed, mouth open, breaths labored, he seemed exhausted by the search for meaning in the bloodless music. He was dressed only in blue Jockey shorts and a sleeveless sweatshirt with the words CHOOSE ME on the front. His body was tanned and muscular, his face handsome but dissipated, capable of cruelty.

I was about to say something to him when I heard another thud, this time at my back. When I turned I saw the figure who had hurtled past the doorway moments earlier.

It was Allison, a hardened version of the sprightly coed whose photograph adorned her mother's desk. She was dressed in an orange leotard made luminescent by the mix of colors from the pole lamp. She was barefoot like her mate, but far from supine. Within the space of the next minute she crouched, sprang, kneeled, leaped, twisted, kicked, and screamed, in agony or ecstasy or something undefined. I could tell she was working hard, because her body was slick with sweat and because the music was insufficient to provoke an emotion more sophisticated than languor.

I leaned against the doorjamb and watched the dance for several minutes more. If not blindingly original, the moves were nevertheless practiced and arresting, out of Martha Graham by way of Merce Cunningham, I guessed, the work of an earnest if not gifted artist. When the tape ran out the dancer collapsed in the center of the floor, the audience opened his eyes, and I stepped into the room.

"Who the fuck are you?" the young man asked when

he saw me, his voice thick, his lids heavy, his eyes dull, as if they were dabbed with salve. His hair was long and sculpted; his jaw jutted; his pose was reminiscent of Truman Capote's on the jacket of his first book.

I told him my name.

"So what?"

"I'd like to talk to you and Allison." I glanced at the dancer.

The girl was panting too heavily to speak. I looked back at her companion in time to see him extract a crystalline nugget from a plastic bag and drop it into the bowl of a tiny glass pipe and touch a match to it. "Crack," he said after absorbing a deep puff. "Want a hit?"

I shook my head.

"Essence of coke, man. The highest of the highs. Al?"

The girl swore and hopped up off the floor. She kicked at an invisible something, took one long look at the recumbent doper, and said, "What if he's a cop?" Then she stomped angrily out of the room. I blinked and followed her.

She led me to a bedroom in the front. The bed was a mattress on the floor, the closet a rope tied from wall to wall, the dresser a pile of clothing in a corner. The sole light was a bulb dangling from a cord in the center of the ceiling. The pull-chain had been extended with a string. A Barbie doll was tied to its end, so that Barbie was in a state of perpetual execution.

Allison marched to the far corner of the bedroom and I lingered in the doorway. She knew I was there, knew I was watching, but that didn't stop her from pulling off her sopping leotard and flinging it at a cardboard box. Naked, she picked a brown towel off the floor and began drying herself off. Her body was tight and stringy, rippling with a dancer's muscles, dark and leggy. Her features bore her mother's royal stamp, but she betrayed them with a vassal's scowl. Still, there was an artist's arrogance to her movements, and a lover's ire as well.

When she finished mopping off her body she pawed

through the pile of clothing and extracted a second leotard and struggled into it. This one was black, to match her mood. When she'd arranged her breasts and buttocks within the clinging fabric she turned on me with hot hostility. "So *are* you?"

"A cop?" I shook my head.

"What do you want?"

"To talk to you a minute."

"What about?"

"Your mother."

That doused her rage, but substituted suspicion. "She send you here to bad-mouth Derrick?"

I shook my head. "She doesn't even know I'm here."

"Right."

"The truth."

Allison frowned uncertainly. "I don't get it. What's the deal? She's not sick, is she?"

"What makes you ask that?"

"I don't know. Some jerk in a sportcoat walks in unannounced and starts talking about your mother, you wonder if there's a problem and he's an insurance guy or something. So? Is there?"

"Not quite the way you think. I'm Marsh Tanner. Your mother works with me. She's my secretary."

"Oh." Allison raised a brow and cocked a hip. "You're him, huh?"

"I'm him."

"Nice to meet you, I suppose."

"Same here."

"She's told me lots of stuff about you."

"Same here."

Her grin slid wider. "From the look of you I doubt very much of it was true."

"Same here," I said, and matched her look. "Is that Derrick in the other room?"

"That's him. Or what's left of him."

"He's an actor, right?"

"He's an actor part-time. Full-time, he's a jerk. So what are you, producing a show or something?"

"What's he on?"

"The pipe? That's crack, man. Rock cocaine. Makes every man a Rambo and every chick a Ramboette."

"Is Derrick an addict?"

"Derrick would be an addict if he could afford to be an addict. Since he can't, he sucks up whatever he can beg off the baby Bernhardts he works with. Since an amazing number of them seem to be cruising along on Daddy's trust fund, once in a while he scores something heavy. Mostly, though, he pisses and moans about being broke and looks at me like I'm Miss Fixit."

"Where's he work?"

"By day he buses dishes at a joint on Union. By night he acts like an actor acting like he's good." Allison crossed her arms. "The question is, why do you care?"

"He and your mother had some trouble a while back, didn't they?"

"He and my mother have had trouble ever since I made the mistake of introducing them."

"There was something about money recently though, wasn't there?"

"Money." She said it as though it was a terminal disease. "In this house there is *always* something about money."

"What was it this time?"

Allison held an internal debate over whether to tell me. Finally she resolved it in my favor. "Derrick, in his lucid moments, wants to open his own theater. The Anthropomorphic Space, he wants to call it. He's got a loft down on Mission already picked out, and he's got some energetic young thespians ready to labor night and day for nothing but the chance to trod the boards and smoke some dope with Derrick, and he's got a review from a Boston paper saying his portrayal of Alan Strang in *Equus* was an inspired leap of unconscious revelation."

"So all he needs is money."

She nodded. "And since my grandfather died and left my mother some, and since Derrick is convinced that half of it is rightfully mine, he persuaded me to put the heat on dear old Mom for a loan. She refused, mirabile dictu, so Derrick made a try for it himself. She refused again, this time with some rather choice remarks that blew holes in various parts of Derrick's ego. The relationship has since been strained, as they say." Her smile was wry and wicked.

"Did Derrick ever threaten her?"

"With what?"

"Physical harm."

"I don't think so." Allison frowned, suddenly serious. "What happened to her, anyway?"

"Did he ever follow her around?"

"Why would he do that? What the hell's going on here, Tanner?" Her foot tapped nervously; her eyes leaped on and off my face.

"Are you here late at night? At one or two in the morning?"

"No, as it happens. I'm not."

"Is Derrick?"

"Sometimes."

"Where are you?"

"I work."

"Where?"

"Is it any of your business?"

"No."

She hesitated. "Okay. Just so we understand each other. I dance at a nudie joint on Broadway. Guys pay to see my interpretation of a dying swan with tits."

"Does your mother know?"

"You mean she hasn't told you of her daughter's fall from grace?"

I shook my head.

"How gallant of her. But why are you asking me all this crap? I'm not saying another word till you tell me."

"Your mother's being harassed by someone."

"Who?"

"I don't know. Neither does she."

"Harassed how?"

"Phone calls."

"Obscene, you mean?"

"Yes. But personal."

"You mean she doesn't know him but he knows her?"

"Right."

"My God." She shook her head. "And you think Derrick might be doing it?"

"It crossed my mind."

She shook her head again, this time in rejection, not amazement. "That's weak, Tanner. Derrick's focused on only one thing lately. If he can't fit it in his pipe, he's not interested. Sex is out. So is theater. Derrick only has eyes for his connection. So I suggest you look elsewhere." She paused and her eyes took on a mist. "Is Mom all right?"

"I think so."

"He didn't attack her or anything, did he? Rape, I mean?"

"No. He scared her once. Shoved her down. But she wasn't badly hurt."

"Tell her to call me if she wants."

"It might help if you call her."

Allison's eyes hardened once again. "Maybe. And maybe we should just leave well enough alone."

I watched her wrestle with obstreperous emotions. "Do you have any idea who'd want to go after your mother like that?" I asked after a minute.

She shook her head. "I don't know enough about her life to know that. I don't *want* to know enough, I guess. Just like she doesn't want to know about me."

"I doubt that's the case, Allison."

"Yeah, well, you don't know, do you?"

"Know what?"

"About me and Mom."

"What about you?"

"We're exactly alike, that's what. Clones. She married

a jerk and I live with one. She makes unreasonable demands on me and I make unreasonable demands on her. She's never wrong and neither am I. We each know what's best for the other, we each think the other's life is a wasteland, and we're each afraid our own life is never going to get any better no matter what. Is it any wonder we hate each other's guts?"

"But you don't."

"Well, we act like we do, so it's the same thing, right?" Allison's tough facade suddenly softened. "Hey. Tell her I've got an audition with Smuin next week. It's a new company he's thinking of starting. They've got money and everything. Tell her if I get in the corps I can keep my tutu on for a change."

"I'll tell her," I said, and turned to go.

"Mr. Tanner?" Her voice was a hollow whisper at my back.

I stopped and faced her. She seemed to have grown a decade younger.

"My mom thinks you're pretty special," she said warmly.

"Not anymore, she doesn't."

"Well, she gets mad sometimes. But she doesn't mean it."

"I hope you're right."

"What I'm trying to say is, if I can help with this I'd like to."

"Good. I'll let you know."

"I'll try to keep an eye on Derrick, just in case I'm wrong."

"Good. There's just one more thing."

"What?"

"Has anyone been in touch with you lately who claims to be your father?"

My words seemed to absorb the air, to erase our previous statements, to leave us in a vacuum. Allison looked as though I'd inquired about a world that was magical and enchanting, a world she dreamed about. "My father?" she blurted eagerly, her sense made dumb and basic by my question. "What about my father?"

"I don't know," I said truthfully. "I just thought it might be possible he was behind your mother's problem."

"You mean you think he's come back?"

"Maybe."

"But has he?" Allison demanded, suddenly intense. "*Has* he come back?"

"Not that I know of," I said.

"But you *must* know something. Tell me what it is. Has Mom heard from him? Is that it?"

Her frenzy was such that I shook my head and held up a hand. "I'm sorry. I shouldn't have mentioned it. I've gotten your hopes up for no reason. As far as I know, no one's heard anything from your father, your mother included."

"Oh."

I apologized again, but within a few seconds her depression lifted and she offered me a sheepish grin. "I guess I haven't quite resolved all that," she said. "I think about him a lot, now that Derrick and I are . . . through. Not about *him,* exactly. Just about a man I choose to call my father. In my mind he looks kind of like Henry Fonda. I don't know why."

Allison and I exchanged what I decided was some sympathy and understanding. "Don't worry, Mr. Tanner," she said after the moment. "She'll be all right. Mom's always been all right."

I hoped she wasn't as blind as most kids are about their parents.

22

Drifting into the night, my thoughts caroming from Allison to her mother and back again, I left the apartment and drove down Delaware to Sixteenth, then cut over to South Van Ness and took it north as far as it went. It was several minutes before I realized that what I seemed to be doing was going back to Peggy's.

When I got to Fillmore I drove around Peggy's block several times, unsure of what I dared to do or even wanted to. Ten minutes later I managed to find a place to park within view of the door to Peggy's building. Suddenly tired, suddenly overwhelmed by futility, I turned off the lights, leaned back, closed my eyes, and waited for events to instruct me.

Ten minutes later, the door to the apartment building opened and Ruthie Spring came out. She was alone and looked displeased, and she turned away without observing me engaged in the nebulous duty I'd assigned myself. She strolled down the block in what seemed to be a huff, in the opposite direction from my outpost, until she reached her red Camaro. A moment later she sped away in a rush, giving the wheels an angry spin. Peggy must have fired Ruthie as surely as she'd fired me.

I glanced up at Peggy's window just as the light in the front room went out. I imagined her in the bathroom undressing, preparing for bed. I imagined our foreplay of the night before, recycled the touch and smell and sight of the bed we'd shared in common, remembered the beginning and the middle and imagined a different end.

I got out of the car. The air was cold but clear, the stars a million reminders of earthly impermanence. As I walked toward Peggy's place I felt reborn or at least recharged.

When I reached the end of the block a car turned onto the street in front of me, a gray Ford that cruised past me with its lights off. When I yelled for the driver to turn them on, he looked at me with what could pass for a lust for mayhem. I inspected him more closely, his face and then his car, and realized I'd seen him at least twice before since I'd begun hovering over Peggy, and one of those times was at a peculiar portion of the night, an hour when normal traffic wouldn't have been on the streets.

I called after him to stop. A second later his brake lights flashed. Though my view was fractured by reflections off the windshield, I thought he turned to look back at me. When I called out again he flipped his headlights on, increased his speed, raced to the next corner, and turned right, disappearing as though he'd been a figment.

On a hunch, I slipped into the shadows of the building beside me and waited for him to reappear. It took three minutes. Two blocks north of where I stood the Ford edged around the corner, lights off once again, a blind behemoth that crept my way with the implacability of a glacier. Still in the shadows, still wondering if this was any of my business, I let him get within ten yards before I stepped into the street and cut him off.

When he saw me his flushed face kindled. In the dark car his eyes were intense reflectors, catching the streetlight and reconstituting it as phosphorescent shrapnel. As I watched him aim the vehicle at my chest I moved onto my toes, ready to jump aside because he looked ready and able to run me down.

From behind his glass shield he waved at me to move aside. When I didn't he smashed a fist against the steering wheel; once, and then again. His teeth and eyes flashed once more, the metallic sheen melodramatic and mad. I held my ground with an infirm defiance. He kept coming, drove toward me until his bumper was a body-length away, then stopped abruptly. As I approached the car he seemed to seethe and scheme.

We looked at each other through the window like prisoner and warden. I made motions for him to roll it down but he held fast to the steering wheel. His face was round and sweaty, a glossy flesh balloon. His eyes were still murderously hot but the hands on the wheel were as white as ivory, as though all his blood had been summoned to flood his face.

"Who are you?" I asked through the glass, my voice heavy and ominous in the night.

"Not your business," he muttered, the words muffled and sullen.

I could feel his resistance more than I could hear it. His lip curled and his jaw bulged. An artery in his neck swelled as thick as a thumb. I tapped on the window with my knuckle, hard enough to hurt.

A car went past and honked at having to swerve around us. We ignored his inconvenience. The driver I was looking at looked at me, then down the street, and back at me again. This time the window drifted down, as slowly as the eyelids on a dying man. "What the hell do you want?" he demanded.

"I want to know what you're doing around here."

"It's none of your goddamned business."

"It is if it's criminal," I said peaceably, aware that the situation was electric, potentially lethal. I wished I had my gun.

"Oh, there's a crime being committed," he said, his eyes still pots of heat. "Only I'm not the one committing it. Who the hell are you, anyway?"

I shook my head. "You first. What's your business around here, friend?"

"That's got nothing to do with you. So get away from the car."

I tried to remain nonthreatening. I knew his face and I knew his car, so I could get to him when I wanted. For now I needed information. "I'm not leaving till you tell me your problem. We could go have a beer or something. You almost made a big mistake a couple of nights ago. You don't want to press your luck."

"Are you nuts? I don't even know who you are. Just leave me the hell alone."

"If that's the way you want it. I'm not a cop, but if I see you around here again I'm going to call one."

"Do that. You just do that."

He was less bothered by the threat than I expected. Which could have meant he was less sane than I expected, too.

"Did she hire you?" he went on, his lip a dismissive curl. "Are you her bodyguard or something?"

"Something like that."

"Well, it won't do her any good. I'll do what I have to do, no matter *who* she hires."

"It's time to put a stop to it, pal. You've had your fun, but enough's enough. An assault charge is more than you bargained for, I think. And that's what it'll be if you fool with her again."

"Assault? I'll show you an assault. You haven't seen anything yet, mister. Just don't get in my way."

He floored the accelerator and the car leaped away in a cloud of smoking tires and a cry of peeling rubber. I jumped aside, but caught my balance in time to read the license plate as he passed under the streetlight at the end of the block. I wrote the number in my notebook, then looked up at Peggy's place again.

It was still dark, its occupant oblivious to what had just transpired. I started back for my car, to set off after the Ford, but a glance told me it was too late. The Ford was too far away, the Marina maze too easy for it to hide in. In any event I was ambivalent: the driver was my second suspect, after all, no more or less fitting than Judson Tomkins, who seemed less fitting by the hour. Without talking to him again I couldn't rationally bring in the police. And even if I could prove he was the spider's alter ego, arrest presented risks. He would doubtlessly be released on bail, and at that point Peggy's jeopardy could escalate as a result of my uninvited meddling.

In a torpor of uncertainty, I waited two hours to see if the Ford would bring its driver back. When it didn't, I drove to the nearest phone booth and called the cop I knew best next to Charley Sleet. I asked him to have a patrol car swing by Peggy's place from time to time for the rest of the evening, on the bogus ground that I was working on a domestic wrangle and that the husband had been threatening my client. I gave him a description of the Ford and the license number, and my friend said he'd take care of it. Then I went home and tried to care for myself. In the process, I wondered who the red-faced man was and what Peggy could possibly have done to him to make him so livid and incorrigible.

23

When the phone rang I was dancing naked with Allison on the Marina Green, a sybaritic pas de deux that in real life would have been bathetic but in dreamland was arousing, elegant, and perfect. The pulsing phone destroyed all that, and by the time I had regained my senses enough to grope for the receiver I was back in my vastly imperfect bedroom, in the grip of an equally imperfect dread of what the call might mean.

"Marsh," she said, her voice thin and sterile. "It's me."

"Peggy?"

"Yes, I . . ."

"What happened?" The question presumed calamity.

"Nothing. I . . ."

"Are you all right? You don't sound all right."

"I'm fine."

I couldn't believe her. "Did he attack you again?"

"No, no, it was just a call, Marsh. Another phone call."

I was thankful and relieved, but as perturbed as ever by the fact of those telephonic confidences. "What did he want?"

She hesitated. "He wants to see me."

I swore. "I hope you didn't agree."

"Well . . ."

Her silence became an elaborate and chilling answer. "When's the meeting?"

"Tonight."

"Where?"

"The Alta Plaza."

"The park?"

"Yes. By the swings. He wanted me to go to some place in Golden Gate Park, but it's so big and isolated I didn't think I ought to do that. And I certainly didn't want him here. The plaza was the only other place we could think of."

The thought of the two of them negotiating a nocturnal rendezvous was infuriating. "You're not going," I said.

"But I told him I'd be there."

"I don't care what you told him, you're not going."

She sniffed twice, then spoke halfheartedly. "But I thought this was what you *wanted* me to do. I thought this was a way of fighting back."

Charley Sleet had suggested that I lay a trap. I had vacillated, but the opportunity had presented itself without my urging. The risks remained, but now they seemed worth taking—even if the ploy was unsuccessful, a retaliatory posture might salvage Peggy's peace of mind and even repair our torn relationship. But I had to make sure what she was thinking, how she saw our roles. "How do you mean, fight back?"

"Well, I thought if you got there first, and hid someplace, then maybe when John came to meet me you could catch him. Or see who he was. Or call the cops. Something."

"Those rescue scenes hardly ever work in real life, Peggy. And when they break down they can make things worse than ever."

"But how else are we going to stop him, Marsh? What else can I do? Tell me, so I'll know what I have to do to get you to stop *looking* at me the way you were last night. I can't take that anymore. I just can't." Her final phrase slid into a convulsive groan.

Her plea ate away my confidence as it augmented my shame. "I know this is a nightmare for you, Peggy. And that there's no easy way out of it. I really do. I know you want it to stop, and it will, eventually. I'll get him. I promise. But not this way. This way's too risky."

"How much time, Marsh? I mean, how long will it be before I can sleep again? Please tell me, so I can have something to look forward to."

I said the only thing I could, which was a slippery evasion. "I don't know, Peggy. I'm working on it, that's all I can say. And Ruthie is, too. Between us we'll figure something out."

Sometime during my speech she made a decision, and it was the opposite of the one I was urging on her. When she imparted it her voice was firm and cocky. "Well, I'm going. I'll go to the park and wait and see what happens. At least I'll have a chance to look at him. Maybe I'll recognize him. Maybe he'll introduce himself and tell me his life story." She laughed bitterly. "Hell, maybe we'll start going steady. I don't seem to have much luck with men I actually go out with. Maybe this is the only kind of relationship that works for me." Her bravado drifted out of reach, and her final words were infirm again. "I don't know what else to do, Marsh. I really don't."

The only way I knew how to respond to her request for encouragement was to tell her about the guy with the red face and the gray car I'd seen outside her apartment that evening, and ask if she had any idea who it was. She said she didn't. She said she didn't know anyone who looked like that. She said she didn't know anyone who drove that kind of car. She didn't say I was wasting my time trying to identify him, but she was thinking it.

Her disclaimer dimmed my hunch to a faint conjecture, but nevertheless I told her I was going to call the DMV in the morning, and that when I got the name of the registered owner of the Ford the whole thing might be over. She didn't say anything and I didn't blame her. One of the few certainties in my world at the moment was that it wasn't going to end that easily.

I thought for a minute longer, then made a decision myself, one that presupposed a gamble. "What time's he supposed to get there?"

"Three."

I looked at my watch. "Okay. I can be there by two-thirty. I'll dig in someplace and wait and see what happens. If he beats me to the park and sees me coming, I assume the arrangement will be aborted and you'll be treated to another lecture on the phone. Or worse."

"I'm prepared for the consequences, Marsh. At least we're doing *something.*"

"Okay. We'll give it a try. But don't make him mad, Peggy. Don't give him any reason to do something that I won't have a chance to prevent."

Her voice took on a bramble. "*That* won't be a problem, will it? I mean, I'm used to doing what he wants. As you well know."

"I'm sorry for last night, Peggy. I don't know how else to say it."

She hesitated, and in the echo of my apology her mood diluted. "I know you are, Marsh. I know in some ways this is as hard for you as it is for me. I know that, but it doesn't keep me from getting mad at you sometimes. The same way you get mad at me, I guess." Her laugh was dry and fragile, but tinged with hope.

"I don't want anything to happen to us, Peggy. I hope you believe that."

"I do. I guess."

"I meant it when I said I loved you. I'm not sure quite how I meant it, but I meant it."

"I love you, too, Marsh. I really do."

We paused beneath the words, without the need to evade or expand them. "We'll get him, Peggy," I said finally. "We'll get him tonight. Just don't take any chances up there. If it starts to go bad—if he has a weapon, or there's more than one of them, or anything else that looks dangerous—just start running and leave the rest to me."

"Okay."

"Maybe I should get Ruthie in on this."

"No," she said quickly.

"Why not?"

"Just don't. Ruthie wants me to be what she is, and I

can't and I don't want to be and I'm tired of feeling I should. You'll take care of it, Marsh. I know you will."

I hung up with her trust ringing like a carillon in my ears, but I found myself wondering if we had meant anything we'd said to each other, or if it had been in the nature of a pep talk, one that would be meaningless once the game had been played.

I threw off the covers and struggled into my clothes, brushed my teeth, grabbed a slice of bread for breakfast, and went down to my car. The night was cold but dry. My breath made momentary clouds; my windshield was a sheet of icy-white geometry.

My engine didn't want to be disturbed and resisted when it was. I gave up trying to start it and coasted down my hill instead, then popped the clutch, pumped the gas, and hijacked the Buick to my bidding. It took six minutes to reach Pacific Heights.

The Alta Plaza was a dozen blocks uphill from Peggy's apartment. It covered an area of two blocks square, and was surrounded by some of the finest homes in the city. The grassy expanse rose in tiers to a gentle knoll in the center, from which three sides of the city could be seen and marveled at. On the east side of the park were tennis courts, and just to the west of them was a play area, with swings, sand, basketball hoops, even a slide and a jungle-gym, all of it sheltered by shrubs and pine trees and supervised by an imitation adobe restroom that was padlocked against both vandals and the incontinent.

I drove around the park two times, looking for a suspicious character or at least a red-faced man in a big gray Ford. When I didn't find either I parked in someone's driveway, hoping they had no errands to run at that hour. After glancing across the empty adjacent streets I strolled into the park, as alert as I could be for other beings. Although I seemed to be alone, and the park benign and vacant, I was edgy and afraid, the way I always am at three A.M.

After hiking to the top of the knoll, I traversed the play

area, mimicking an insomniac on a soporific stroll. No one appeared to challenge or converse with me. When I reached the opposite street at a point out of sight of the playground I doubled back the way I'd come, as silently as I could manage it. This time I was looking for a hiding place.

The one I found was deep within a lilac thicket, behind a huge magnolia, not far from the swings where Peggy was to meet her menacer. As I eased into the tangled bush I convinced myself that from where I was I could put a stop to anything. The conviction was evanescent.

From my nest I could see the entire play area and, nailed to the trunk of a tall tree in the center of the playground, a sign of the litigious times: USE APPARATUS AT OWN RISK. The sign was a reminder that on this evening the risk was not mine but Peggy's, a reminder that intensified the chill in the clear night air.

I snuggled deeper into my brittle lair, curling into myself for warmth. The wind caused the pines overhead to stir uneasily, as though they too were leery of the evening's tryst. Beyond the fringe of the park the lights of the city spilled away from me. I felt on top of the world, which meant among other things that I was in a position to fall off.

Although I spent some time trying to imagine what was likely to happen over the next hour, I couldn't come to grips with it. Peggy and the spider. "Tea for Two." *Brief Encounter. Sunday in the Park with John.* The stuff of song and story, except this rendezvous was perverted, sullied and extortionate, a coerced union. The possible product of the meeting was so disturbing I tried not to think about consequences, tried instead to think of tactics.

Something crackled, then rustled, then fell silent. I looked toward the sound but didn't see anything beyond windblown shadows and the skeletal arc of the frame that held the swings.

A cloud crossed the moon. The breeze picked up, usurping other sounds. I rearranged my limbs and wished I'd brought a flask of brandy. Then I saw a problem.

There were two sets of swings. I'd stationed myself near the westernmost, the first I'd noticed, the ones for tiny children. It was the most private end of the playground, the one farthest from the tennis courts, the most likely setting for what the spider had in mind, but it was still possible that instead of being close to the action I had placed myself too far away to be effective.

Dismayed by my predicament, I didn't see or hear her approach. But suddenly she was there, standing in the center of the little playground, a blue and yellow slide to her left, a trash barrel to her right, facing this way and that, looking for her tormentor or maybe just for me.

She was dressed in black—shoes, coat, gloves, scarf—not casually but stylishly, as though a minute earlier she had been sipping cocktails and exchanging gossip and getting slightly drunk. Her hands plucked at the buttons on her coat as though they were insects that infested her. Her eyes were wild and overzealous, seeing more than could possibly be there. I wanted to go to her and call it off and take her away from all of it, the cold and the hour and the danger that was as likely to occur as not, but I stayed in my prickly cave.

"John?"

Her voice was small, tentative, shoved almost beyond my hearing by the wind.

"John? Are you there?"

Someone answered her. I couldn't make out the words he used, but they came from somewhere east of me, from the bushes below the tennis court or the trees beyond the silver swings, the larger swings, the ones far too far from me. I cursed my stupidity and my untenable position. In the meantime, Peggy repeated the spider's name.

He answered a second time. Once again I could only hear an uninflected hum. Peggy turned his way, which put her back to me. I considered moving closer to my target, but detection was likely if I did so, and at that point I was prepared to ruin the setup only to put Peggy out of a clear and present danger. And I still wasn't certain where he was.

Peggy must have heard something else, because she shook her head and backed away, as though frightened by what he said. Then he spoke again, louder this time. The only word I heard was *promised*.

As chastened as if he'd slapped her face, Peggy stood stockstill, slumped, head down, a docile servant. Once again it was a struggle not to go to her and take her home.

A further word, peremptory this time, caused Peggy to straighten and look quickly to her left and right. To look, I guessed, for me. When I refused to let her find me she abandoned her earthly search and looked to the sky, as though her final hope resided there. Then she began to unbutton her coat.

She did it slowly, her fingers gloved and cumbersome, her stare fixed firmly on the sand beneath her feet. When the buttons were undone, she shrugged the garment off her shoulders, extended her arms to the rear, and let the dark wrap slide slowly to the ground. She hesitated, then undid her scarf as well and tossed it onto the woolen heap of coat. The gloves were next, each peeled slowly from her hand, each dangled from between two fingers before she flipped it toward the growing pile behind her back.

Her dress was basic black, knee-length, short-sleeved, set off by a celestial string of pearls. It was testimony to my flayed and battered senses that I didn't realize what was going on until she twisted an arm behind her back, grasped the talon of her zipper, and tugged it to her waist. The sound that reached my ears seemed a perfect duplication of a cry for help.

24

My heart assailed my chest; my lungs threatened to absorb the wind. I didn't want to watch, except I couldn't do anything else.

The zipper parted to reveal a V of powdered flesh. The loosened fabric flapped softly in the breeze, caressing her shoulders like the fluff of a feather boa. The thin black band of her brassiere bisected the wedge of epidermis like a draftsman's precise slash.

She was stripping for him, had known all along she would, had possibly even originated the idea in the hope that the prospect of seeing her stark naked would cause him to grow careless in the heat of dense desire. What must she be imagining—a stage, a band, a drunken, urging crowd—and what seamless desperation must have brought her to this point. With alternate glances I searched intently for the spider and admired her every move.

Peggy leaned forward, and the black bodice fell off her shoulders and onto her outstretched arms. Washed by a spot of moonlight, her neck was a pristine stem, her shoulders a bank of morning snow. She lifted one arm and then another free of the encircling sleeves, and gathered the bodice at her waist. Seconds later she had loosened her belt and tossed it aside as well, another doffed encumbrance. Had we been in one of my old Broadway haunts—the Chi Chi or El Cid—the band would have moved to "Night Train" and the customers would have begun to cheer her on. For an instant I felt like cheering her myself.

Free of the belt and tugged by upraised arms, the dress floated like a magician's trick above her head, catching momentarily on her chin, then soaring free and clear and shaken loose of twists and tangles. When the dress was fully off and in her hands she folded it and placed it carefully on the ground beside her. Knees bent, thighs sandwiched, torso twisted to conceal her private parts, her shyness made sublime what would have been indecent.

When she stood up straight she wore only the pearls, the black brassiere and panties, and her black high-heeled shoes. She looked around the park again and lingered when her eyes caught the twisting helix of the gaily painted slide, as though it brought back memories or reminded her how far she was from youth. For an instant her face froze in a mask of abject panic, and I thought she was going to give it up. I wanted her to, almost begged her to, but instead of surrendering she set her chin and firmed her jaw and raised one arm above her head and posed a wanton pose that was incongruous in the middle of the children's soft white sand.

From somewhere beyond the farthest swings her audience barked an order, impatient and dictatorial. I tried to pinpoint its source but couldn't. Peggy stiffened, then crossed her arms and bowed her head, awaiting his instructions. The spider spoke again, and again she did his will. I still didn't know where he was, but I knew he wasn't near enough.

Arching her back, Peggy reached to the center of her spine and unclasped the black brassiere, struggling at first, then subduing the tricky hooks. Bowing once more, she rounded her shoulders until they were free of the twin black straps, then extended her arms before her and bent forward at the waist to let the bra slide slowly down her arms, a stunt that must have made the spider boil. Because she tossed the silken halter negligently behind her, she didn't see it fly to the top bar of the little junglegym and dangle there, a comic gloss on the simple toy, and a brutal hint of what might one day lay in store for the next little girl who frolicked there if she was as unfortunate as Peggy.

Naked from head to waist but for the pearls that ringed her like an owner's collar, she stood uncomfortably in the center of the park, awaiting the spider's further urge. Her hands fluttered to her breasts and down again, uncertain whether to camouflage or anoint their resting places. Moments passed, the spider in a swoon no doubt, Peggy more and more abandoned to a self-cast spell.

"Don't stop," he ordered suddenly, the loudest words to date. "All but the shoes. You can keep the shoes."

She started to shake with shame and cold and the image of what she looked like and the definition of what she had become. Still, she lowered her hands, hooked her fingers through the waistband of her dusky panties, tugged them away from the sharp ledge of her hips, and rolled them down her thighs until they fell to her feet as noiselessly as leaves. As though she walked a tightrope, she lifted one leg out of the silken hobble, then raised the other so that the panties dangled for a moment from the pointed toe of her left shoe before she kicked them toward the bushes. Naked to me and to her enemy, she straightened proudly and defiantly, daring the spider to demand more.

"Turn," he said sharply, and so she did, a careful pivot that displayed the whole of her so gracefully I had to remind myself again that this wasn't for my benefit, that we weren't continuing our foreplay of the other night, that this was not my treat.

That fact was enough to prick my trance. I tore my eyes from Peggy's flesh and searched for a place to move to, a spot closer to the spider, a nook from which I could effect a rescue and put an end to the evening's long debasement. But before I could make a move the spider issued another command: "Tease me. Pose for me, like in a magazine."

She responded fitfully, uncertainly, afraid she would disappoint or even anger her instructor. Her hands darted like butterflies around her body, lighting here and there, remaining briefly before they flew away, skittish and awkward oddities. Her hips slid one way and then the other, her legs bent and straightened; her toes stretched her upward then brought her back to earth. Biting her lower lip, her brow knit with memory and with effort, she clasped her hands behind her head, thrust her chest, and rotated her torso left and right, a movement borrowed from aerobics or remembered from a stag film.

When she finished with the stretching twists, her hands slid down her ribs and came to rest beneath her breasts, then moved to hide and then to knead them. As she pursued her ministrations her head leaned back to prohibit her eyes from seeing how she used herself.

The breeze became a gust; the trees became a rooting throng. I took a breath and left my perch and scurried toward a second clump of bushes, this one behind the restroom, ten yards closer to the man I hated as I absorbed his crime. At the same time the spider spoke again, and his voice helped conceal my progress as it told me where he was.

When I reached the new position I waited, giving Peggy but a glance to see what she was doing. Her head was cocked to hear him better, and after the rumble of distant words she asked a question. I was thankful not to hear it. The next thing she said was throaty and alluring, but the spider stayed hidden out of sight.

I used the sounds to move once more, this time to a cypress tree. When I reached its trunk I turned to see Peggy moving farther from me, toward the swing set across the playground. I swore beneath my breath and watched to see where she would stop.

She went directly to the swings, leaned against the slack strap seat, lifted her legs above the sand, and began to pump, her hands grasping the rusty chains as though they were descended from the heavens and would therefore lead to rescue. Back and forth, higher and higher, she drove the swing seat up until her hair streamed out behind her and her legs raised toward the moon that loomed before her, yet another onlooker. In a moment she was almost horizontal, a marble eagle soaring above us all, compelled to fly still higher until the stars made room for her to join them. Like meteors, her shoes flew to the ground and buried partway in the sand.

It was now or never. At the top of her next arc the chains slacked and bucked and Peggy uttered a frightened squeal. I took advantage of her risk and left concealment, running headlong for the bushes where the spider's orders had been issued. My feet crunched twigs and leaves and gravel, my legs snapped fronds and branches, my noisy journey dispossessed the other sounds of night and warned my quarry that I was coming.

I heard him swear, heard him thrash to escape his hiding place, heard him curse the woman in the swings and heard him cry out in anticipation of defeat. I ran faster. Ahead of me, the bushes parted for a moment and I could see a shadow turn and scramble toward the other side of the hedge and safety. I veered, and in the process met my fate.

My foot caught under an upraised root and I hurtled headlong into a pile of leaves and pine needles that had been gathered by the tender of the space. I landed on my shoulder and my hip, and when the latter tried to pulverize a stone I groaned. As chorus to my cry, the spider cursed once more, somewhere far beyond my sprawl. Above the laughing pines I heard the clatter of his quick escape and his final, frantic dictate: "Think of me, Margaret. *Think of me!*"

By the time I was on my feet and chasing him he was a blur in the dark distance, a creature in full flight, topcoat flapping, arms flailing to maintain his balance. I ran as fast as I could without falling once again, but I trailed too far behind. As I reached the crest of the grassy knoll I could see a car door flash open, a figure duck inside, the interior go back to black and the whole shape lurch crazily from the curb like a rabbit flushed from a hidden warren.

The car disappeared down the Pierce Street hill. It was a black sedan, no machine I knew. I came to a stop in the middle of the empty park, panting like a racer, my nerves a tangle, my head a void, my senses bloated to the point of failure. When I could harness my lungs and distinguish time between the thumpings of my heart, I turned and walked back toward where it had all gone wrong.

25

Peggy had dressed but for her shoes and was sitting on the edge of one of the benches that lined the walk, waiting for me, waiting for the night to end, waiting for someone to condone what had just gone on inside the halcyon little park.

When I made enough noise to interrupt her introspective scan, she looked up. She was huddled like a pariah beneath her coat, its collar atop her head, its sleeves across her chest, but there was light in her eyes until she sensed my message. "He got away," she observed lethargically, as though her life was an unrelieved fiasco.

I nodded and sat down beside her. She leaned my way until our shoulders touched, then reached out a hand and took one of mine. "Unbelievable, huh?" she murmured, her body a warm compress, a quick reminder of its earlier labor at allure. I was determined to divert us from all that, but I didn't know how. Memory is not easily avoided, especially when its wellspring is fresh and its ramifications tarnish essential assumptions about oneself.

"Not unbelievable," I said. "Just unfortunate."

"Hootchy-kootchie," Peggy went on dully. "Like some two-bit carnival attraction. Like those places up on Broadway, the ones with the barkers out front and the women rolling around naked on the floor and the little Japanese men scurrying in and out in their shiny black suits."

"Like the places Allison works," I said, my intention better than my phrasing.

Peggy stiffened and withdrew her hand. The warm spot

on my shoulder quickly cooled. "When did you see her?" she demanded.

"Earlier tonight. About a thousand hours ago."

"Where?"

"Her apartment."

"Who . . . What happened?"

"Nothing that I can prove had anything to do with this."

"Was Derrick there?"

"In body but not in spirit."

"You mean he was stoned."

"Getting there."

"God*damn* that boy. What did Allison say about him?"

"She said he was a part-time actor and a full-time jerk."

"That's being charitable, believe me."

Peggy shivered and I put my arm around her shoulders and pulled her to me once again, to thaw both my body and my dismay at having consented to the events of the past hour.

I decided to keep Peggy focused on anything but the park. "Have you seen Derrick around your apartment in the past few weeks? Other than the time he put the dun on you to back his theater project?"

"You know about that."

"Allison told me."

"Do you think I was wrong to refuse him the money, Marsh? I mean, I didn't do it because I wanted it for myself. It's in trust, for Allison. Payable five years from now, but only if she's shed Derrick by then. If not, I'll keep postponing the distribution till Allison comes to her senses."

"Sometimes they never come to their senses."

Peggy breathed deeply. "But I have to believe she'll straighten out sooner or later, don't I? Or I have to stop being her mother. What other choice is there?"

"How much money are we talking about, anyway?"

"In trust? About forty thousand. It's all Allison's. And

that's the way it should be. But I will *not* have that boy picking her bones bare. I just *won't.*"

"That trust arrangement gives Derrick a motive to want you out of the way, you realize. To keep you from adding amendments that keep the money out of reach."

"But no one knows about it."

"Not even Allison?"

"Well, I . . ."

"Let me guess. You got mad at her one night, and told her how much it was worth to her if she dumped Derrick out on his lantern jaw, on the assumption that her avarice would overcome her lust."

Peggy sighed. "Something like that."

"And kids being kids, that made Allison all the more determined to keep Derrick around, jerk or no."

Peggy's sigh blended with the music of the trees. "Parenting is hell, Marsh. When they're little we raise them to have certain values, and then we're shocked when they grow up and actually exhibit them." Peggy chuckled a brief twitch. "I'm trying to think of the last time I did something right, and you know what? I can't. Not one single thing. I harped and harped at Allison to be independent and strong and honest, attributes my ex-husband and I both lacked with a vengeance at that age. And now she's using those very traits against me and has been since the day she left home. There's not many things in my life I'd want another chance at, but mothering is one of them." Peggy looked skyward, and was mocked by the playful stars. "Ah, hell. What am I *doing* here, Marsh? What the hell am I doing here?"

Peggy's question drifted out of reach, leaving me without an answer. "Well, you put on a real nice show tonight, Gypsy Rose," I joked, because I decided we had to face it or be its victim, because humor was the only device I could think of that would ease the task.

"Please. Don't even think about it."

"Seriously. It was brave and it was effective and if I

hadn't fallen on my butt like a Keystone Kop I'd have caught the bastard. I'm sorry I'm such a klutz."

"I should never have come."

In retrospect I agreed with her, but it wasn't what she needed to hear. "Maybe you've given him what he's been after all along," I said instead. "Maybe now that he's had a good look at you he'll move on to someone else."

Peggy looked at me from beneath her woolen cowl. "You don't really believe that, do you? What he's going to be is furious at me for trying to trap him."

"Maybe," I admitted. "That's why you're coming home with me."

Peggy started to stand up but I held on to her. "Oh, no I'm not," she protested as I forced her back to the bench.

"Oh, yes you are. You are if I have to tie you up and kidnap you."

She started to object once more, then fell silent. We listened to the wind and smelled the trees and watched the lights of the city watch us, a million bright eyes, all of them turned our way, wondering what entertaining enterprise we'd concoct next. "I have to go by my place and get some things," Peggy said finally.

"That's not a good idea. He could be waiting for you."

"I can't help it. I need my things. If you don't let me get them I'm not going."

"Okay. But in and out. Quick like a bunny. And I go in with you."

She looked to her left, toward the bay and the Golden Gate, the route out of the city, the escape. "What about my car?" she asked absently, her thoughts elsewhere.

"We'll leave it. I'll bring you back out here tomorrow. I'll even pay the ticket."

"But—"

"We do it my way or we spend the night right here," I interrupted. "From the way you're trembling I'd guess you're not prepared for a night in the park."

"Okay," Peggy surrendered. "I'm too tired to argue."

I stood up and reached out my hand and helped her to

her feet, which were still bare. We walked out of the park arm-in-arm, Peggy clutching her shoes and purse like a basket of goodies for Grandma, me on the lookout for the Big Bad Wolf.

The night was still clear, the stars still bright—a match for the man-made sparkle below them. The sky seemed lower than usual, as though the solar system had contracted for a better look at Peggy's lithe performance.

My car was still in someone's drive, but ticketless. We got in and I drove toward Peggy's apartment. The road was all downhill, on one of the steepest streets in town.

I parked in the yellow zone in front of Peggy's building. We went inside without exchanging another word, lost in each other's thoughts and bleak conclusions.

As we were mounting the stairs I heard a noise from down below, the garage area it seemed. I looked down the stairwell but couldn't see anything. The noises continued—a clatter, a bang, then the scrape of shoes on concrete. "Mr. Mendosa?" I called out.

The noises stopped. "Hello?" I called again.

"Who is it?"

The accented words floated to me out of the dark depths, spooky echoes off the plaster walls.

"It's Tanner," I said, as loudly as I dared. "I'm here with Ms. Nettleton. I talked to you a couple of days ago and I'd like to talk to you again for a minute."

"It is four-thirty. I was only preparing the cans for the garbage men. I am not yet dressed."

"I'll see Ms. Nettleton to her apartment, then come down to your room. If it's okay. It'll only take a minute."

"Since it's Ms. Nettleton, I will wait."

I thanked him and turned to Peggy. "I'll check your place out, then you get your things together while I talk to Mendosa, then I'll come get you and we'll go to my place and catch a few hours' sleep. How long will you be?"

"Five minutes."

"Fine."

We climbed the final flight of stars, pulled open the fire

200

door, and entered the dark hallway. I motioned for Peggy to stop, then listened for indications that we weren't alone. All I heard was the buzz of my inner ear and the whisper of Peggy's careful breaths behind my back.

I walked toward her door and motioned for her to follow. When I got there I checked the lock for signs of tampering, then pressed my ear to the door and listened. Nothing. Not even Marilyn.

I backed away from the door and held out my hand. Peggy fumbled in her purse, then dropped the key in my palm. I inserted the key in the lock, then motioned for Peggy to move to the side, out of a theoretical field of fire. I moved to the side as well, and pushed the door open. The hinge squeaked, the door scraped across the carpet and banged against the wall. I waited. No one shot at us, no one scrambled toward the windows in the back.

I told Peggy to stay where she was and went inside. The smell of fresh flowers was a vivid presence. I took in a lungful of their spice, and then another, then flipped on the light and looked around. There were no signs of disturbance. Marilyn hurried over and rubbed against my leg. I looked through the remaining rooms in the apartment, found nothing more alarming than evidence that Peggy had tried on several costumes earlier in the evening, before selecting the one most likely to seduce the spider.

I went back to the hallway and beckoned her inside. "I guess it's okay," I said. "Get your stuff together as fast as you can. I'll be back in five minutes. You can go to work from my place, or I'll bring you back here."

"My car."

"Right. I'll take you to your car. Tomorrow. Not now."

Peggy wandered back toward the bedroom, looking idly around the apartment, her expression bemused, as though it was the first time she'd been in the place. I went through the door, made sure it had locked behind me, then trotted down the stairs, entered the garage, and crossed its empty darkness to Mendosa's room.

The door opened immediately after my knock. He was

dressed in his work clothes but he had traces of shaving cream beneath his ears. His hair was mussed and there was a cup of coffee in his hand, but his eyes told me he was more awake than I was.

"Why are you here at this hour, Mr. Tanner? Has there been more trouble in the building?"

I shook my head. "I wanted to ask you if you'd ever seen a certain man hanging around the area in the past few days."

"What man?"

I described the red-faced man and the clothes he wore and the car he drove. Mendosa grew grave with recollection. "I believe I have seen this person," he concluded finally.

"Where?"

"In his car. In front of the building."

"Parked?"

"Yes."

"What was he doing?"

"Watching. Only watching, until he saw me watching him."

"Then what did he do?"

"He drove away. Quickly."

"When was this?"

"Perhaps a week ago. Perhaps a few days longer."

"Did you see him again after that time?"

"Once. Driving past. When he noticed me in the doorway he drove faster."

"Did he ever say anything to you about Ms. Nettleton?"

"No."

"Did you ever see any of the tenants talking to him?"

"No. I thought he was one of Miss Smith's visitors, to tell you the truth. Perhaps one who wanted her to leave her life of sin."

"Did you talk to Miss Smith about it?"

He shook his head. "She knows what I think about her life, so she avoids me. It is the way we both wish it, though

I would be happy to introduce her to my priest if she was willing to call on God."

Mendosa spoke with such fervor it seemed impossible for a whore or anyone to refuse his offer of salvation. I asked if he'd seen any strangers loitering nearby other than the man in the Ford.

He shook his head. "No."

"Why are you up so early, Mr. Mendosa? Did anything unusual occur in the building in the past hour? Noises, loud conversation, anything?"

"I am awake because this is my normal time to begin the day. The garbage is today, plus I wish the building to be warm when the tenants arise. But I did hear something. Not long ago someone ran up the stairs. They ran fast, with heavy steps."

"When?"

"Thirty minutes ago, perhaps."

"Any idea who it was?" I asked.

He hesitated. "I should not guess. My son, he tells me what happens when a witness makes a guess. It is, how do you say it, objectionable."

"We're not in court, Mr. Mendosa. I won't quote you, or even object."

"Mr. Tomkins makes a disturbance like that some-times," Mendosa blurted finally. "When he is drunk and angry."

"Did you see Tomkins go out last night?"

"No."

"Did you see him at all yesterday?"

"No."

Mendosa looked at his watch and then looked behind him, back into his apartment where unspoken duties awaited. I thanked him for his time, then remembered a duty of my own. "Ms. Nettleton says to tell you she's sorry about the mess she made on your floor," I said.

Mendosa frowned. "There was no mess on the floor; only on the stairs."

"Well, she's sorry about that, too."

26

I decided to take a peek down the hallway on each floor. The first two corridors were empty, but for the buzz of imagined snores. I walked to Tomkins' door, listened for a moment, knocked softly, waited, knocked louder, but heard no response. I envisioned him in a masturbatory frenzy, surrounded by his admiring, airbrushed girl-friends. I got rid of the image as quickly as I could.

The third floor, Peggy's, looked empty as well. After making sure of that I tapped on Peggy's door. When she asked who it was I told her, then said I'd be back down in two minutes. She said fine. I went to the stairs again, and this time climbed toward four.

Halfway to the intermediate landing the fire door above me opened, banging against the wall with the sound of a gunshot. Footsteps began to descend, in an ominous cadence. I retreated to the darkness of the doorway on level three and waited to see who else was abroad at that eerie hour.

He rounded the landing rolling in a robust swagger, a broad smile on his face and a lusty glitter in his eyes. One hand shoved his shirttail below his belt, the other fumbled for the talon to his unzipped fly. When I stepped into his path I startled him out of his vulgar reverie.

"What the . . . ?" His eyes bulged, red seeping into white, tiny bloody bandages. His hands dropped away from his clothing and made a pair of doughy fists. He squinted in the gray light, and finally focused. "Christ. You again."

Although his sneer was real and slanderous, there was a casualness to it that indicated that I was less threatening than whomever it was he had expected to encounter.

With elaborate nonchalance he unwrapped his fists, uncinched his belt, retucked his shirt, and buckled up again, a boastful grin underlining his flushed features like a wormy slit across an apple. "Come back to take another look at my pictures?" he asked when his fly was finally fixed. "I got some new ones since you stopped by the last time. Young ones. Hairless."

For the second time that night I courted a homicidal impulse. "What were you doing up there?" I gestured toward the door he'd just emerged from.

"What do you think?" Tomkins rolled his eyes and let his tongue hang stupidly from his mouth. His left hand cupped his genitals and he made a suggestive gyration of his hips.

"I don't believe you."

"Hey. Look around and try to guess who cares."

Tomkins bent over and brushed what looked like sand off his trousers. Much as I tried to dismiss it, when he straightened he had the soft, smug look of the satiety he was claiming to have just achieved.

"Who were you with?" I demanded.

Tomkins' smile rolled toward a semicircle. "A gentleman never kisses and tells."

"Come on, Tomkins. Where the hell have you been?"

"What's it to you?"

"Just curious."

"Curiosity played hell with the cat, pal." His laugh was as foul as the rest of him.

I glanced down at the floor, at the pile of silica that had fallen there. "Where were you earlier this evening?" I demanded.

Tomkins hesitated as he was about to edge past me. "I told you before where you can stick your questions, Tanner. You need a reminder?"

With a final grinning insult he powered by me and

started down the stairs. The only way I could have stopped him was with a right cross or a two-leg takedown, and at that point I didn't have a right to do either, given the rather strict and specific requirements for a valid citizens' arrest.

As I watched him lumber toward the second floor I thought about Tomkins' past, and about his earthy allegation. If he had truly enjoyed a sexual encounter on the fourth floor earlier in the evening, one of the two possible partners was Peggy Nettleton's best friend. I tried to imagine a reason for Karen Whittle to let Judson Tomkins have sex with her. I couldn't even come close.

On my way to the top floor I spent another twenty seconds trying to put together a circumstance that would explain that union. I was deep into unlikely exchanges and desires before I decided I was being paranoid, that the obvious explanation for Tomkins' dalliance was a certain Miss Smith, the same Miss Smith everyone in the building assumed to be a whore.

I tapped on number 44, waited, and tapped again. After a creak of bedsprings, footsteps approached the door. "Who is it?" a wary voice demanded.

"My name's Tanner. If you're name's Smith I'd like to talk to you."

"Do I know you?"

"No."

"Then who are you? A cop?"

"Private investigator."

"What do you want?"

"If you'd let me in I could tell you in about two minutes and I wouldn't disturb anyone else on the floor."

"I don't let people in my apartment at this hour," she said firmly. "No matter what they call themselves."

Her voice was rich and cultured, not at all the brazen scratch I'd expected. I began to doubt Miss Smith was the harlot Tomkins declared her to be. "It's about a man in the building," I said.

She hesitated, and I expected to hear her retreat into her apartment, but she finally spoke. "What man?"

"Judson Tomkins. He lives down on two."

Her laugh was brief and hard. "I know him, sad to say. So is that it? Is that what you want to know?"

"I was wondering if you just had a more, ah, intimate relationship with him."

She paused again. "Look, mister. I've had a lot of grief in my life and I don't need any more. I know Tomkins well enough to know he could be in any kind of trouble in the world, trouble I don't even want to think of, which means the only smart thing for me to do is stay out of it. Which is what I'm going to do."

"I'm used to keeping information confidential," I said. "No one needs to know we've talked."

She laughed again, this time more warmly. "I'm used to keeping my mouth shut, too, Mister Investigator. And that's just what I'm going to do right now."

"But I only—"

"Look. I know what people in this building say about me. Tomkins, and little Mendosa down there. Well, whatever I may have been or done in the past, it's not true anymore. Get it? I have friends and they come see me and we have a little fun and once in a while maybe we get a little loud. But that's it. I know the vulnerabilities of a whore, Mister Private Eye, but I'm not one and there's no way you can prove I am. So take your questions elsewhere. There's no way you can lean on me. No way in the world."

"That's none of my business," I said quickly. "All I need to know is if Tomkins was with you a few minutes ago."

"I learned a long time ago not to answer questions about who I was with and when. So I'm going to bed. If you've got any sense you'll do the same."

"It's important," I said.

"Not to me," she answered, and her footsteps took her away from the door.

I was looking at my watch and wondering if there was

anything more I could do when the door to the apartment across the hall opened and Karen Whittle's face appeared in the narrow space above the chain. "What's going on?" she asked.

She was wearing a housecoat and her hair was in curlers but she seemed fully awake. As she brushed back a wayward curl her housecoat fell open to reveal a lacy camisole that stretched like a drumhead across her abdomen. "I was wondering if you and Lily were all right."

"Why wouldn't we be?"

"I just saw Judson Tomkins come down from this floor. He had a look on his face that inspired my concern. I was just asking your neighbor about him. I'm sorry I disturbed you."

She frowned and bit her lip. "I'm no more disturbed than usual," she said with a hint of wildness that revived my suspicion of a link between her and Tomkins.

"How's Lily?" I asked.

"She's asleep, which is where I'm going when you start quieting down. What are you *doing* here, anyway? It's five A.M."

"I was down at Peggy's."

Karen Whittle raised her brows. "Is that supposed to explain what you're doing outside my apartment?"

"I told you. Tomkins and Miss Smith. I was checking on them."

"Why?"

I shrugged. "Tomkins is a guy who needs checking on."

She frowned, then yawned. I wasn't certain she was as sleepy as she pretended. "I'm not supposed to understand, am I?" she said.

"No." I started toward the stairway, but then turned back. "What does your ex-husband look like?"

Apprehension iced her features. Her eyes flicked at each end of the hallway, and her hand squeezed her housecoat at the base of her throat so tightly she seemed intent on strangling herself. "Why? What about him?"

"I saw a man hanging around. I thought it might be him."

"In the building?"

"No. Outside."

"When?"

"Yesterday."

"Oh." Her hand slid away from her throat and her lips stretched into an easy smile. "Well, Tom is tall, dark, and handsome, or he was when I married him. When we divorced he was short, fat, and bald. At least he looked that way to me."

"Red hair? Red face?"

She shook her head. "I was the one with the red face," she said, "when I realized what a bastard I'd married."

I grinned at her arid joke and told her good night and listened as she shut the door on what I'd thought was a good idea.

A minute later I tapped on Peggy's door. "Who's there?" she asked for the second time that night, her voice still dry and strained, her mood still delicate.

"Me."

The door opened six inches, but a chain still stretched across the gap. We looked at each other through a narrow column of air that reminded me of the times I'd talked to people through the bars of a jail cell.

Her preparations for the trip to my apartment included changing into what looked like a cotton jumpsuit. "Let's go," I said. "We can have you in bed by six if we hurry."

"I'm not going." Her chin jutted and her lips thinned to the diameter of wire.

"Come on. Don't be difficult."

"I'm not going, Marsh. I'm here and I'm fine and I don't want to leave and you can't make me because I'm not going to let you in."

"It's not safe, damnit. You don't know *what* that guy will do."

"Yes, I do."

I looked at her. "Did he just call you? Have you talked

to him since you got back here? You have, haven't you?"

In response to my inquisition she moved out of sight behind the door.

"Did he threaten you?"

"No. He was very understanding. He—"

"Crap and double crap. Come *on*. You're not staying alone tonight, not where that psycho can get at you. I mean it, Peggy."

She didn't answer or appear.

"You know what he did, the son of a bitch? Huh? You know what your precious phone pal did? He bugged the office. Not my office; *your* office. He put a little bug in that picture behind your desk and he's heard every single word you've said for months. Still think he's harmless, Peggy? Normal? He'll do anything to get you where he wants you. *Anything.* Don't you realize that by now?"

My outburst left me winded and defeated. Peggy didn't respond for several hollow seconds. I was mad enough to grant her wish and leave her when she sighed a whistle that curled at me from her hidden refuge. "Where is it now?"

"The bug?"

"Yes."

"In my desk. Why?"

"I was just wondering if it was still working."

"I put it in a vitamin bottle. I'm saving it, because if I ever find the bastard I'm going to feed it to him."

Peggy fell silent once again. I leaned against the door-jamb, closed my eyes, and ultimately surrendered. "See you tomorrow," I said wearily. "Please don't do anything stupid."

"He asked to speak to you," she said softly.

"What?"

"He wanted to talk to you."

"By name, you mean?"

"Yes."

"What did he want to talk about?"

"I don't know. I guess to tease you about tonight.

About not catching him or something. He laughed about it. He asked if you hurt yourself when you fell down."

My face reddened around my fury. "What else did he say?"

"Nothing."

"Tell me, goddamnit."

"He said I had a glorious body. He said he'd like to see it again, in more suitable surroundings. He offered to take me to Carmel sometime. To the Highlands Inn." Her voice was light and affectless, a weatherwoman laughing at a cyclone.

"Did you make a date with him, for Christ's sake?"

My bitterness brought her out from her hiding place and caused tears to fog her eyes. "Good night, Marsh," she whispered sadly.

"Peggy, I—"

"Good night, Marsh. I'll see you in the office later this afternoon. I'd appreciate it if you could be there around five. There's something I want to talk to you about."

"What is it?"

"I'll tell you then. Now go home and get some sleep."

She closed the door on my next entreaty. I had an urge to knock again, to bang and bang until my frustration was immersed in the exchange of pain for sweet destruction, but I backed away until I calmed down. When I knocked again it was for a different reason.

This time she opened the door only wide enough to reveal her cheek and eye. "I'm not going with you, Marsh. There's no use trying to persuade me."

"This is something else."

"What?"

"It would be more comfortable if I could come inside."

"No."

"Why not?"

"You wouldn't leave, and right now that's the only thing I want from you."

I put my hand against the door to keep her from closing

it. "Just one more minute. You know that guy Tomkins? The one with the porn collection I told you about?"

"What about him?"

"I just saw him."

"At this hour?"

I nodded.

"Where?"

"Coming down from the fourth floor. Is there any chance he was up there visiting your friend Karen?"

The eye slid away from the opening. "No. Don't be absurd."

"Are you sure?"

"Of course I'm sure. You've met her. You know it's impossible. Karen despises him. Every woman in the building despises him. And that's without seeing his girlie collection."

"Okay," I said. "Here's something else. Tomkins was brushing sand off his pants. There was sand in the play area at the park, and probably sand scattered all over the bushes as well, by the wind and kids tossing it at each other and the like. Plus the janitor says Tomkins just got here a few minutes before we did. So there's a chance Tomkins is our man."

"No."

"I know you want to believe the spider's a romantic Don Juan, Peggy, but in real life these guys turn out to be repressed, perverted pipsqueaks with green teeth and runny noses and urine stains all over their pants. Tomkins fits that to a T. He's a registered sex offender, for God's sake. He exposes himself to kids. So get your head out of the clouds and deal with this, Peggy. Help me figure out how to stop him."

By the time I finished she was shaking her head with my every word. "It's not Tomkins. It's not."

"Humor me. Assume it was. Is there any possibility your friend Karen might be instigating the whole thing? Does she have any motive at all to torture you like this?"

Peggy shook her head again. "No. That's crazy, Marsh.

212

Karen's my best friend. She wouldn't do anything like that. She'd have no reason to."

"You didn't take a man away from her at one time or another, did you?"

"No."

"Her ex-husband, maybe?"

"No. They lived in Arizona when they were married. Tucson. I've never even *been* to Tucson."

"Could she be a lesbian? Maybe you insulted her when you didn't pick up on her advances."

"Don't be silly."

I tried to make sense of the night or any little part of it, but all I came up with was a perfect image of Peggy's wanton pirouette in the middle of a covetous stand of pine trees. "I'm tired of standing out here in the hall," I said. "Think it over, Peggy. This thing better end soon or it's going to get completely out of hand. He's already seen you naked, and if he's got any blood in his veins at all he's not going to be able to get that vision out of his mind. It'll make him even more obsessive, Peggy. His demands will become more intimate and extreme. So you've got to start helping. You've got to come to grips with a motive for what's going on."

"But there isn't any. At least not one that's sane."

"Maybe. But maybe it's more than that. Maybe it's calculated, an attempt to drive you crazy or frighten you until you leave town or something. I suggest you give some thought to what might be behind all this."

I turned on my heel and left Peggy behind the door she had locked to keep me out.

By the time I got home it was after six. I undressed and lay down on the bed and tried to sleep. But my brain pushed anxieties at me with the subtlety of a line of chorus girls with nothing on their minds but seduction and nothing on their bodies but G-strings and cheap perfume. By the time seven rolled around I was a sleepless hodgepodge of wonder and regret, and I left the bed as thankfully as I'd entered it.

After breakfast at Zorba's, I put in a call to the service that has access to the DMV records. I gave them the red-faced man's license number and they told me they'd get back to me in an hour. Then I called Ruthie Spring.

She answered right away. Like me, she's a poor sleeper, and like me, the reasons lie deep and out of reach. "What say, sugar bear?" she asked. "You still at Peggy's?"

"Nope. Home."

"Problem?"

"Several. We set a trap for the spider last night. Or tried to."

"Who's we?" she asked, her voice arch and chilly.

"Peggy and I."

"Oh. I thought maybe you'd put me on the second team."

"You know better than that, Ruthie."

She paused. "I hope I do, sugar bear. So did it work?"

"No better than the last time."

"Too bad. Anyone draw blood?"

"Lucky for me, pride doesn't show when it's wounded."

Ruthie laughed a hacking rasp. "So what do you want from me?"

"There's one thing you can do that might help. The guy in her building, name of Tomkins, apartment twenty-three. I'd like you to clamp a tail on him, just to see where he goes and what he does. I'd particularly like to know if he does anything with a woman named Karen Whittle."

"That's the friend that lives upstairs. Borrowed some ice the other day."

"Right. She's hiding something, and she may be in cahoots with this Tomkins for some reason, so if you could keep an eye on him a lead might turn up. I thought about having Charley Sleet roust the guy on the theory that it wouldn't take too much to scare him out of town. But if the Whittle woman's involved, then that wouldn't put an end to it. What we're really looking for is a motive, I guess."

"I thought it was sex."

"Yeah, but I think there's more to it, somehow. Or maybe I just want there to be."

"I know where you're hailing from, Marsh. Miss Peggy turns out to be not quite the filly you thought she was when she was in the show ring instead of back in the barn. Happens all the time. Hell, my first husband was such a lizard I get a hot flash every time I think I was dumb enough to let him slither into my bed, to say nothing of my twat."

"I didn't know you'd been married before Harry."

"Well, it's not something I write on toilet walls."

"Okay, Ruthie. Pick up Tomkins when you can. He works at a porn store on Turk. But be careful. He's warped, he's tough, he's facing a jail term, and he's been out on the edge of trouble for a long time. Try not to let him catch the tail."

"Will do."

"You need to get paid, Ruthie? Looks like I'm your client now, not Peggy."

"When I need your money I'll send up a smoke signal, sugar bear. Till I do, I'd as soon you not bring it up."

Ruthie would be faint from hunger before she'd ask me for a dime, and she knew I knew it. I thanked her and told her to call me if anything turned up. "And I don't think it's Peggy who looks different in the ring," I added. "I think it's me."

I hung up the phone and the DMV search service called a minute later. The red-faced man's gray Ford was registered to a rental company that had a dozen offices in the city. They wouldn't give out information about their customers to me but they would to Charley Sleet. I put in a call to the Central Station but Charley was out and no one knew where he was. No one ever knows where Charley is till Charley wants them to, and that only happens about twice a day. I left a message for him to call, then left the apartment and strolled down to the office and checked the mail.

The only item of interest was hand-scrawled on a sheet

of yellow legal paper: *Thanks for ruining my life. One day I'll return the favor.* I wadded it up and threw it in the trash, then went to the wastebasket, got the letter, uncrumpled and smoothed it, then put it in the drawer of my desk on top of the seven other letters of its type I've received over the years, the ones that might someday explain why I had turned up in the morgue.

27

I fooled my way through the morning until I thought enough people would be up and about at Peggy's apartment building to make another visit worthwhile.

When I got there it was just after eleven. I circled the block, lingered in yellow zones and in front of fire hydrants, and made various other essays at finding a place to park. When one finally opened up I eased my Buick into the slot and wondered how long it would be before there wasn't a single place in the city to put a car.

I stayed in the Buick for an hour, watching traffic come and go or loiter the way I had moments earlier. None of the cars was the gray Ford that belonged to the red-faced man. None of the drivers was anyone I knew. No one I was interested in went in or out of Peggy's building. By the time the hour had passed I was almost asleep. Then a horn honked at me because someone thought my presence in the car meant that I was about to yield my space, and I made myself get on with it.

The climb to the fourth floor wore me out, but the woman who answered my knock revived me quicker than CPR. She was surprisingly attractive for one in the business she allegedly plied, not beautiful, not cute, but big and handsome in a frank, unstudied way, a way that featured a thick hood of auburn hair, blue-green eyes, and lips the color of a zinfandel. When she saw me she was neither pleased nor the opposite. She studied my face, ran it through her memory, and waited for me to state my business.

She was still dressed for bed, but instead of teasing lingerie she wore a night shirt decorated with the logo of the Oakland Raiders and the number 44. When she saw me admiring it she crossed her arms above her heavy breasts and grinned. "This is a genuine game jersey, friend, in case that's what you were wondering. Knew a guy who played for the Silver and Black once," she added after a moment, her voice suddenly warm with nostalgia.

I asked who it was, not because it was important but because I was a fan.

She smiled again, this time to herself. "Oh, he was a superstar; you'd know his name in a minute. But he's retired now. Married. Moved back home to Mississippi. Settled down or so they claim. Hard to believe he could ever settle *too* far down, though," she added fondly. "Those were good times. Good, good times. I hope Al Davis rots in hell for taking the boys down south. I get him alone some time I'll leave him half a man and all a Christian." She backed up a step and looked at me more closely. "I don't know you, do I?"

I shook my head. "I was up here last night. You wouldn't let me in. I . . ."

She pursed her lips and nodded. "I'm short two hours' sleep because of you. At my age I need all the rest I can get. Of course at my age I can rest anytime I want to, more's the pity." Her smile was friendly despite her mild complaint. "What's your name?"

I told her.

"And you say you're a private eye?"

I admitted it.

"You don't happen to know a cop named Charley Sleet, do you?"

I smiled. "Sure. Charley and I go way back."

She nodded. "I thought I'd heard your name before. Charley says good things about you."

"I say good things about Charley."

"I do too," Miss Smith said softly. "I do, too."

I raised a brow. "You know Charley pretty well?"

"Yes."

"A long time?"

"Since his wife died."

"I, ah . . ."

For the first time she flashed a frown. "You think he should spend the rest of his life in mourning, I suppose."

"No, not at all."

Her lips hardened. "He loved her. Hell, he *still* loves her. He doesn't love her any less because he stops by to see me from time to time. Or used to," she added with definite disappointment.

I tried to repair the damage. "Next time I see him I'll tell him we talked. I'll give him your best."

She shook her head quickly. "No. He knows where to find me and he knows how I feel about him. I don't want to get in his way if he doesn't want me there."

Memory filled the doorway for a moment, remnants of both our lives, memory that had in common a friend and a world that frequently inflicted pain on those the least deserving of it.

After she disposed of whatever portion of the past that had visited her, Miss Smith looked at me. "What do you want?"

"I need to know about Judson Tomkins. The guy down on two. He came up to see you last night."

She raised a brow that was plucked so thin a needle would have hidden it. "What makes you think so?"

"He told me he did."

She pursed her lips. "You know Tomkins personally, Mr. Tanner?"

"I've talked to him a couple of times, which is as personal as I want to get."

"Then you know he's reprehensible."

"Yes."

"And you know he's even more twisted than most people when it comes to the game that's played between the legs."

I nodded.

"So when he tells you he was here with me you know enough to know that's not necessarily the truth."

"Are you telling me it's not?"

Her face became a schoolmarm's. "I told you last night that I was smart enough to stay out of it. I haven't grown stupid overnight."

"So you won't talk about Tomkins?"

She shook her head. "Sorry."

"Would you talk to Charley about him?"

"I'd talk to Charley any time of the day or night. But not about Tomkins. What me and Charley had didn't have anything to do with business. His *or* mine."

I tried a different tack. "Do you know Peggy Nettleton? Lives down on three?"

"Know her to say hello to."

"She works for me."

"Doing what?"

"Secretary."

"Is she good?"

"She's great."

"Well, that's nice. I like her. She's one of the few people in this place who can bring themselves to acknowledge my existence. So treat her good, boss man. Treat her real good. You want some tips on how, come by and see me." Her smile was a tad lascivious, and gave me a hint of how it had been used for profit not too long ago, and why of all the women in the city Charley had picked this one to comfort and sustain him.

Miss Smith put her hands on her hips and looked up and down the hall. "So is that it?" she asked when she didn't see anyone. "If so, you'd better go."

I guessed she had a friend due any minute, but there were a few more things to ask. "How about Karen Whittle? Lives across the hall down there."

"What about her?"

"You know her very well?"

"No."

"Not even to speak to?"

"I speak; she doesn't. She's a very cautious lady."

"Any idea why?"

"She's afraid her ex is going to run off with her kid, is what I heard. I don't know if it's true."

"You see any strangers hanging around the building in the last few days, Miss Smith?"

She smiled. "You mean other than the strangers who live here?"

I nodded.

"No one more outrageous than usual. Why? Are you working for the Whittle woman?"

I shook my head. "Some guy's been hounding Peggy. Mostly by phone. But he lay in wait for her in the stairway one night. Pushed her down. Scared her. I'm trying to put a stop to it."

She shook her head. "That's the trouble with the world these days. You never know where the trouble's coming from. There's crazies behind every tree."

"You're an expert on the subject," I said. "Why do some guys talk dirty on the phone? Why would they do that rather than visit someone like . . . visit a prostitute, for instance, if they couldn't find a woman on their own?"

Miss Smith frowned. "Because they're scared of women. Or hate them. Or both. Because it's more demeaning, at least in their minds, to hassle someone impersonally, to make them obey you even though they can't see you. Plus they can let their imaginations run wild, they can believe the woman's Marilyn Monroe even if she's just Plain Jane. Plus it's safer, psychologically. They don't have the risk that the woman will fight back. It's safer physically, too. You'd be surprised how many women beat up on their men these days. One friend of mine, his wife has broken his nose five times."

I asked my next question while Miss Smith was still remembering the battered husband. "You have any idea how a woman could scare a guy like that off? What she could do to keep him from harassing her anymore?"

She chewed a nail and thought about it. "That's a tough

one. Because something that might make him stop the calls might make him mad enough to do some real harm, if you know what I mean. If he was upset enough he might want to shut her up for good. If it was me, I'd try to trap him."

"We did that. It didn't work."

"Well, try it again."

"Maybe. Thanks for your help, in any event."

"That's okay. Any friend of Charley's is a friend of mine. And I've changed my mind. If you do see Charley, tell him I said hello. Tell him I sent a kiss."

She blew a sample my way. I told her I'd deliver the message. She closed the door and I went across the hall.

As before, a youthful voice answered my knock, but this time she didn't let me in, not even after I reminded her who I was. "Is your mother here?" I asked after Lily had denied me entrance.

"No."

"When will she be back?"

"I don't know."

"Could you let me in?" I asked again. "Just to talk for a minute?"

"What about?"

"Your father."

"I don't have a father."

"I mean the one you used to have."

"What about him?"

"Well, I was wondering if you had any pictures of him."

"I don't think so."

"Are you sure?"

"I'm *pretty* sure. I've never even *seen* a picture of him, I don't think. I've never seen *anything* of his. Mom threw all that stuff out."

"Do you remember what he looked like, Lily?"

"Not really."

"Nothing at all?"

"He was tall, I think."

Everyone's tall to a child. "What else?"

"He was real handsome. That's what *I* think, anyway. Mom says he wasn't."

"What else?"

"He was mean to us. And he wants to steal me away and take me someplace where I'll never see Mommy again."

The blurted prospect made me shudder, as did the conditioning that produced it. I wondered if there was a substantial likelihood of such a fate, or whether it was just another form of warfare in the bitter aftermath of a long-lost love.

"Have you seen your father recently, Lily?"

"No."

"I mean in the last month or so."

"I haven't seen him since I was a baby."

"Has your mom seen him?"

"I don't think so. But maybe. She's afraid he's in San Francisco someplace, I know that. That's why I can't go anywhere. That's why I don't have any friends."

"Peggy's your friend, Lily."

"I know. I mean friends who play with dolls and stuff."

"I'll bet Peggy would play dolls with you if you asked her. Why don't you give it a try?"

She hesitated. "Mom doesn't like me to play make-believe. The last time I played dress-up with Peggy she bawled me out."

"Maybe next time she won't."

"Mom says when little girls play make-believe then they forget to be careful sometimes. She says the most important thing to be in life is careful."

In the face of that cold caution there seemed nothing better to do than say good-bye. I started to leave but the voice called me back after a single step. "You know where Mom went?" she said.

"Where?"

"She went to school. She said after Christmas maybe I can go to a *real* school."

"That's great, Lily."

"Do you think I'll make some friends at school, Mr. Tanner?"

"I know you will."

"Do you think they'll like to play with dolls? To play Mom and Dad and stuff?"

"I'm sure they will."

"Christmas isn't *too* far away, is it?"

"Two months."

"This is going to be the best one ever."

After leaving Lily I retreated to Peggy's apartment and knocked on her door. She didn't answer. I wondered if she was at the office, or with Karen Whittle, or with the spider on another stolen date. I returned to the stairs and went down to the second floor.

After three knocks on Tomkins' door I took a credit card out of my pocket, shoved it between the door and jamb, and ran it up the seam until the latch slipped back and the door flipped open. After peeking inside to make certain he wasn't sleeping, I slipped into the room and shut the door.

The place was pretty much as I'd seen it last, the bed back down out of the wall, as tangled and dingy as before. If anything, the number of sultry women on the walls had multiplied, as though exhibitionism was infectious. I poked around the corners of the room, until I spied a pile of dirty laundry. I kicked at the clothing until I uncovered the pair of trousers Tomkins had been wearing the night before.

I bent down and patted the pockets. Nothing but a stained and crusty handkerchief. I moved to the cuffs. When I turned them inside out a tablespoon of a coarse mixture of dirt and sand spilled forth, leaving a gritty splash across the floor. I pawed through the other garments as well, but found nothing else that would indicate Tomkins was the man I had chased from the park nine hours earlier.

The only other source of information was the desk beneath the window. The drawers were filled with files of one kind or another, correspondence mostly, fan letter responses from movie stars and country singers, all of them female, all of them buxom, all of their letters stilted and impersonal, run off on a machine and signed the same way. A few publicity photos were stuck in the files as well, but presumably since the subjects were fully clothed they didn't merit a slot on the wall.

I was ready to leave when I noticed a manila envelope on the far corner of the desk, on top of a stack of back issues of *Hustler*. The envelope was unmarked. It looked like the one that had been lying on the floor when Tomkins and I had come in the apartment the day before, only it was no longer sealed, its flap torn open in a jagged rip of urgency.

I picked it up. There was something inside, and they felt like photographs. I reached inside and pulled them out.

There were three of them, Polaroids, color snapshots of Lily Whittle, taken in her mother's apartment in the bright light of day. She was lying on the floor on top of a gaily patterned quilt, bathed in the morning sun. She was lying on her back. Her eyes were closed, her hair was splayed across the blanket, her legs were lax in a peaceful arc of sleep, and she was naked. I put the envelope and pictures in my pocket and left the apartment and the building.

By the time I got to the Buick I was sifting through so many improbabilities I decided it was time to work on something else. I started the car, but as I was about to pull away from the curb I noticed Ruthie Spring's Camaro parked at the end of the block. I shut down the engine and got out of my car and strolled that way.

Ruthie was sitting in the driver's seat, sipping coffee from a thermos. When I tapped on the window she looked at me and grinned. After she unlocked the passenger door I slid inside.

She offered me coffee and I took a sip, then returned the

cup. "Slow day so far," she said, simultaneously eyeing me and the door to the building.

"Tracking Tomkins?"

Ruthie nodded.

"He been out yet?"

She nodded again. "Baker's Beach."

"Why there?"

"For the view, I guess. He strolled around, checked out the beach and the picnic area, kicked some driftwood and pocketed a few shells, or maybe they were just used rubbers, then came back here. He's in the garage, working on his car. I've had more exciting times in my closet."

I gave thanks for surviving a close call. "He meet anyone at the beach?"

"Nope."

"You sure? A woman, maybe?" I mentioned Karen Whittle.

"He didn't talk to a soul, Marsh. I had him in sight the whole time."

"Did he make you?"

She elbowed me in the ribs. "Hell, Marsh. I learned the ropes from Harry. The same way you did, don't forget."

"Sorry, Ruthie. I'm grasping at straws in this thing. I think I'm going to get away from it for the rest of the day. Maybe something will come to mind if I leave some space for it."

Ruthie nodded. "Got a call from Miss Peggy early this morning," she went on casually.

"And?"

"She wants me to call her at the office at five-thirty, sharp. If no one answers she wants me to call again every five minutes. If no one answers by six she wants me to come down there and see what's going on."

"She say what's she's up to?"

"Nope."

"You going to do it?"

"Sure. Unless you know a reason not to."

I shook my head. "I'm supposed to be there at five myself. Looks like Peggy's taken charge of her own case, doesn't it?"

"Sure does," Ruthie agreed. "Been better off if she'd done it all along."

28

I drove to Sausalito, for lunch at Angelino's. After lunch I played a game of chess in the No Name Bar with a man I'd never seen before. We didn't exchange a word during the entire match, which ended in a draw in terms of both skill and reticence. By the time I headed back toward the city I was a counterweight to the unbroken cable of commuters that lapped across the Golden Gate.

When I got to the office it was ten minutes to five and Peggy was waiting for me. She gave me a brief smile but continued with her task, which was posting debits and credits to the ledger.

I went into my private office and reviewed the calendar for the following week. I had done a good job of cleaning the slate. The expanse of time included nothing to divert me from Peggy and our problem.

I glanced at my watch. Five till five. Time was apparently going to remain perversely plodding. In a nervous buzz, I went back to the outer office, to question Peggy on what she had in mind. As I hovered over her desk she looked up, smiled enigmatically, then looked back at the ledger. I hovered a minute more. If Peggy sensed my mood she didn't care to improve it. I went back to my desk.

Ten minutes later I had decided to force the issue, but as I was about to invade her domain again Peggy came into my office and sat down on the couch. "Have you got some time to talk?"

"Sure."

"Can we do it out there?" She gestured toward the waiting room.

"If you want. It's more comfortable in here, though, isn't it?"

She nodded. "But I have to wait for something to happen and it's easier to do it there."

My question lapsed unspoken. "Whatever."

I followed Peggy to the outer office. She sat at her desk and I sat on the couch opposite her. She wore a new brown suit, at least it was new to me. With its herringbone help she looked more confident and more aloof than the day before. After a minute she put away the ledger and looked toward the door to the hallway as though she was expecting someone to come through it.

I followed her glance. Nothing happened, as far as I could tell. After staring at the glass panel in the door for several seconds, she looked at me. "We're a mess, aren't we, Marsh?"

"I guess that describes the situation."

"I hope when this is over we can get back to the way we were."

"Me, too."

"I think we'll only get better if you put it out of your mind," she went on. "We have to pretend neither of us saw or heard anything that happened in the past four days. If you can do that over the next hour or so, we may be back to normal again. Do you think you can?"

Because she was up to something I withheld my concurrence. "What's going to happen in that hour, Peggy? What makes you think it's going to rescue us?"

Her look was stiff and circumspect. "You'll find out soon enough."

I was worried, and was forming a blunt demand that she let me in on what she was up to, but ten seconds later she brightened, her aspect much less worrisome. "In the meantime, what shall we talk about?" she asked cheerfully.

"Whatever you want."

"Okay. Let's talk about why you're not married." The statement was perky, the hyper-happy prattle of psychotherapists and tour directors.

"Why would you want to go into that?"

"Because I'm interested and you never bring it up. I tell you all about *my* involvements, tacky though they are. You never tell me anything. You're an attractive man. Most attractive men are married, or at least have been. Why not you?"

"Are you serious, or should I try for a one-liner?"

"I think I'm serious."

I grinned. "By any chance does this mean that you think *we* ought to get married?"

"No. Not necessarily."

"Okay. Just checking."

This time her smile was wry. "Not that I'm not willing to discuss it."

"Of course."

Our looks were sly and bordered on the provocative.

"Marriage," Peggy prompted.

I sighed. "Well, I came close a couple of times. The girl who gave me my office chair was the closest."

"What happened?"

"She traded me in for a concept."

"What's that supposed to mean?"

"She decided she wanted to be rich and famous, and that I was an encumbrance since I didn't share her dream."

"Do you see it as a failing? That you've never married?"

"Well, it doesn't seem like an accomplishment, so I guess if it has to be something it has to be the opposite."

"Why were you the closest with the one who gave you the chair?"

I had asked myself that question a hundred times, but had answered it only to myself. "I think it had to do with the date."

"What date?"

"The chronological date. It was a good year for love."

"I don't understand."

I caught myself smiling. "Those were beguiling times. It was 1969. The world bulged with diversions. Everyone was in love in the sixties. There was always somewhere to go, something to see or hear or do that was new and different and just a little naughty. We were never home, never watched TV, never sat around feeling bored or frightened or inadequate or any of the other states of being that rear their ugly heads when there's too much time to think. We wandered North Beach and Haight Street and the park for hours on end, went to rock concerts, art happenings, street dances, the whole thing. We were together more than a year before we slowed down long enough to realize we weren't meant for each other. Nowadays, we would have realized it in a week."

"Why?"

"Because these days the most exciting thing in town is a restaurant menu, or at least it seems that way. So everyone concentrates on their bodies and their relationships, and not many of either can stand up to continual scrutiny." I sighed. "Basically, it came down to this. For a while what we had between us was the most important thing in either of our lives. For a while we would have given up anything we had or were trying to get rather than give up each other. Then one of us wanted something more than to be married to the other, and the whole thing fell apart."

"Where is she now?" Peggy asked softly.

"I haven't the faintest idea. She called me once, about four years ago. She was living in Santa Monica with a self-styled movie producer. I gathered things weren't going well with him, but we didn't have anything much to say to each other. At one point in the conversation we both apologized, but we weren't sure quite why."

"And she's the only one you've felt that way about?"

"Pretty much."

"Why do you think that is?"

"I don't know. I think you have to be able to live with

yourself before you can live successfully with someone else, and by the time I got to where I could live with myself I decided I kind of liked it."

"With you and the girl with the chair," Peggy said. "Who found something they wanted more than they wanted the other? You or her?"

"Both, I guess."

"What did she want?"

"A Jensen Interceptor and a house at the beach."

"How about you?"

"All I wanted was some peace and quiet."

Peggy started to say something else but turned toward the door. A sound had worked its way to us from the hallway, and a moment later a shadowed silhouette passed beyond the glass, a large and human shadow. It tapped lightly on the door, then moved on.

Peggy looked at me and smiled. "Richard," she said. "He's such a nice guy. He's been checking on me every hour or so since you put the speaker system in. That was his sign that he's leaving for the day. After today he won't have to worry about me anymore," she added, a blithe and specious afterthought.

I felt a muscle harden. "What the hell are you talking about? What are you going to try to do?"

"You'll see."

"When?"

She looked at her watch. "In a minute. What else shall we talk about?"

"I don't know. What?"

"Let's talk about sex."

"Why?"

"Because that's what's wrong between us, isn't it? I mean, if John was calling me and asking me about my views on modern poetry you wouldn't be upset, would you?"

"I don't know. It depends on what you think about John Ashberry, I guess."

"Now, Marsh. You know what I mean, don't you?"

I nodded, and decided to fill some time. "You want to hear my theory about sex?"

"Sure."

"Well, I think the reason we're all screwed up about it, the whole world is, I mean, is that it's so unnatural, our attitudes. And here's why. A long time ago, when a girl hit fifteen and a boy seventeen or so, the neighbors would have thrown a big party. And after the party the boy and girl would have held hands and smeared themselves with mud and jumped over a rope or something, and then they would have gone off to a tent and screwed till dawn. And the neighbors would have sat around getting drunk and rooting them on. And if a baby resulted, fine. The old people in the neighborhood would have helped the young kids raise it, and everything would have been great. But then one day one of the boys had been such a jerk all his life he couldn't get anyone to go off to the tent with him. And when he heard from the other guys how much fun the sex thing was he got pissed off and decided, Shit. I'm going to put a stop to *that*. I'm going to grow up and be a priest, and then I'm going to say that the gods told me to put a stop to all that fornicating. I'm going to tell everyone it's wrong. It's a *sin* for boys and girls to have that much fun so early in life. I'm going to make them wait. Wait for years. Maybe ten. And I'm going to say that if any of them get caught doing it in the meantime they have to be called names. Like slut and stuff. And if a baby is born it'll be called a bastard. And I'm going to declare it shouldn't be fun, and if it is you should feel bad about it. And lo and behold this kid did what he threatened to do, and here you and I are a couple of thousand years later, looking at each other with the evil eye because that snotty little kid couldn't get a girl to go off to the tent."

By the time I was finished, Peggy was laughing. "Where on earth did you read that?"

"I just made it up," I admitted. "Now when is your little plan going to spring into action?"

Peggy looked at her watch again. "Right now."

I leaned back in the chair. "I'm waiting."

She shook her head. "You have to go back in your office. And not come out till I tell you. No matter what you hear happening out here."

"What am I going to hear?"

"It's not important. Just go in there and hide, and wait till I call you."

"What's Ruthie got to do with this? Why's she supposed to telephone here in a half hour?"

"You're just delaying things, Marsh."

"Should I get my gun?"

"I don't think you'll need it."

"I think I'll get it just the same. You're not going to do anything stupid, are you?"

She shook her head. "I'm going to do the only thing that will put an end to it. The only thing that will let you and me trot off to that silly little tent ourselves some day. If we decide we ever want to."

The set to her jaw was a bar to further discussion. I took my two hundred pounds of concern and disbelief into the private office.

"Close the door," Peggy ordered.

I did as she asked, but not quite all the way.

29

Despite Peggy's disclaimer, I got out my weapon. It smelled of oil and benign neglect. The barrel was clean, but not clean of the psychological residue left from the times I'd used it. I spun the empty cylinder, loaded it except for the chamber beneath the firing pin, placed the gun on the exact center of my desk, and contemplated it as I would a miracle medicine, wondering if it would perform as advertised or would create more problems than it cured.

"John?"

The voice was Peggy's, but I hadn't heard anyone enter the office. I tiptoed to the door and looked through the crack.

She was still alone, apparently talking to herself. For a moment I feared for her sanity, but then I understood. In her effort to end the nightmare, Peggy had seized upon the one established link between her and the spider: the bug he'd planted in the picture behind her desk. She must have taken it from my drawer and was using his own device to talk to him, to lure him to her once again, this time on her terms. I returned to my desk, looked down at my gun, then picked it up.

"John? It's Margaret. Margaret Nettleton. I know you can't speak to me, but if you can hear me I wish you'd listen. I want you to come to the office. Now. I'm alone. Marsh has gone for the evening. So we can talk. . . . I suppose it's stupid of me to do this, but I can't deal with the situation impersonally, the way everyone wants me to.

I have to talk to you about it. To explain and to get an explanation. . . . I know there's more to this than people think. And I want to understand. And I want you to understand me. So would you please come down here? So we can talk? It will be much better in person, John. Really, it will."

I stuck the gun in my belt, eased my chair away from the desk, and stood up. I didn't know whether Peggy's plan would work, or how long it would take him to get here—I didn't even know whether the spider was monitoring the receiver. If he wasn't, Peggy was speaking only to me and to the ghosts in her imagination, but if he was listening, and if he responded to her invitation, he wasn't going to get away from me again.

I had edged around the desk and started to tiptoe to the door when I noticed something that brought me to a stop. The bottom desk drawer was open, and I could see that the bug, the little transmitter young Manchester had dug out of the picture frame behind Peggy's desk, was still in the vitamin bottle where I'd tossed it on the day of its discovery. Powerful as it was, it couldn't possibly be picking up Peggy's soft soliloquy. Which meant the mystery was solved, and Peggy had narrowed the field to one.

"John? I recognized you in the park last night. When you ran away. I didn't know it was you when I went up there, or I wouldn't have let Marsh try to trap you. I would have waited till we talked, until you had a chance to explain. I want to know why you've been doing this to me, John. I know there's a reason. A reason I can understand. So please. Come talk to me. I think I deserve that much, John. After all you've done."

A minute wriggled by, then another. I took the bug out of the bottle, tossed it in the air and caught it, and wondered all the while if Peggy could possibly be as commiserating as she sounded.

"John? I'll only stay two more minutes. If you're not here by then I'll have to assume you don't want to talk, and I'll have to go to the police. I can't live the way I have been since you started calling me, John. . . . That doesn't mean I want to stop our talks. I mean, I think maybe we could keep on. Maybe. But we have to put them on a different basis. No more threats; no more vulgarity. And I have to know when they're coming. I have to be able to *sleep* at night. Surely you understand. If you've been watching me all these weeks, you must have seen how exhausted I've become. So I have to have some sort of agreement from you. You have to promise to take my needs and my schedule into account. . . . The terrorism has to stop, John. Today. If you tell me it will I'll believe you, but I have to see your face, to know if I can trust you. If I can't trust you, I'll have to go to the police and I don't want to do that. Not unless that's the only way to get you to stop driving me crazy. So come down here. Please. Let's do it this way, just between the two of us."

I didn't know whether I wanted her to succeed or fail. I was tempted to get on the second line and summon Charley Sleet and have him put the arm on the spider the minute he stepped out his door. But Peggy had a method to her madness, or I had to assume she did, a method she thought would reassemble her scattered life, and I had to let her work it to its end.

It took four minutes. I had about decided to call a halt, to tell Peggy her gambit had misfired, when the door to the hallway opened with its characteristic squeak. Much as I wanted to join the party, I hurried to a place where I couldn't be seen from the outer office.

Footsteps sounded, each more vivid than the last, until they were joined by a voice. "So you know."

Peggy didn't answer immediately. I envisioned the encounter, each inspecting the other's aspect, searching for auras of threat or trick. "Yes," she said finally. "I know."

"Only since last night?"

"Yes."

"And your proof is your own eyesight? In the middle of the night? Through thick woods?"

She hesitated. "Not just that."

"What else then?"

"Something you dropped when you ran away."

"What?"

"I'm not telling you. Not yet."

"I see," he said, still assured, still the manipulator. "And what do you intend to do with this so-called evidence?"

"I don't know yet. It depends on what you have to say for yourself over the next few minutes."

"So you have not yet called in the authorities."

"No."

"And you may not, if I satisfy you in some particular during this conversation. Is that your position?"

"Yes."

He paused. "What about your employer?"

"What about him?"

"He seems to fancy himself a rather righteous individual. What if he overrules you? What if he decides I deserve to be punished? As if my whole life has not been punishment." His voice broke for an instant, and he coughed to cover it.

"He won't call in the police unless I ask him to," Peggy said.

"You are certain of that."

"Yes."

She was far more certain of it than I was.

"You say you are alone," he went on. "I'm afraid I don't believe you. Unfortunately, you have a recent history of resistance in this matter, of enlisting aid. Even though you had no need to."

"Not this time," Peggy protested, but casually, the spider's suspicion of no concern. "If you don't believe me, look around. There are only two rooms, this one and that one. Marsh has gone home—he plays poker on Fridays and tonight he has to bring the beer. He gets it from a former client in Mill Valley, so he had to leave early. But go ahead and look. I'll wait as long as you want."

I was considering a series of imperfect hiding places

when the phone rang. After the second ring I looked at my watch. Five-thirty on the dot. Ruthie, by prearrangement. I heard Peggy pick up the receiver.

"Hello. Yes, Marsh. Yes. It's in the mail. No. He said to call him next week. Okay. Have a nice weekend. You, too. I will. Don't be such a worrywart. Five more minutes. And don't draw to an inside straight. 'Bye."

She hung up. A whoosh of air told me the spider had abandoned his inclination to search the office and had taken a seat on the couch across from Peggy's desk. "So?" he began, the word smug and self-important. "What do we do now?"

"I ask some questions."

"I've told you many times, Margaret. I ask the questions. You answer them."

Peggy's voice stiffened. "If you're going to be like that I'm going to call the police."

"Why?"

"Because from now on it has to be different. If you don't do what I say, I'll file charges against you, no matter *what* you threaten to do to me."

The spider hesitated. "What is your question?"

"I have many. The first one is, why me?" The words were earnest, the question genuine.

"For several reasons," the spider said abruptly. "Because you were nearby and I could observe you closely, to compare your answers with my observations. And because you are beautiful. And intelligent. And have lived life the way it has come to be lived in this day and age. You should feel complimented that you were the one selected, Margaret. Believe me, I gave the matter much thought. I considered many possibilities before selecting you."

Peggy's laugh was as edgy as my forebearance. "If you think my life is some sort of a model, then you don't know me at all."

"Come now. You have married, and had a child. You have a skill that pays you a living wage. You see men. Several of them. You've been divorced along with half the

239

others in the land. You have several women friends and you work for a man you respect and who respects you. In sum, when I formulated my plan you seemed quite typical of the type of woman a man like myself can expect to encounter these days. Typical enough to teach me."

"Teach you what?"

"The truth about women."

The silence that followed his response was long enough to memorialize the occasion.

"I still don't understand," Peggy said finally. "I need to know why you did what you did. It made me feel totally ashamed, you know. It made others feel ashamed for me. It ruined the last two months of my life, and it may have ruined my job, and I think I have a right to know why you did all that to me."

He didn't melt but he softened. "The explanation is simple. If you open your mind, if you really wish to understand, you can."

"Tell me. Please."

"May I assume you will keep it confidential?"

"On certain conditions."

"What are they?"

"If you promise not to call me in the middle of the night anymore. Or follow me. Or come to my apartment. Or attack me. Or do anything except talk, politely and calmly, and that only when it's convenient for me to do so. Do I have that promise from you, John?"

"I will conform if I can. Unfortunately, my need is such that I can't promise that I—"

"We can work it out," Peggy offered quickly. "If you want to. If you try to understand my position."

"I will try. I promise that."

"First, tell me something," Peggy said suddenly, as I dueled with my anger at her easy accommodation with the spider. "How did you learn my new telephone number so fast?"

His chuckle was round and smug. "I simply read it on your Rolodex. When you were away from your desk. You

240

entered the new number quite promptly, I must say. Presumably so your Mr. Tanner would know how to reach you in an emergency. I was happy to benefit from your efficiency. I only missed one call."

"And your voice. You sound so different in here than you do on the phone."

"They have many magical machines these days, Margaret. Voice boxes, they call them. The one I used breaks down every element of speech—pitch, timber, inflection, rhythm. It can completely defeat a voiceprint comparison."

"Marsh told me there was some sort of spy bug in my picture frame. Did you put it there?"

"Yes."

"When?"

"Last Christmas."

Peggy gasped. "You've been listening to me that long?"

"Yes."

"My God. That's almost worse than the phone calls."

"I heard nothing outrageous. Believe me."

"You don't understand. It's the violation. The *invasion.* It's the same as learning I've been spied on by a peeping tom."

"It's not like that at all. I—"

Peggy broke through his easy rationale. "You've got to learn respect for people, John. There are certain things you just can't *do* to women. Or to anyone, for that matter. Privacy's the most fundamental right there is. I think you'd better remember that."

"I didn't mean to do what you think I did. My motives were pure. Believe me."

"The end can't justify the means. Not with this. I . . . There's one more thing I have to know."

"What is that?"

"The last time we talked, you hinted that you'd had something to do with my friend Lowell's death. The pilot. Is it true? Did you?"

"No."

"How can I be sure?"

"Check with the authorities. I'm certain they have no reason to suspect foul play. I hinted at complicity because I wanted you to believe I was all-powerful. So that you would not feel able to resist me. I was glad to see him out of your life, I admit that. But I was not the agent of removal."

"I hope not, John. Because if you were I'll see you jailed for life, if it's the last thing I do. I mean it. Now tell me why you've been torturing me for so long."

"It *wasn't* torture, Margaret. At least it wasn't meant to be. Please believe me." He hesitated once again. "I . . . this is not easy for me. I have been obsessed with this subject for so long, it has assumed such elephantine proportions, I scarcely know how to begin."

"You seem to feel more comfortable on the phone. Maybe if I turn my back. Maybe if I hold this ruler like a telephone, and you pretend you're calling me, the way you used to. There. Is that better?"

"It is ridiculous, that much is certain. But you are right. Already I'm more at ease. You see? You *are* special. It is just that sensitivity I hoped to tap by choosing you as my mentor."

"I'll try to remember that," Peggy said, with a twist of sarcasm and perhaps a trace of pride.

"I'm afraid you will find the problem is ludicrous, Margaret. You see, I want a child."

"What?" Peggy sounded as startled as I was.

"A child. Progeny. An heir to the wealth and beauty I've so carefully assembled over the years."

"But—"

The spider ignored her. "My possessions are my life—my art, my home, my car, my clothes. I have devoted my every waking hour to the creation of beautiful environments—my office, my apartment in the city, my homes in Glen Ellen and in Cap Ferrat, my gallery. I will be forty-five next month. I'm in good health as far as I know, but who can say for certain. In the past I have engaged in practices that recent revelations indicate entail a greater than normal risk of premature demise. I—"

"Do you mean AIDS?"

"Among other possibilities. Those escapades were several years ago, but the incubation period of the virus is uncertain. I . . ." His voice trailed off.

"Go on. You mentioned a child."

"Yes. I want a child. Badly. It has become my *idée fixe*. I was an only child myself, you see. My parents are not living. I have no heirs. None. And I can't bear the thought that my entire fortune would simply escheat to the state upon my demise. The prospect is anathema to me. Worse than death itself. I will do anything to avoid that eventuality."

"You could leave it all to someone else. A friend. A colleague."

The spider uttered something like a laugh. "Unfortunately, the few people I call friends could be counted on to sell everything I bequeathed to them before grass started growing on my grave."

"I can understand that, I guess," Peggy said. "But I don't understand how I fit in."

"It's quite simple, actually. Simple and laudable, I believe. If I am blessed with a child I want it to be raised in a wholesome atmosphere. By that I mean I want no divorce, no separation, no messy wrangle over either the child or his inheritance, no single-parent, divorced-father, broken-home type of arrangement."

"No one wants their marriage to end in divorce. But wishing isn't enough sometimes."

"I know that. It is not a perfect world, or at least those of us who inhabit it are not. But I operate under a handicap that substantially lessens the odds that any marriage of mine would succeed. A handicap that explains why I've not wed before now."

"Since you mentioned AIDS, I assume you're gay."

"A natural assumption, but no. True, I have engaged in homosexual affairs from time to time, though not recently.

Mostly as an experiment. At one point I thought I *was* homosexual, actually, but several years of intense personal scrutiny have convinced me I am not. No, the situation is more complex. I am asexual, nonsexual, unsexual. A gelding. A neuter. Call it what you will. The medical terms are abstruse and unenlightening."

"I still don't understand," Peggy said.

"It's very simple. Sex is a foreign tongue to me, its energies and excitements as unfamiliar as Sanskrit. My libido is a shrunken cinder, not a raging flame. I have no erotic impulse, none whatsoever, toward anyone. Things, yes. Sculpture. Painting. Music. I embrace such glories with a vehemence many call obscene." He spat a bitter laugh. "But alas, none of my treasures are fecund; none can present me with a child. Do you begin to sense my problem?"

"You don't know what to do with women."

"Correct. I haven't the *faintest idea* how to proceed, especially in the erogenous sense. The few times I have made an effort I have been laughed at, ridiculed, worst of all, pitied. I have read the how-to books and watched the films of the Mitchell brothers and worse, and on occasion I have even tuned in to the amazing Dr. Ruth, but I still don't understand. I don't know what things *mean.* Sexy clothing, for example. And exotic sexual practices and devices. I don't know how women feel about such things, and so I don't know what to do to ensure that the sexual component of my marriage would support a lengthy union. So I came to you for help. I selected you to teach me what I felt I had to know."

"You could have just asked," Peggy said softly.

"Hah. I tried that with others, the candid exchange of views, but honesty was lacking from the first. Everyone lies about sex, in my experience. Everyone. No, after much trial and error I concluded that the phone, the threats, the inquisitorial approach, were all essential to achieve anything approximating truth. You *were* truthful with me, weren't you, my dear Margaret?"

"Yes. I . . . yes. I was."

"So you see, it worked."

"At quite a price, at least to me."

"Yes. I'm sorry for that."

Peggy's voice stiffened. Her chair squeaked as she turned back to face her nemesis. "If you're asexual, why did you have me perform that vile striptease? Why did you have to *humiliate* me?"

"That was not my intent. Not at all. I—"

"I don't believe you, John. I don't believe this whole thing was just a course in the feminine mystique. You *enjoyed* tormenting me; you were too brutal, too overbearing. You treated me like a Nazi, John. Torturing out of me the most embarrassing details of my life, then reveling in my shame. I have to tell you that I think you're totally lying about your motives."

"No. *No*, Margaret. It is as I said. I merely wanted to learn."

"No, John. It doesn't fit. There's much more to it, whether you know it or not. You want me to believe you're the meek John Smith, and maybe in real life you are, but on the phone you're a criminal, John. And I'm still suffering from your crimes."

"No."

"Yes. There's something *driving* you to behave that way. A need to dominate women. To degrade them. Something. Have you ever been in analysis?"

"How dare you suggest that."

"I think you need it."

"Nonsense."

"It might help, John. If you're being honest with me now, your problem is bigger than you think. I want you to get help. I want you to promise to see someone. That is, if you want us to continue our talks. That's the only way I could even *think* of agreeing to it."

"No. I can't do that. It would be—"

"Your resistance only proves your need, don't you see that? Well? Will you do it?"

"I don't know. I don't know if I can."

"Try. Just try. That's all I ask."

"I'm not sure I can live with what might result, Margaret. I'm not sure I *want* to know what lies behind my behavior. I have my suspicions, of course. And they are all unbearable."

"Try it. Therapy. Just once. To see what it's like."

"I will if I can. Truly. I will do my best. But you don't understand. You act as though I have never tried to improve my lot. On the contrary, I have been *desperate* to alter the situation. You mentioned the striptease, as you call it. It was another, perhaps my final, effort to summon forth my lust. I thought if you, the woman I knew better than any other, were to tantalize me in forbidden, bizarre circumstances, perhaps my desires would finally awaken from their slumber."

"Oh."

"You seem disappointed. But you should not be. My passions *were* aroused, my blood spurted, my palms grew damp. Alas, I realized it was because you reminded me of my sculpted family, my bloodless brood, my plaster panoply. Do you see? I was inflamed by your form, not your function. And of course any possible evolution of that fervor was destroyed by your clumsy attempt to apprehend me. I was angry at you for that, Margaret. I was not a danger to you. Ever."

"That was impossible for me to believe, John. Surely you can see that."

"I suppose I can. I apologize for your trepidation. Truly."

Peggy paused. "Have you decided who is going to bear your child?"

"I have a candidate. I doubt that you know her. I met her in New York, at a tax conference. She is a CPA. I intend to propose on my next trip east, in three weeks' time."

"Congratulations." The word was flat and sour, but the spider seemed not to notice.

246

"Thank you. But my knowledge remains incomplete. I am not yet confident of my amatory skills. And I am not yet certain I can interpret women's actions and intentions accurately enough to judge if Judith is the appropriate selection. So I am hoping you will continue my lessons."

Peggy laughed helplessly. "It's absurd, you know."

"Please."

"I have to think about it. But whether I help you or not, the harassment has to stop. Right now. Before I lose my mind."

"Yes. I went too far. I see that now. But I was desperate. I hope you understand."

"And I need time. To get my own life back to normal. To patch up some relationships of my own that have suffered because of you."

"Please. You need not remind me. I am sorry, I say again. My methods will change."

"If they don't I will go to the police. I hope you believe that."

"Yes. I do." For the first time he sounded chastened and contrite. I wondered if it was just another con or whether he was serious. I wondered if Peggy could possibly be serious herself. And I wondered what I would do if she told me that she was.

"You must leave me alone until I contact you," Peggy was saying.

"But when will that be?"

"By the end of next week I'll call. And let you know whether I'll go on with this."

"Thank you. It's more than I deserve."

Peggy laughed again. "You're right. I just wish I understood why I think I'm going to let you walk out of here without *doing* anything to you."

"You are an empathetic person. I knew that from the first. You have suffered in life, and you recognize a fellow sufferer."

"Maybe that's it. Or maybe it's just because I want a man to talk to when I'm lonely."

30

I stepped into the room the moment he was gone and I heard the microphone switched off. Peggy was sitting at her desk, head bowed, hands clasped. "So he's the one," I said. "Good old Arthur-from-down-the-hall."

Peggy only nodded. Her eyes were deeply lidded, as though the confrontation had been too bright to bear without a filter.

"And he's just going to stroll out of here scot-free."

She nodded once again. Her hands retreated beneath the desk, in what might have been a flinch from the unspoken corollary to my accusation.

"And I'm supposed to sit here and let him go," I added roughly.

"Yes." The word was crisp and challenging. "Yes, you are."

"And stand by like a eunuch and let you get mixed up with him all over again."

"It won't be like it was."

"How do you know?"

"He promised."

"So what?"

"He's an honorable man. I mean basically."

"Nonsense. He's just the opposite."

"You don't understand, Marsh. You never have."

"Okay. Indulge me. What if he doesn't *keep* his precious promise?"

"I call the police."

"Really? What if he doesn't give you the chance?"

"I don't know what you mean."

"I mean what if after he leaves here he decides you're far too dangerous running around loose? That knowing what you know gives you too much sway over his future. What does he do then?"

"I don't know."

"I do. He tries to kill you."

She recoiled, her body leaning away from me, her hands emerging once again, this time to mask her eyes. "No. He wouldn't do that."

"You thought he wouldn't shove you down the stairs, but he did."

"He wouldn't try to kill me. I know he wouldn't."

"You don't know him *nearly* that well, Peggy. You know only what he wants you to know, what he wants you to believe."

She didn't respond. Her palms dropped away from her eyes, laying bare their reddened, dampened surfaces.

"What if I go to the police myself?" I asked. "What if I call Charley right now?"

"You wouldn't go against my wishes like that."

"I would if I thought I had to do it to save your life."

"But it's not that *severe*. He's Arthur *Constable*, Marsh. He's worked down the hall for years. He's the guy you make fun of all the time. He's got a problem, but you know him well enough to know it's not *that* kind of problem."

"I don't know any such thing. You don't, either."

"Please, Marsh," she pleaded with what seemed to be her final store of energy. "Let me do this my way."

"I don't know, Peggy. This whole thing makes me nervous. It has from the beginning and it sure as hell does now. It's the stairs business that doesn't fit. You could have been seriously injured in that fall. You keep saying he's not violent, but his conduct runs counter to your thesis. What's this evidence you've got on him, by the way?"

She shook her head. "I was lying."

"Christ. So all we really have is your testimony."

"You were there, too."

"I know. But I didn't see him. Not close enough to identify him, at least. If I have to I can always lie, I suppose. It wouldn't be the first time."

Peggy found another cell of strength. "But don't you see? I won't have to *give* any evidence. If I agree to keep talking to him, the way we talked before, he's bound to get tired of me after a while. Sooner or later he'll get everything I have to give and we can all get back to normal."

"What about the next woman he picks on?"

"No. Don't you see? He thinks *I* have all the answers. When I don't have any more to give him he'll go ahead and marry his sweetheart in the East and have the baby and that will be the end of it. Really, Marsh. I'm sure of it."

"I wish I could believe you."

"Why can't we just give it a try?"

"Because he's nuts, Peggy. He's going to marry a CPA for Christ's sake. He may be nice but he's nuts. Which means he's unpredictable. Which means he's dangerous as hell."

"He's a professional man, Marsh. He makes scads of money counseling people about their taxes. He's not going to jeopardize all that just to play some silly game with me."

"He already jeopardized all that the first time he picked up the phone and called you. And if you're trying to convince me he's normal, you're going to have a tough time. I think we should go to the cops. Let the shrinks and the DA decide whether he's safe enough to let out on the street."

"During the Usser case you were always telling me no one can predict what someone's going to do in the future."

"It's true; they can't. And neither can you."

"Well, I'm not going to the police, I'm going home." She pulled out a drawer in the bottom of the desk and took out her purse and placed it in her lap. "I'll see you on

Monday. Have a nice weekend." Her words were laced with ridicule, as if I was incapable of the task.

"I want someone to stay with you tonight," I said quickly. "You stirred him up. It's not safe for you till he has a chance to cool down."

She shook her head. "We already tried that, remember? It does more harm than good."

"If you don't agree to let me or Ruthie stay with you, then I'm going straight to Charley."

"No." The word was quick and angry.

"I can understand that you don't want me around your place tonight. Or Ruthie, either. We haven't been very consoling during this thing, I admit. So how about Allison? She could come stay with you, or you could go down there."

"I can stay with Karen."

"No."

"Why not?"

"Allison or me. Which?"

She didn't like the choice, but she finally said, "Allison. If she can."

"Call her. If she can't help, I'm taking you to a motel down the peninsula. I won't stay with you, but at least you'll be where Constable can't get at you."

She picked up the phone and dialed a number. After an uneasy opening, she began to talk in low tones about the night's arrangements. I sensed an instant of resistance, but then Peggy's voice softened and the pauses were longer. When she hung up she smiled and told me Allison would come to her apartment after work. I said that was fine. She said Allison thought I was a hunk.

Peggy began to gather up her things. I sat down on the couch and watched her. When she sensed my inspection she stopped stuffing her purse and looked at me.

I put on my crony's smile. "What's *really* going on with you and this guy, Peggy?"

She looked startled by the question. "How do you mean?"

"I mean here he's made your life miserable for months, and physically assaulted you, and now you're finally in a position to put him away and you don't. Not only don't you put him away, you agree to prolong your relationship with him. Which is exactly the attitude that got you in trouble in the first place."

"So?" Peggy asked in a huff. "It's my business, right?"

"So I don't get it. Surely you know it'll be the same old story, the one that's already driven you to the point of breakdown. He'll convince you to try to help him with this hollow libido he claims he's got, but all he's really going to do is keep you under his thumb while he gets off on hearing you talk some more about your sex life. You'll end up in the same shape you were before, only this time voluntarily, so you won't be able to prosecute him even if you want to. What I want to know is why you're *doing* all that."

"What difference does it make?"

"The *difference* it makes is that I can't stand to see you hurt."

I wanted her to reciprocate or at least respond, but she only shook her head despondently.

"You said you wanted us to get back to how we were," I went on. "Well, if I can't understand why you're doing this, then I don't see how that's going to be possible. Because the woman that would let this guy toy with her again, after all she's been through, after everything he's done to her, is not the woman who's sat behind that desk for the last eight years."

"I—"

"Agreeing to talk to him some more is not only a lousy idea, it's pathological, and I think you know it is, and yet you're still going to do it. That doesn't make sense, and you're a sensible person. The most sensible person I know, or you were until two months ago. So what did he do that I don't know about? What the hell did he *do* to you to make you lose your mind?"

252

She closed her eyes. "Nothing." The hush succeeding the word was a fatalistic chasm.

I tried to find encouragement in the sliver of affection that was left between us, but I couldn't. My sadness mated with anger, and produced a skeptical reaction. "I don't believe you, Peggy. What was it? Allison? Did he threaten to harm her if you didn't cooperate?"

She shook her head. "No. He never mentioned Allison."

"Then what *was* it, damnit?"

She shook her head but didn't answer. I simmered with frustration and tried to think of a new approach. I hadn't come up with one when Peggy said, "I have to go. I have to feed Marilyn."

I gave up. "You will let Allison stay with you tonight, won't you?"

"Yes."

"Okay. You win. After I drop you at home I'm out of it. From here on it's between you and Constable and the cops. You know the number at the Central Station. I strongly advise you to call them, but I suppose you won't. I've done all I can do. I won't try to contact you this weekend, and I won't hang around outside the apartment, so you don't need to worry about me messing up your plans with Arthur. I'll see you here on Monday afternoon, if you still want to work for me. As far as I'm concerned it's back to strictly business between us, Peggy. Just the way you want it."

31

We left the office in a steely silence, our bonds more frayed than ever. It seemed to take a year to reach the parking lot. Peggy waited impassively while I unlocked the car door for her, then slid inside. Once I was behind the wheel she removed herself as far from me as she could. In the icy blast from her cold shoulder, I drove through the city in a storm of debate and confusion, wanting to say something that would reverse what we had become, afraid of making what we were far worse. Then Peggy rearranged my life even more than my dejection contemplated.

"I think I should resign," she said as I emerged from the Broadway Tunnel.

"Why?"

"Because it's not the same anymore."

"You meant the job or you mean us?"

"Us."

"It can be if we want it to."

"But that's the trouble. You still don't know what you really want."

"So it's all my fault?"

"I didn't mean that. But I can't change the past, Marsh. I can't make what's happened between Arthur and me disappear, not from *your* consciousness, at least. The point is, if you can't come to terms with what I've done with Arthur, and what I may be doing with him in the future, then there's not much reason to fool ourselves about the course of our relationship."

"I admit I'm having trouble with all this, Peggy. But don't I get some time to try to deal with it?"

"You can have all the time you want. But it'll be better for both of us if I'm not around to get in the way of your deliberations. I know a law firm that needs a temp for a month. I think I'll tell them I'll take the job, and then we'll see where we are when the month is up."

"What about *my* stuff?"

Peggy smiled tolerantly. "I'll get someone to replace me before I go. Don't worry."

"A trial separation, is that it? Do you know of one that ever worked?"

"They must, once in a while."

"In my experience those temporary arrangements always end up being permanent."

"Well, if that's what happens to us it'll be because we want it to, right?"

"Not necessarily. Some diseases are inevitable, but others don't need to happen if you take sensible steps to prevent them. It's like people who think having an affair will improve their marriage, when really an affair is terminal. But I guess you already know how that works," I said bluntly. "That affair you had, by the way. I was wondering who you had it with."

"My boss," Peggy spat angrily, and looked away from me.

I'd been cruel to bring it up, intentionally and flagrantly so, but the situation was so delicate and our past so current and compressed that Peggy seemed prone to excuse it. "Is that what we have, Marsh? A disease?"

"I think so."

"What's it called?"

"Third-degree disenchantment."

"Just like I warned you."

"Just like you warned me," I acknowledged.

I drove another block before I spoke again. "Are you definite about resigning?"

"I think so."

"No point in even talking about it?"

"No. Not now, at least."

"Will you think about it for a week?"

"The other office needs someone by Monday. I should let them know."

"Okay. Monday. Don't make up your mind till then. Give things a chance to cool off."

"What if they only heat up?"

"We've already been through the worst, Peggy. It's just a matter of adjusting to the experience."

"You make it sound easy."

"It's simple, not easy."

We completed the trip in silence. Peggy looked out the window at the passing scene, absently, as though it was a trackless waste. I wondered if she was thinking about me or thinking about Arthur Constable. Then I wondered if it was too late for it to make any difference what she thought about either of us.

I pulled to a stop in front of Peggy's building and got out and opened her door. "Thanks for the ride," she said as she got out of the car. "I'll call you Sunday night and let you know what I've decided about the office."

As I waited for her to join me on the walk I looked up at her building. As I did, I thought I saw a curtain fall across a window on the second floor. "I'll walk you to your door," I said.

Peggy closed the car door and looked at me. "You don't need to."

"You're more certain of Constable's surrender than I am. He could have been handing you a complete fabrication, that business about his sexuality. He could already be planning to pull the phone freak thing on someone else, and planning how to get you out of his way so he'll have a free hand."

She shook her head. "I know him better than that."

"The only thing you know is what he *wanted* you to know."

"I . . . Okay, Marsh. I guess you're entitled to one last

gesture. Walk me to my door and then leave. I'll give you a good night kiss if you don't try to come inside."

In the wake of her chiding smile I stood by while she unlocked the street door and preceded me into the lobby.

Her ankle was still tender enough to make her summon the decrepit elevator. As it rumbled to life behind the etched brass doors, we waited as though it was bringing down a coffin.

After a thud and a clank the doors swung open and I stood aside to let Peggy enter the cage. She was already two steps inside before I noticed it was occupied.

"Hello, Tomkins," I said into the path of his oily grin.

His bow was courtly, sarcastically genteel. "Tanner. Miss Nettleton. Been out to dinner? A damned good idea. I'm the same way—never like to fornicate on an empty stomach."

I raised a fist in front of his face. "Shut your mouth, Tomkins. And keep it shut. I'm not in the mood for your brand of filth tonight."

Tomkins only extended his leer. "Yeah? What's the matter? You two have a lovers' spat?"

I edged to the side of the elevator and kept my hand on the door to keep it open. "Are you getting out, or not?"

Tomkins' expression sobered. "I'm going to the garage. The same place you're going."

"We're not going to the garage."

"That's what you think."

Tomkins reached beneath his jacket and pulled out a handgun and pointed it at me. When I took a step toward him he shook his head and cocked the gun. "We're going to take a little stroll, Tanner. So get out. Both of you. Now. You move over there beside him, sweetheart, so I can keep an eye on you both. Real slow, now. Keep your hands where I can see them, Tanner. That's right. Now turn around, hands against the wall. Come on, assume the position, hotshot. I mean it."

Because he was too far away to grab and Peggy was too close to be out of danger, I did as he ordered. When he had joined us in the lobby, Tomkins patted me down for a weapon with as much roughness as he could muster. When he didn't find one he grunted with satisfaction and moved back against the opposite wall. With his revolver he gestured toward the door to the garage. "There. Go on. Open it."

When I hesitated, Tomkins came toward me, the gun carefully out of my reach, and grasped a handful of my jacket lapel. With a grunt he tugged me away from the wall and shoved me through the door and into the dark dungeon of the garage. After I staggered to a stop I turned and watched him do the same to Peggy. "Take it easy, Tomkins," I warned, but he only laughed.

"What the hell, pal. I'm going to get a lot more familiar with her than that before the night's over."

"Is that what this is all about, Tomkins? Another chapter in your pathetic sex life?"

"You don't need to worry what this is about, because you're not going to be around long enough to do anything about it even if you manage to find out."

"Don't be dumb. Your past problems with the police will seem like a traffic ticket if you do anything to her."

"Shit. They're threatening to violate my probation. All because I watched some kids play ball in a goddamned schoolyard. Even my lawyer says I won't beat it this time, and since Mommy cut off my money he's not even going to try. They don't like sex offenders in the joint, you probably heard that. They even cut up Tree Frog Johnson the other day. The probation guy tells me all about the stuff they do to guys like me, thinks that'll make me stop eyeballing the little kids. Well, I'm not going to take a chance on serving time. No way. I'm taking off. The lawyer says I ain't done nothing bad enough to make them look for me too hard. And I got enough bread to get me set up down in Houston. So I got it covered, except I got some things to take care of first. You two, then the other two, and then I'm out of here. But I figure I might as well

258

get some jollies in before I go. And this is one jolly I've been thinking about for a long, long time."

Tomkins eyed Peggy's breasts with a clear implication. I looked up and down the oppressive confines of the garage, but saw only a stark expanse of grease and shadow that indicated we were entirely alone.

Tomkins noticed my glance and laughed. "If you're looking for that swish Mendosa, he's off tonight. Goes to see his grandkids or something. We got the whole place to ourselves. Now get moving. The boiler room on the left down there. Open the door and go inside."

We crossed the slippery floor, then veered toward the door marked FURNACE. "Go on," Tomkins repeated. "Open up."

I turned the knob and pushed the door open. A rush of warm air met me, along with the hissing sounds of imperfectly confined steam. I moved inside, and heard Tomkins shove Peggy along behind. "Over against the wall," Tomkins ordered. "Just stand there and don't try anything." I did as he asked because I couldn't risk anything else. The gun was lethal and Tomkins was clearly at ease with it.

There was no room to maneuver in the small boiler room, and only the light from a single bulb to see from. The walls were lined with tools and equipment, shining somehow in the middle of the dim bower, doubtlessly thanks to Mendosa's careful maintenance. Somewhere beyond the light the boiler and the furnace moaned and sighed, mating in snug delight.

To the left of the furnace the incinerator gave off a molten glow around the edges of its iron door. If Tomkins had wanted to preview our descent to hell, he couldn't have done a better job.

When he saw me looking at the fiery chamber he nodded. "You got it right for once, Tanner. You and your sweetheart are going to have your final fling in there. Should be a hot one."

I was frightened, but I was also puzzled at the reason behind Tomkins' deadly task. While I tried to find the key to his motivation, I stood with my back to the brick wall and waited for Peggy to join me. When she had, Tomkins eyed us cheerily. "Damn. I can do this quick or slow, and hell if I know which would be more fun."

"Why do it at all?"

"Because I got to."

"Why? We haven't done anything to you. That harassment thing I was asking you about the other day has been resolved. We know who did it and the cops do, too. We won't be bothering you again."

"That's real nice to hear, but the main reason you won't be bothering me is that dead people don't bother *anyone.*"

Peggy shuddered at my side. I moved closer to her, but slowly, so Tomkins wouldn't be alarmed. "I don't understand, Tomkins. Why kill us?"

For a moment he looked as witless as I felt. "It's the story of my life, pal."

"How do you mean?"

"I mean I got into something a little too deep and all of a sudden this is the only way I can think of to get out of it. Happens all the time. Things just never seem to turn out the way I thought they would. Life's a bitch that way, right, Tanner? Lucky for me I got the time and money to get right again. Then I'm free to screw up all over." Tomkins' eyes clouded. "They think I can help it. You know that? They think I want to do this stuff. Shit. Who'd *want* to do the stuff I do? Huh? Tell me. Who the hell would want to?"

Tomkins laughed, mordantly and pathetically. Peggy leaned into me and took my hand and squeezed it. I squeezed back, to give her more hope than I had myself.

Tomkins blinked his eyes and waved the gun. "I think I'll take it slow. Slow and easy." He gave Peggy a chilling grin. "So what say, honey? Why don't you just take them off."

Peggy's hand contracted around my own. "No."

"Strip, damnit."

"Never."

"Why not? It won't be the first time, I'll bet."

The threatened reprise of her mortification at the hands of the spider made Peggy a martyr. "Not for you. Not ever."

"Well, hell. I'm a reasonable man. Since you're a little shy, I'll just help you out."

Tomkins took two steps toward us and reached for the buttons to Peggy's blouse. As his hand passed below my nose I lashed out and slapped it away. With a bitter curse he backhanded my face. When I put up a fist to counter his punch he shoved the revolver against my cheek, hard enough to break the flesh. "Don't even think about it, Tanner. I'd just as soon take you out right now. But you don't want me to do that, because in about two minutes me and the little lady are going to put on the juiciest fuck show you've ever seen. It'll make my videos seem like a rerun of the Sermon on the Mount. It'll be a hell of a treat, Tanner. That is if you like sex. You do like sex, don't you? I know you like the weird stuff. Hell, if I had a camera I could shoot me a snuff film. Make a fortune off of guys like you."

Tomkins laughed and withdrew the pistol from my face. As he did I noticed a crack in the grip that reminded me of the pistol on Karen Whittle's wall.

A tear of blood dripped down my jaw, then fell onto my shirt. I debated a mad attack, to let the chips fall where they may, but it had no chance of success. I squeezed Peggy's hand again, and waited for a gift.

Tomkins backed to the opposite side of the room and began looking for something, I wasn't sure what. Peggy leaned toward me and whispered, "Are you all right?"

"So far."

"Why is he doing this?"

"I have an idea, but there's no point going into it unless we get out of here."

"Maybe I should do what he wants."

I shook my head. "I'll think of something," I whispered. "But it might help if you could flirt with him a

261

little. Divert his attention somehow. Give me a chance to jump him."

Peggy nodded as Tomkins came back within earshot, looking at his watch along the way. "Time's awasting," he said. "Get 'em off, honey, and let's get this over with. Not that I don't intend to enjoy it." He paused and looked me in the eye. "Bet you're thinking you'll have a chance to take me out when things get hot and heavy, right, Tanner? Well, look what I just happened to bring to the party."

Tomkins reached in his pocket and brought out a circular disk that was thin and white. He fumbled with it for a moment, then drew out a strand of what I finally realized was adhesive tape. "Turn around and put your hands behind your back. Come on. Do what I tell you or you're going to have a lump on your head the size of Russian Hill."

With a sudden crack, the barrel of the pistol banged against my skull, not hard enough to knock me unconscious, just hard enough to convince me he was serious. I did as he asked, trying to separate my hands as he applied the bandage, trying to leave room to maneuver, but he was good at the task and by the time he was finished I was trussed up like a turkey on the way to the oven.

When he finished with my hands, Tomkins spun me back around and forced me to the floor, then began to do my ankles the way he had done my wrists. When I put up some resistance he banged the pistol against my kneecap, hard enough to make me groan.

When both my hands and feet were securely bound, he tore off a long strip of tape and tipped me to my side and taped ankles and wrists together behind my back so I was virtually immobile, a ridiculous horse rocking on my stomach. Clearly I should have risked anything not to get myself in this position. And clearly it was too late for hindsight and regret.

"There we go," Tomkins said as he finished up. "Now, I'm going to do you a big favor, Tanner. I'm going to let you watch." He twisted my body so it was more or less reclined against the wall, my head facing forward, my neck and back bent in painful, opposing arcs.

While Tomkins had been wrapping tape around my ankles, I noticed that Peggy was looking around the boiler room for something, presumably an object that would serve as a defensive weapon. In between passes of the tape, Tomkins kept an eye on her as well, however, and only when he was finishing up the final wrap did Peggy have time to turn and pluck something off a rack of implements that was hanging on the wall. I couldn't see what it was, but as she stuffed it into the back of her skirt I was hoping it was our salvation.

When he was finished with me, Tomkins backed away and turned to Peggy. "Okay, honey. It's show time. Off with the clothes. Don't worry about getting nothing dirty. You won't be needing them again."

Peggy canted a hip and adopted a brassy sneer. "You expect me to make love to you right here on this filthy floor?"

"Sure. Why not? If it hurts too bad I'll let you ride on top."

"It's not very romantic."

"Romance takes time, honey, and I don't have it. Now come on. Let me see those tits."

"Not here."

Tomkins brandished the gun in her face. "You think this is a bagel or something, lady? When a guy has a gun you don't make demands, you do what he says."

"Not here," Peggy repeated. "If you want to make love to me you have to get me something soft to lie on. There's some old mattresses in the storeroom down the hall. Go get one, and—"

"Get *this,* bitch," Tomkins roared, and slugged Peggy on the side of her jaw with the butt of the pistol.

Peggy slumped to the floor, stunned but conscious. I started a cockeyed roll toward her but Tomkins kicked me in the side hard enough to stop me.

Peggy groaned and sat up, rubbing her jaw and shaking

her head. Tomkins stood over her like a slave master. "You want it rough, huh? You like to pretend you're putting up a fight. Good enough. How's this?"

Tomkins reached for Peggy's blouse and ripped it at the shoulder. Peggy scooted away from him as far as she could, but Tomkins followed her to the corner she retreated to, reached down, and grasped another piece of blouse. This time two buttons popped away and Peggy's chest was bare but for her black brassiere.

"Wait," Peggy said, holding up a hand to prevent another grope. "Wait. If we're going to do it let's make it nice."

"Now you're talking," Tomkins said, and stepped back to let her get to her feet. "Maybe I should go first," he added, and reached for his belt and tugged it free of the buckle.

Peggy stepped closer to him and reached out a hand. "Shall I help?"

Her question was flirting, tantalizing, suggestive, and commanded Tomkins' full attention. I struggled with my bonds, and thought I felt some give, then heard a piece of tape begin to tear. Encouraged, I strained harder, and felt my muscles surge, then cramp into painful knots. I rested a moment, then began again.

Tomkins eyed Peggy as though to measure the sincerity of her offer. "Okay, honey. Help yourself." He raised his hands above his head, to let Peggy have free access to his clothing.

With her right hand, Peggy reached slowly for his fly, her body making the gesture a promise of more to come, her eyes dripping tears that contradicted her debauched display. I strained at my bonds again. When they didn't yield I struggled to sit up.

"Tomkins. Hey. I stole your pictures."

Tomkins raised his eyes off Peggy's fumblings and looked at me. "What the hell are you talking about?"

"The pictures. Of Lily Whittle."

Tomkins froze. "What about them?"

264

"I stole them from your apartment this afternoon."

"Like hell."

"If I didn't, how would I know they existed?"

The pictures were clearly crucial to him. He turned, putting Peggy at his back. I summoned all my strength and applied it against the strands of tape. Nothing gave me faith. Tomkins took two steps toward me.

"Where are they?" he demanded.

"Not till you let us go."

He shook his head. "But I'll make it easier on you if you tell me."

"Sorry. If I go, so do the pictures."

"Shit. I bet you got them in your pocket. I bet you're keeping them for yourself."

He came to where I lay and stood over me, then reached for my jacket to search the pocket for his treasures. His attention was so diverted he didn't notice Peggy raise her hand behind his shoulder. An instant later she plunged a screwdriver through his neck.

Peggy screamed in terror at her own commission. The cross-hatched head of the Phillips blade penetrated Tomkins' throat and emerged through the other side, as bloody and blunt as a bullet. A ragged plug of flesh dropped to the floor, to make way for a rush of blood.

Tomkins dropped his gun and clutched his throat, his cry a muffled gurgle through a flooded larynx. His head rolled from side to side to dislodge the spear, but Peggy held fast, the tool thrust to its hilt. As he fought to force the probe to reverse its course, Tomkins sank to his knees and inclined at the waist, a final, desperate prayer. Exhausted by her effort, Peggy fell to the floor beside him, her eyes unseeing, her breaths as heaving as Tomkins' own.

I rolled, not toward the two combatants but toward the gun that had fallen between them. Because they were too engrossed in life and death to think of it, I was able to press the pistol beneath my body, then maneuver enough to grasp it in my fingers behind my back before Tomkins realized what I was doing. With a strangled curse he released his throat and dove for me. Unclamped, the severed artery spewed forth a crimson geyser that showered us both in thick, sweet syrup as we struggled for title to the weapon.

Despite his wound, Tomkins was strong enough to overpower me and my still-joined limbs. Avoiding my attempt to knee and then to butt him, he rolled me to my side, ripped the gun from my hands, lumbered to his feet, and leveled it at me. "You bastard. At least I'll take you with me." With his penultimate burst of energy, he drew the hammer back and focused on my chest.

At his side Peggy began to crawl toward him. It seemed to be happening in slow motion, in a fourth dimension, but that must have been a defect in my senses because before Tomkins could accomplish his mission Peggy extended her arms, wrapped them around his knees, and struggled for leverage to topple him.

When he felt her embrace, Tomkins kicked at her until he broke her grip and forced her back. Then he backed to the wall across from me, leaned heavily against its stiff support, and trained the gun again. "Say good-bye to the world, Tanner. You and me are back on the elevator. And this one's going all the way to the bottom."

The discharge made the room implode. Dirt and dust drifted down from the ceiling, jarred by reverberating echoes. Tomkins' body slammed against the wall behind him. Steam roared even above the gunshot, and a fresh white stream canted across the room and condensed on Tomkins' face in tiny droplets that gradually became a splash. Tomkins' smile became beatific, as though my death would gain him paradise.

I must have been hit, but it caused not a specific pain but only a general slump of lethargy. As I felt my strength slip away, Peggy rolled across the floor, moaning, as though she too were wounded. I started to yell for her to watch out—that he was still dangerous, still had his gun—

when Tomkins toppled onto me and spilled more blood across my face.

As I writhed to get him off me, I heard a raucous jeer. "Why didn't you tell me you folks were having an orgy down here? If I'd known I'd have been on time."

32

In the aftershock of the blast and the steam and the screams, I thought for a moment I'd been blinded. Then I blinked and knew it was blood that blurred my vision, and that everyone was apparently all right except for Tomkins, and that Tomkins was dead because Ruthie Spring had shot him. I rolled out from under Tomkins' hemorrhaging corpse and called for Ruthie to come cut my bonds.

It seemed to take a year, but finally I heard her boots echo across the concrete floor like the beats of an empty heart. I asked her to wipe my eyes. When she did I could see that her crack about the orgy had been a rough reaction to the aftershock of homicide, that Ruthie was as capable as the rest of us of stark chagrin.

With eyes as vacant as I'd seen them except on the day of Harry's death, Ruthie bent over me, examined my bondage, then reached into her purse and pulled out a knife big enough to skin a bear and sharp enough to shave with. A second later she had flicked through the strands of tape without a catch.

When I was free of my restraints and had rubbed some circulation back into my limbs, I looked up at Ruthie. "You okay?"

She managed a weathered grin. "I'm not sure, sugar bear. Feel a little like I did in Korea the first time they tossed a sucking chest wound on the table."

"You ever kill someone before, Ruthie?"

She shook her head. "That was one pleasure I was hoping to get through life without."

"Well, you still haven't. Tomkins was dead before you pulled the trigger."

"Didn't look that way from where I stood."

"Oh, he had enough left to take me out with him, and he would have if you hadn't come along. But you shot a dead man, Ruthie. If you don't believe me, go look at what used to be his throat."

Ruthie stayed where she was. My claim of Tomkins' prior demise didn't dissolve her daze. She replaced the knife in her purse, then took out her gun and looked at it, then replaced it as well, and left my side and went to examine Tomkins. When she straightened up again there was more flicker than fear in her eyes. I decided she was stable enough to leave, so I crawled toward Peggy.

She had burrowed into the corner like a wounded spaniel, so close to the furnace the heat was stifling. Tomkins' kick had evidently caught her ribs, the ones already tender from her fall, and she was groaning with each breath. I draped her tattered blouse around her shoulders, then took her hand and rubbed it. She seemed eased by my ministrations, but when I asked if she was okay she gave me a startled stare, as though in the circumstances such an inquiry was wicked.

"You saved my life, kiddo," I said softly.

Her eyes stayed wide and defenseless, locked on the evil hulk of the incinerator. Whatever she saw there obliterated me, so I tried again.

"I'd be dead if you hadn't stabbed him, Peggy. You would be, too. And you'd have wanted to die a long time before he killed you. What you did was brave and necessary. Do you understand?"

I thought she nodded, but given the pain that laced her body I couldn't be sure it wasn't a flinch.

"You saved my life," I said again. "I can't let someone resign who saved my life. In fact, I think I have to give you a raise. I think it's a state law, that if an employee saves your life you have to give them a raise. Talk about your oppressive government regulations."

Despite my dingy humor, she stayed curled in her muggy cave. I bent toward her and spoke when my lips were six inches from her ear. "Ruthie shot him," I whispered harshly, not loud enough for Ruthie to overhear. "Do you remember that? Tomkins was going to kill me and Ruthie came in and shot him."

That seemed to focus her. "Ruthie?" she said. "Is Ruthie here?"

I gestured behind me. "She saved us. *Both* of you saved us. You make quite the dynamic duo."

"She shot him?"

"Right in the chest. Right before he had a chance to shoot me."

"Good," she said. "Good."

I asked her where she hurt, but she didn't answer. "Can you stand up?"

Lapsed again, she made no movement to rise. I put my arm around her shoulders and gave her a reassuring hug, but she was unyielding.

"I'll carry you," I said mildly, as though we were confronted only by a puddle. "We'll go up to your place and wait for Charley. Okay? Do you understand what I'm saying?"

Long seconds passed, then she nodded. I went to where Ruthie stood staring down at Tomkins' freshly lacquered body. "I think we should get out of here," I said. "We've already seen enough to last a lifetime."

Ruthie didn't move. "I've seen a lot of dead ones, Marsh," she said hollowly, "but this is different. With the others, hell, even with the Chi Coms, I felt like maybe where they were going was better than *this* crummy vale of tears. But not this one. This one's on his way to purgatory, Marsh. And I don't like to think I sent him there."

"He was in hell long before you shot him, Ruthie. He was a prisoner of his perversions, and you didn't have anything to do with that. You just did what you had to do to save my life. I owe you, Ruthie. Big."

Ruthie didn't acknowledge the debt. "I was outside

staking him out," she explained, as though giving a statement to a cop. "I saw you two go in the building. I thought I saw Tomkins look out his window as you got out of the car, but I wasn't sure. I waited a while, but when you didn't come back I decided I'd better check it out. I buzzed until someone let me in, and noticed the door to the garage was ajar, so I decided to come in and look around. I hung around till I heard some kind of noise. Seemed like it came from in here so I wandered over for a look-see. Didn't appear there was any time to chat, so I opened fire. *Damn*. He's as dead as anyone I've ever seen."

"You keep trying to take credit and I keep telling you you can't."

"I know what you told me. It helps a little but it doesn't help enough."

"If you hadn't shot him I'd be dead."

"That helps a little, too. That one will probably get me through it."

For the first time Ruthie looked at me instead of at her fallen target. When she gave me a glimpse of her sassy grin I thought I could stop worrying about her. "Damn, you got a lot of blood on you," she said as she looked me over. "Any of it yours?"

I shook my head.

"Good. I'd hate like hell to have to prove what a lousy nurse I am by trying to bandage you up. How's Miss Peggy?" she asked after I'd patted her back and kissed her cheek.

"In shock, I think. He knocked her around a couple of times. She could have broken something."

"I'll go call a doctor," Ruthie said.

"Better call Charley first. Tell him what happened. Tell him I'm getting Peggy out of here, then going home and changing clothes, then I'll be back to tell him what it was all about." I took out my notebook. "And ask him if he's got anything on a gray Ford rental car with this license number." I tore off the page and gave it to her.

Ruthie raised a brow. "You sure you know what the score is, Marsh?"

"I think so. If I'm right I'll bring some props that will tell the story. For now, let's get out of here. I don't think Peggy can walk, so I'll carry her. You get the key from her purse and we'll go up and put her to bed. If you can stay with her, I'll go clean up and be back in half an hour."

Ruthie nodded. "I'll call a sawbones, too."

"Good."

"Anything else I should do?"

"Well, it'd be good if no one left the building."

Ruthie put her hand on her purse, the place where her gun was stashed. "Who else is in on this?"

"Tell you later."

"Damnit, Marsh Tanner. You—"

"Later."

Ruthie shrugged. "Okay. I'll call in someone to keep watch on the front door. Hell, maybe little old Caldwell can come over. He's been wanting to stick his nose in my business ever since we met. And I don't mean *that* business, so you can wipe that grin off your face."

I laughed until I took another look at Tomkins.

I went over to where Peggy was lying and placed her arms around my neck and slid my arms beneath her legs and torso and lifted her off the floor. She groaned again. I worried I might be aggravating her injuries, but her eyes were still glassy with shock and I didn't think it would abate as long as we were in the boiler room. With one last look at Tomkins, I carried her out the door.

Although I was as careful as I could be, by the time I got Peggy to her apartment she was sticky with Tomkins' blood and even more in pain. The only thing I could think of was to put her to bed. On the way to the bedroom we passed a mirror. When she saw herself she screamed, then fainted.

I took her into the bedroom and lowered her to her bed. After covering her with a blanket I backed out of the room and joined Ruthie in the kitchen. "She passed out," I said.

"You better stick close by. If you can't find someone to guard the door, don't worry about it. Nothing's going to happen that's not remediable."

Ruthie frowned. "Am I supposed to know what that means?"

I shook my head. "If she comes to, you might help her clean up, and do whatever else might help bring her out of it. But I don't have any suggestions how to do it."

"Don't worry, sugar bear. I've handled battle fatigue before. Takes some time, maybe, but it usually melts off, sooner or later."

"Try to make it sooner, Ruthie. I'm going to need her to confirm my hunch on why Tomkins tried to kill us."

"You still keeping it under your hat?"

I nodded. "I'll tell you about it when I get back. I'll even bring along some milk to help you wash it down."

"Make it Jack Daniel's and you're on."

I started toward the door, then stopped. "Ruthie?"

"Yeah, sugar bear?"

"In case you've got any reluctance to help Peggy get through this, I thought I'd mention that I'm not the one who shoved the screwdriver through Tomkins' throat. She is."

"Yeah?"

"Yeah."

"You think that makes a difference?"

"To me or you?"

"Take your pick."

"It shouldn't, should it?" I said.

Ruthie shook her head. "But we both know it does, don't we, sugar bear?"

33

Tomkins' blood lay on me like a dark stigmata, emblazoned by a higher power, emblematic of my sins, imprinted in my flesh forever. After ten minutes of scrubbing, in the hottest shower I could stand, I finally looked clean, though I didn't feel clean at all. Five minutes later the only thing that had vanished was the store of warm water. I climbed out of the shower, tossed my bloodied clothes in the trash, put on a new outfit, and drove back toward the Marina.

The grocery store on Chestnut was a typical mom and pop operation, the kind my parents had run when I was young, the kind that drains and drains and finally empties its owner of everything but exhaustion. I waited in line for a cart behind two young trendies who were conversing with animated artfulness, doubtlessly about the preferred brand of Brie or the proper temperature for broasting garlic. As quickly as I could, I made my way to the dairy case and examined its contents.

One by one I loaded my cart with the appropriate articles, until I had a complete set. When she saw the accumulation the checkout lady cracked a joke about cats and the woman behind me said something about a cow. My response to both was lame.

By the time I got to Peggy's there were three black-and-whites parked out front, surrounding the coroner's black van. I lifted my grocery bag from the trunk and went inside the building and asked the uniform at the door where I could find Charley Sleet.

The patrolman was young and arrogant and he lectured me on improperly interfering with a homicide investigation. As he was about to send me on my way I told him I was the one who had called it in. Then he groused about leaving the scene of a crime, the consequences of the destruction of evidence, and the necessity of hot pursuit. I told him the person who had pulled the trigger was still in the building, and suggested it might be something Charley Sleet would want to know. He summoned a full load of truculence and directed me to the garage.

I was hoping I wouldn't have to go inside the boiler room to find him when I saw Charley lumbering across the greasy concrete toward me. When he saw me he waved. I waited for him to join me, and we entered the elevator together. "Where to?" I asked.

"Wherever you're going."

"Peggy's."

"Fine by me."

I pressed the button. The elevator made sounds that made me look for a certification of inspection.

"You know what went down in there, I hear," Charley said as the box began its irregular ascent.

"Yep."

"You do the shooting?"

"Nope."

"The screwdriver?"

"Nope."

"What the hell. You buy a box seat, or what?"

"That's about it," I admitted.

Charley eyed my bag. "What's that?"

"Evidence."

"You serious?"

"Partially."

"Going to let me see it?"

"Not yet."

"Why not?"

"I have to set the stage."

"Playing Nero Wolfe, are we?"

"Might as well give it a try. He was a hell of a lot more successful than I am at this business."

We spent the rest of the trip discussing why so many of San Francisco's leading citizens were turning out to be crooks.

I knocked on Peggy's door. A moment later Ruthie answered. When she saw Charley she grinned. "Hey, big guy. Where you been keeping yourself?"

"Here and there," Charley said.

"I know that place on Eddy Street you hang out. Person could expire just from the fumes."

"I go for the atmosphere, Ruthie, not the food."

"Atmosphere my ass. Last time I was there three drug deals went down before the waitress took my order, and that didn't count what was happening in the john. You want a decent meal you should come up and see me sometime," Ruthie invited, mimicking Mae West.

"I will if you tell that boyfriend of yours it's strictly platonic. I hear he's kind of a hothead."

"So you know about me and little old Caldwell, huh?"

"Some."

"Is there anything happening in this burg you *don't* know, Charley?"

"Well, I don't know who's going to play cornerback for the Niners next year," Charley said, and gave me a look.

"And I don't know who gives a shit," Ruthie answered. "And I'll tell you one more thing. These days Caldwell only gets hot when I take off my jeans."

"Hell, Ruthie," Charley drawled, "you let enough people watch that, we could do away with nuclear power."

Ruthie laughed and slugged him on the arm.

"One other thing I don't know is what happened down in that boiler room," Charley went on, his words suddenly thick and serious. "Someone around here care to enlighten me?"

Ruthie looked at me to see if she should tell him. "How's Peggy?" I asked her.

"Better. Woke up about five minutes back, came out

and said hello, then went in to take a hot bath. Water stopped running a couple of minutes ago, so she should be ready any time. You bring dinner or something, Marsh?" she added, eyeing the paper bag.

"Just the drinks."

"Damn. You know I like my hootch, but you got enough bourbon there to drown me and Charley both."

"Not bourbon. Milk."

Ruthie and Charley exchanged wordless disclaimers of abstinence. When they started to ask questions I shook my head and guided them inside the apartment.

I told the others to wait in the living room, then took my props into the kitchen. It took me a while to set them up the way I wanted them, and when I was done I could hear enough snatches of conversation to indicate that Peggy had finished bathing and had joined Ruthie and Charley. I walked to the door and listened for a moment, to see how she sounded. I thought she sounded good enough for what I had in mind.

When I walked into the living room I went to Peggy's side. She was wearing her white silk robe. Her feet were bare and her hair was wet and she was pale enough to play Camille, but her jaw was firm and her eyes were clear and animate. "How you doing?" I asked.

She gave me a weak but plucky smile. "Okay. Sorry I checked out on you."

"That's okay. I wouldn't have minded checking out for a while myself. You feel like talking about it for a bit? Charley needs to know what happened down there."

Peggy nodded. "I know what happened, but I don't know why. That man was a despicable creature, but I can't for the life of me think of what I did to make him want to kill me."

"He was just an agent, Peggy."

"Whose agent?"

At that point Charley Sleet edged closer to us. "You ready to reveal all, Nero?"

"I guess so. If everyone else is."

Three heads nodded their concurrence. I motioned for them to sit down, all except for Peggy. But before I could get into it, Charley asked a question. "Is the dead guy the one who's been hassling Peggy on the phone?"

Peggy looked at me quickly, her eyes wide with surprise, but I couldn't tell if she was pleased or perturbed that I'd told Charley about the spider.

I shook my head. "The dead guy's name is Judson Tomkins. And he doesn't have anything to do with that at all. The phone business is a separate thing."

Peggy had been anxious, but my answer seemed to calm her down. Then Charley revived it one more time. "Is it still going on? The phone stuff?"

I shook my head again. "It's taken care of."

"By you?"

"By Peggy, mostly. She found out who it was and convinced him to lay off."

Charley looked at Peggy and gave her his Papa Bear grin. "You want to press charges?"

She shook her head. "No harm, no foul; isn't that what you guys say all the time?" Her laugh was only slightly forced, which was a healthy sign.

Charley nodded. "Well, if he needs any more convincing, you know where I am. I'm about the best convincer in town, or so they tell me."

Peggy smiled and thanked him. Then all eyes turned back to me. I took a breath and clasped my hands and ran my theory through my mind, just to test it one last time. When it still seemed right, I plunged ahead.

"This whole thing started when Peggy went to the grocery store on Tuesday night."

Peggy's look was skeptical and disbelieving. "But nothing happened at the grocery store. Tomkins wasn't even there."

"I know that."

"But—"

"I told you, Tomkins was just an agent. A hired gun, working for someone else. But before I give you a better idea of what happened next, I think we should take a break. Have a little hot chocolate, maybe. Peggy, why don't you go out to the kitchen and fix us some?"

Peggy looked at me as though I'd grown an extra ear. "Fix some yourself," she snapped.

Ruthie watched us both, then said, "I'll do it, Marsh. Only I'm making mine bourbon and branch."

I shook my head. "Let Peggy handle it."

Peggy started to bark at me again, but held back. With a quizzical wrinkle across her forehead, she marched to the kitchen without another word. A few seconds later she peeked around the corner and glared at me. "What's this all about?"

"Look them over," I said. "See if you see anything familiar."

"Look *what* over?"

"The evidence."

Peggy hesitated, then disappeared again. Ruthie looked at Charley and Charley looked at me. They both had questions, and Charley spoke first. "Can we at least go over the mechanics of what happened downstairs?"

"Sure," I said.

"Okay. You didn't shoot him or stab him, or so you say. So who pulled the trigger?"

"Ruthie."

He looked at her. "That right?"

Ruthie nodded.

"Where's the weapon?"

Ruthie patted her purse. "Got John Henry right here."

"Remind me to take it for ballistics when I leave. How about the screwdriver? Who used his neck like a two-by-four?"

"Peggy," I said.

"Now this is turning into Agatha Christie, for Christ's sake. How'd you all get down there in the first place?"

"Tomkins was waiting for Peggy and me when we got here," I said.

"You mean waiting to kill you?"

"I think so."

"You and Peggy. Where was Ruthie?"

"Out in her car, staking out the building."

"Why?"

"I'd asked her to keep an eye on Tomkins for a while."

"Why?" Charley said again.

"Because I thought he might have something to do with Peggy's telephone problem. He didn't seem to fit, really, but he was too good a possibility to let roam around loose."

"So you and Peggy got here. Where from?"

"The office."

"And you went inside, and . . ."

"Tomkins looked out the window and saw us coming and met us in the elevator. He pulled a gun and herded us to the boiler room and got ready to kill us. But first he decided to have some fun and games with Peggy."

"You mean sex?"

"Yep."

"He get the job done?"

"Nope."

"Any thanks to you?"

"Nope."

Charley nodded. "There was a bunch of tape wadded up down there. Who'd he use that on?"

"Me," I admitted.

"Way to go, Nero. So he had you taped up like a sprained ankle, and was getting set to assault Miss Nettleton. Then what happened?"

"When he was wrapping me up, Peggy grabbed a screwdriver off the wall. Then when I got him to come after me with a little diversion, she stuck him in the neck."

"Bled a little, didn't he?"

"Old Faithful," I said.

"Then what?"

"He decided to take me with him."

"You mean kill you."

I nodded. "If it was the last thing he ever did. Which it would have been," I added.

"And then?"

"About two seconds before he pulled the trigger, Ruthie saved the day. Or at least my portion of it."

"She shot him."

"Right between the lungs."

Charley looked at Ruthie. "What was he doing when you fired?"

"Pointing a gun at sugar bear, over there. Telling Marsh he was going take him with him on the elevator, or some crap like that."

"Any doubt in your mind he was ready to shoot?"

"About as much doubt as I have that fucking's a lot more fun than fishing."

"So—"

Charley's question was interrupted by Peggy's return from the kitchen. This time she carried something with her, and she placed it on the coffee table in front of all of us. After we looked at it for a minute, mine was the only face that didn't wear a frown.

It was rectangular and waxed and held a half gallon of milk. On the side that was turned toward me, the word MISSING was printed in dark, bold letters. Beneath the word were two pictures, both of children—one boy, one girl. Beneath the girl's picture was the relevant data: Missing since 3/3/83; From Albuquerque, NM; Date of Birth 3/3/80; White Female; Eyes Blue; Height 36"; Weight 29 lbs; Hair Brown. Below the data was the phone number to call if you'd seen her: 1-800-843-5678. It was the number for the National Center for Missing & Exploited Children.

Peggy's eyes and mine met above the carton. "It's Lily," she said.

I nodded. "I thought so, but I only saw her once so I wanted to be sure."

"It says she's missing. It says she's been missing for over three years. And it says her name is Linda Wilson."

I looked at Charley. "That's what this is all about, folks. The girl whose picture is on that milk carton."

Charley thought a moment. "Where is she now?"

"Upstairs, I think. If not, she should be easy to find. I don't think anyone knows we're onto the situation yet."

"Back it up," Charley said. "Start at the beginning."

"Okay," I began. "Peggy's best friend in the building is a woman named Karen Whittle. She lives up on four, with her daughter, Lily. Lily's six years old. Her mother teaches the child at home, barely lets her out of the house, goes crazy if strangers come to call, all because her ex-husband is supposedly trying to kidnap the child and steal her away. But this milk carton proves that the husband isn't the kidnapper, the wife is."

"You don't know that," Peggy blurted. "I want to talk to Karen. I'm sure there's an explanation."

"I'm afraid I'm right, Peggy," I said. "But it's easy to check to make sure." When she didn't say anything else I went on. "Anyway, the husband—I think his name is Tom Wilson, but you can check that with the Albuquerque cops—has presumably been looking for his daughter all this time, and this week he zeroed in. I saw him around the building several times, each time more angry than the one before. He's been driving a gray Ford, a rental. I think you may have found it abandoned somewhere near here yesterday or today," I said to Charley.

Charley frowned, then nodded. "Ruthie asked me about it, and we did have a sheet on that. They found the Ford down by Fort Mason. Why abandon the car?"

"Because I think Wilson's dead."

Charley gave me a narrow look. "Who killed him?"

"Tomkins. I think he buried Wilson at Baker's Beach. Early this morning Tomkins had sand on his clothes, and Ruthie trailed him out there a few hours later, when he was probably checking to see that his nighttime burial detail didn't leave any traces. If you take some men out and give it a good search, I think you'll find Wilson's body."

"I still don't get it," Charley went on. "What's Tomkins have to do with all this?"

"He was working for Karen Whittle. Pure and simple."

"What did she have on him that made him kill for her?"

"She had money enough to get him out of town, and she was willing to barter with her body as well. I caught him coming out of her place early this morning. He'd clearly just had sex with her, but it seemed so absurd I didn't believe it at the time." I was all too aware of the additional inducement—the three snapshots of Lily in my pocket— but I decided not to mention them, just as I decided not to mention that I'd assumed the woman Tomkins had been visiting was Charley's friend in the apartment across the hall from Karen Whittle's.

"So the Whittle woman was behind it all," Charley said, still putting it all together.

I nodded.

"But why did she want to kill *me?*" Peggy asked. "What did I have to do with it?"

"You ran into her at the grocery store that night. She saw you buy some milk. As it happened, the milk you bought had Lily's picture on it, as part of the Missing Children thing. Lily was a lot younger in the picture, but she hadn't changed all that much. Plus, when the two of you played dress-up you'd seen her in a brown wig, which was her natural hair color, and the color of her hair in the picture on the carton. She knew if you ever looked at the milk carton closely you'd realize Lily had already been a victim of a kidnap and that she was the perpetrator. She couldn't take the chance you'd turn her in, friend or no friend, so she ran back here and changed her clothes and put on a ski mask and waited till you got back and pushed you down the stairs. Not to kill you or even hurt you, just to have a chance to get the milk carton away. You'd told her about the problem you were having with the telephone calls, so she used the words that convinced you your attacker was Arth—was the spider. Then over the next few days she kept checking back to see if you'd gotten any

283

more milk—first to get some margarine, then some ice, always showing up with a reason to look in your refrigerator. The pressure got too much for her eventually; she decided it was too risky to let you live. So she convinced Tomkins to help her out. She'd lived in fear of discovery for years. Her nerves were shot even before her husband showed up, and when he arrived on the scene she completely flipped out, decided to do anything in the world to prevent her daughter from being taken away and herself from being thrown in jail. And the world has always included a lot of murder."

The room rang with my declamation for a time, then Charley broke the spell. "That takes care of her. But why would Tomkins go that far, even for money?"

"He's a convicted sex offender, and remember they've got him nailed on a probation violation. His probation officer has been regaling him with stories of what the cons do to sex offenders in the joint, because he thought it would be some sort of deterrent. Tomkins was so petrified of serving time he decided to take off. Since his mother cut off his allowance, he needed money to finance his escape, a lot of it and soon. Karen Whittle provided it."

I looked at Peggy. Her eyes were closed against my disclosures. For yet another time I was going to have to hurt her.

"You said sex, too," Charley reminded.

"No," Peggy blurted fiercely. "I can't believe that. Not Karen and Tomkins. You must be wrong, Marsh. You have to be."

I could have pulled the pictures from my pocket, or I could have reminded Peggy about her own involvement with a faceless predator, but I didn't do either. "Maybe I got that part wrong," I said. From the look on Peggy's face it seemed to help.

"Anyway," I went on after a moment, "first Tomkins got rid of the husband, then he tried to get rid of Peggy. And me, since the Whittle woman apparently figured that since I'd seen Lily and was a friend of Peggy's and was in the law enforcement business in a sense, I was a threat to her as well." I looked at Peggy, then at Ruthie. "And if these two hadn't come to my rescue, he would have gotten the job done."

Peggy lowered her head to her hands. "Karen," she said. "My God. She was my very best friend. We talked for hours and hours. I thought I knew her better than I knew anyone in the world. How could she *do* something like . . ." Her voice trailed off, silenced by a world whose propensities had grown impossibly enlarged.

"Kids," Ruthie intoned simply.

Charley and I looked at each other. "Guess I'd best go get her," he said finally.

I reached in my pocket and pulled out the envelope containing the photographs of Lily Whittle and handed it to him. "Give this to Mrs. Wilson," I said.

Charley looked at me. "I need to know what it is?"

"No."

He shrugged. "I'll take your word for it."

"That's the reason I gave it to you."

34

"So," Peggy said.

"So."

We were alone. Charley had gone to question Karen Whittle, refusing Peggy's request to accompany him. Ruthie had gone outside to find Caldwell, who was somewhere in his car, watching the door to see that no one escaped. I'd stayed behind because violence produces reactions, sometimes immediate, sometimes delayed, sometimes both, and my own reaction was that I didn't want to be alone again until I had to be.

"I guess it's over," Peggy said.

"It is if you want it to be."

"What's that supposed to mean?"

"Nothing, I guess."

"You're not thinking about Karen and that Tomkins creature, are you?"

"No."

"Well, I am."

"I know."

Peggy crossed her arms and hunched her shoulders, as if a cold wind had just blown through the door. "She was a good friend to me, Marsh. I know what she did was inexcusable, if she did it, but I feel terrible that she got herself so backed against the wall the only way she could think of to save herself was murder. It's like a Greek tragedy or something."

"It's too bad. I agree."

"What do you suppose will happen to Lily?"

"A relative, probably. If there are any."

"There's a sister, I think. In Wyoming, or somewhere like that."

"Then Lily will probably end up there. If the sister wants her."

"What happens in the meantime?"

"A foster home, I guess."

"Do you think that could be me?"

"I don't know. Why don't you call the DA's office and find out? I think there's an agency called Social Services that handles things like that."

"I'd like to think I could adopt her for good, but I guess that would be asking too much."

I shrugged. "The requirements are a little more flexible these days, I think."

Peggy sighed. "I'm not sure my motives are all that pure, to tell you the truth. Maybe I just want to prove I can do it more competently than I did the first time."

I smiled. "Some things are imperfectible, you know. Almost everything but bowling, actually."

Peggy matched my look. "Says you."

"Well, you don't have to make a decision now. Talk to the social services people tomorrow. Find out what your rights are. Then decide."

"Procrastinate, you mean."

"Deliberate. Cogitate. Evaluate. Negotiate. I'd say this is something that shouldn't be rushed into."

The subject drifted away from us and we relied on silence and the sense that something fundamental had been altered by the day's events. Peggy stared into the space above my head, at the still life of apples and pears and a wine bottle that hung there.

"God," Peggy said abruptly. "I still can't absorb everything that's happened. Every time I start to think of it my mind gets, I don't know, stiff or something. Hardened. Like it's becoming numb."

"Defense mechanism. Reflexive nonchalance."

"You mean it happens that way with you?"

"Sure. The trick is not to let it become a permanent condition."

"So how have you managed it?"

"I'm not sure I have."

"No. You still care about people, Marsh. Sometimes I think you're the only one in the world who does."

"Well, if I do it's probably because I'm underemployed. If I made more money and had more toys, I'd probably become devoted to them."

"You're talking about that awful slogan you see all over the place, aren't you? 'He who dies with the most toys wins.' That's just so . . . *wrong*, Marsh. Isn't it?"

"I hope so."

"If it isn't then we really are meaningless, aren't we?" Peggy laughed at her own bleak synthesis. "Do you want a drink?"

Since the question seemed ritualistic, I said, "I think I'd better go."

I waited for an objection. When I didn't hear one I asked Peggy if she'd be at work on Monday.

"I . . . Do you want me to be?"

"You know I do."

"Why?"

"If I have to say it I won't get it right. If I could talk nice I'd still be a lawyer, for crying out loud."

"But you think we can put all this behind us."

"I think we already have."

Peggy grinned sheepishly. "Well, I know this much. If I have to kill someone to get back in your good graces, we'd better not get mad at each other very often."

"That didn't have anything to do with it."

"I think maybe it did. Just a little."

I knew she was right, in ways I couldn't entirely fathom, but I knew that it was only a shortcut, not the sole solution, that we'd have been all right anyway. Eventually. But she spoke again before I could tell her so.

"I think I can help us become friends again, Marsh," Peggy said softly.

"How?"

"By telling you why I let Arthur Constable go on doing what he did to me. Why I told him I'd be willing to talk with him some more, even in light of what he's done. Do you think that might make it easier for you?"

"I don't know. Would it be easy for you to tell me?"

"Not easy. But I can do it now. Yesterday I couldn't, but now I can. I feel whole again, somehow. I think it's because I saved your life. Or I tell myself I did, at any rate."

"You did. No question."

"That's nice of you to say. And I warn you, I'm going to keep believing it. I may even mention it at parties."

"Fine. Maybe I can get the *Chronicle* over here and give you a spread. Or at least a line in Herb Caen."

Peggy smiled easily, then closed her eyes and leaned back against the couch. When she spoke her words were flat and toneless, appropriate for reciting statistical irrelevancies. "One night, while he was pecking at me the way he did, Arthur got me to talk about the one thing in my life I'd hidden from everyone, Marsh. And I do mean everyone. I've done lots of things I'm not proud of, but this one was by far the worst. This baby was locked away deep, for thirty years. I was always afraid to let it out, afraid of what people would think of me if they knew, afraid of what I'd think of myself if I relived it. But with John—Arthur—it didn't matter. I didn't *care* what he thought; I didn't even know who he was. And he knew so much about me anyway, this other thing wouldn't be such a big deal. Plus he was clearly a basket case himself. I didn't know how, precisely, but I knew he wasn't normal, so he couldn't very well criticize *me* for abnormality. You know what I mean?"

"I guess so."

"And the funny thing is, it's *not* such a big deal. I mean, it's far from a unique experience in this day and age—the papers are full of it. But it's unique to me. It was the biggest deal in my whole, entire *life*. And it stayed so horrible I refused to ever mention it because there was never anyone I felt I could trust enough to tell about it. Finally someone came along. Someone I could trust or at least be safe from."

"The spider, you mean."

"Yes. First the spider. Now you. You and Karen."

"Quite a trio."

Peggy looked pained. "Don't be that way. Please."

I grinned. "Sorry. I just never thought I'd be flattered to be lumped in with a pervert and a killer."

"Well, you should be. In this instance."

"Okay, I'm flattered. Now what's the big secret?"

Peggy lapsed into an inward stare. Marilyn hopped into her lap and curled into a furry ball. "Now that I've built it up I feel kind of silly. It's like a play everyone tells you is so great, and by the time you see it you're inevitably let down."

"I promise not to be let down."

"It doesn't matter. You can fall asleep in the middle if you want. But I'm going to tell it, anyway."

"Good."

She leaned forward and met my eyes. "You remember I told you about my father? How bad I felt that when he got Alzheimer's and had to be put in a nursing home I didn't go back and take care of him or bring him out here to live with me or anything? How I just let him rot in an institution back east?"

"I remember. Though I hardly think you let him rot."

"Well, that was rough for me. That ate a pretty big hole in my self-esteem. But what I didn't tell you was I really didn't have a choice."

"Why not?"

Her eyes deepened and her voice grew grave and purposeful. "Because despite his trouble I couldn't let myself get close to him again, and the reason is he abused me when I was a child. For about three years, between when I was ten and thirteen, he used to crawl in my bed and fondle me and make me do the same to him, or fondle myself while he watched and told me how to do it."

She looked to my soul for my reaction, my response, my judgment, to see if any of them came wrapped in flippancy or revulsion. I couldn't tell if what she saw was comforting.

Suddenly she laughed, a sarcastic cackle. "He only had one testicle. Isn't that a strange thing for a ten-year-old girl to know about her father? And when I was old enough to fondle other men, and found a man with two, I thought *he* was the one who was abnormal. That was good for a laugh, let me tell you."

She broke into tears, silent ones, tears that came from ancient lakes and timeless glaciers. I reached out and patted her knee, but nothing changed until she reached up and swiped at her eyes and sniffled above a willful smile. "It was horrible, needless to say. Just horrible. I mean in those days the whole sex thing was pretty much secret anyway, you know? Not like today, where you're bombarded with innuendo every six seconds. Back in the fifties even normal sex was a forbidden, frightening subject to a young girl. And sex with your very own father, well . . ."

"Did you tell anyone about it at the time?"

"No. No one."

"Not even your mother?"

"Especially not my mother. See, when it started I wasn't even all that sure it was wrong. I mean, what did I know? I thought this was something fathers and daughters did together. It sounds impossibly naive in this day and age, but that was the way I was. Then, after a year or so went by, and I knew it was bad, I hated my mother *worst of all*, for letting it happen, somehow. Then after a while it seemed too late to do anything. Because I'd let it go on for such a long time. I thought *I'd* be the one they'd punish, not Daddy."

"And so it just started and stopped?"

She looked away, at the bedroom doorway. "Well, I kind of helped it."

"How?"

"I came up with a plan. One night when Mom was gone he came in to me earlier than usual. I waited till he got close and I grabbed my hairbrush and hit him as hard as I could. Without warning. Just hauled off and slugged him. By accident I hit him right in the solar plexus. He went down like a tree. I actually thought I'd killed him, and at first I was immensely relieved but then I started to cry. Hysterically. I guess I sensed I'd done something irrevocable. That things would never be the same."

"What happened then?"

"When he got his wind back he just looked at me for a long time, and left my room without a word, and never came back. He barely spoke to me after that. It was like he'd moved out of the house. And in a way that was as hard to deal with as the other."

"How do you mean?"

"I don't know, Marsh. The psychology of it is strange. He was my father. And I'd hurt him. Never mind how he'd hurt me, at that point I was overwhelmed by the possibility that I'd made him a different person, a lesser being. Talk about mood swings. Fear to guilt to anger to shame to maybe even a little repressed desire, who knows? Up the spectrum and back again. I was a mess. And really, I've been a mess ever since, at least with men. That's why I go through so many, I think. I want them to be different from my father, and they are, of course, but sooner or later, no matter how benign they are, they do or say something and I see my father in them and so I break away. Slug them also, so to speak. Then time goes by and I try again, and then again. It's pretty standard stuff, I know."

She looked at me hesitantly, to see whether I'd demean her confession. "Things like that are never standard, Peggy. Not to the one that suffers them."

Over a silent minute she seemed to relax, to finally

accept my reactions as appropriate. "Well, the important thing is that I'd never, ever talked about it till John came along, and when I did I felt this tremendous sense of relief. It didn't last long, of course, since a minute or two later I started feeling ashamed all over again, about the rest of the phone business, but still in all I owed him something. I still do. Which is why I told him what I told him this evening. When he told me why he'd done what he did to me, I sensed he was a lot like me, in a way. A victim of something he didn't fully understand and couldn't talk with anyone about. I thought maybe I could help him the way he helped me. Can you understand any of that, Marsh? Am I making sense?"

"I think so."

"But do you believe me? I mean, do you think it's rational for me to feel that way about it?"

I nodded. "I know studies that compare the various kinds of therapies that litter the world today almost always conclude that the only thing any of them really do for a person is get them to talk about their problems. The rest of it's a bunch of hooey, but talking actually helps. I think that means what you're saying makes sense."

"Good."

"And I'm flattered that you told me."

"Good."

I grinned. "And I'll expect you to be in the office on Monday."

She hesitated before she answered. "Okay."

"And we'll talk about this again, whenever you want."

"Okay."

"We can even talk more about it now if you want."

She shook her head. "I think we've been through enough for one night, don't you?"

I nodded. "You look exhausted."

"I am."

"I'll let you get some sleep."

"I think I will tonight. For the first time in a long while."

"Good."

The knock on the door was startling. We looked at each other, quickly fearful, momentarily leery that someone out of the past few days was out there to endanger us.

"Allison," I remembered after a second.

Peggy slumped in relief. "I'd forgotten."

I stood up. "So I'll be going. Get lots of sleep."

"You, too."

"I hope we're okay again."

"Me, too."

"I . . ."

She smiled like the Peggy I had learned I loved. "Good night, Marsh."

"Good night, Peggy."

"Thanks for listening and everything."

"Hey. I'm the one who should be saying thanks. About three hours ago you saved my life. Compared to that I ain't done nothing."

"I think you have. I think maybe you've done enough."

"Then can I make a suggestion?"

"What?"

"Why don't you tell Allison what you just told me?"

35

When I got home the phone was ringing. I picked it up and said hello.

"Tanner?"

"Yes."

"How you doing?"

"Okay."

"That's great. Know who this is?"

"No."

"A friend."

"You don't sound like either of them."

"Funny. I—"

"If this is business, call me at the office on Monday."

"This isn't business, this is just a friendly chat. I wanted to ask if you got my note."

"What note?"

"What's the matter, don't you read your mail?"

"Halliburton."

"Give the man a door prize."

"Okay, Halliburton. What can I do for you?"

"The question is, what can I do to you?"

"What's that mean?"

"I mean I was wondering if you could suggest how I can pay you back for fucking up my life? See, since the trial started my wife left me, they repossessed my Porsche, I got a notice of foreclosure on my house, my lawyer filed suit against me for some sort of fees he claims I owe. Pretty much clears the slate, wouldn't you say? Only thing I got left is some worthless coins some guy told me came out of a sunken treasure and a case of French wine that got ruined when they turned off the electric."

"Too bad."

"You sound real sorry about it."

"Maybe you should have thought a little more about the consequences when you defrauded the Arundel Corporation."

"Maybe. And maybe you should have left well enough alone."

"I was just doing a job, Halliburton. If not me it would have been someone else."

"But it *was* you is the thing. And you know what?"

"What?"

"I'm going to pay you back. I'm going to ruin you the way you ruined me."

"How?"

"I don't know yet. But I'm a sporting man, so I'm letting you know up front that I'm out to get you. That's a better deal than you gave me. Right?"

"Seems to me your quarrel is with the Arundel Corporation, not me. I'm just a hired hand."

"Yeah, well, your days as a hired hand are numbered. I don't know when, and I don't know how, but one of these days I'm going to destroy you, Tanner. I'm going to make you as miserable as you made me."

"I'd probably be worried if I thought you had what it takes to get the job done."

"You're such a cool customer you make me sick. The jury bought your whole story, you know that? One of them told my lawyer you were the one that convinced them I was crooked. So you'll be seeing whether I've got what it takes or not. In the meantime, I think I'll give you a call from time to time, just to let you know I'm on the job. Every time the phone rings, you'll be wondering if it's me. You'll be wondering if I've done anything yet, wondering if someone's calling to tell you you're deep in a pile of shit when all the time you thought it was under control. There you'll be, wondering when I'm going to strike, thinking maybe I've given up, then one day, out of a clear blue sky, I'll bring you down. I'll find out what's the most important thing in the world to you, and I'll destroy it, Tanner. I'll make you wish you were dead and buried."

"I'll tell you something, Malcolm. If you pick a week like this one, that won't be all that hard to do."

ABOUT THE AUTHOR

Stephen Greenleaf was born in Washington, D.C., and grew up in Centerville, Iowa. He has received degrees from Carleton College, Northfield, Minnesota, and from the Boalt Hall School of Law of the University of California, Berkeley. After serving two years in the army, including a year in Vietnam, he practiced law for five years before beginning to write fiction. Five of his six previous books feature private detective John Marshall Tanner of San Francisco. His fifth book, *The Ditto List,* was Mr. Greenleaf's first nonmystery novel. Mr. Greenleaf lives in Oregon with his wife, Ann, an author of children's books, and his son, Aaron. He is currently working on another novel.